JLA JSA
VIRTUE AND VICE

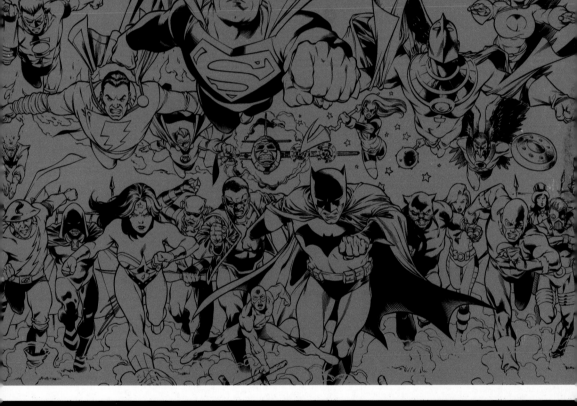

WRITERS: DAVID S. GOYER • GEOFF JOHNS

PENCILLER: CARLOS PACHECO   **INKER:** JESÚS MERIÑO

LETTERER: KEN LOPEZ   **COLORIST:** GUY MAJOR

COVER PENCILLER: **CARLOS PACHECO** • COVER INKER: **JESÚS MERIÑO** • COVER COLORIST: **GUY MAJ**

Jenette Kahn, President & Editor-in-Chief • Paul Levitz, Executive Vice President & Publis
Mike Carlin, VP-Executive Editor • Dan Raspler, Group Editor • Stephen Wacker, Associate Edi
Amie Brockway-Metcalf, Art Director • Georg Brewer, VP-Design & Retail Product Developme
Richard Bruning, VP-Creative Director • Patrick Caldon, Senior VP-Finance & Operatic
Terri Cunningham, VP-Managing Editor • Dan DiDio, VP-Editorial • Joel Ehrlich, Senior VP-Advertis
& Promotions • Alison Gill, VP-Manufacturing • Lillian Laserson, VP & General Coun
David McKillips, VP-Advertising • John Nee, VP-Business Development • Cheryl Rubin, VP-Licensing
Merchandising • Bob Wayne, VP-Sales & Marketing

DC COMICS

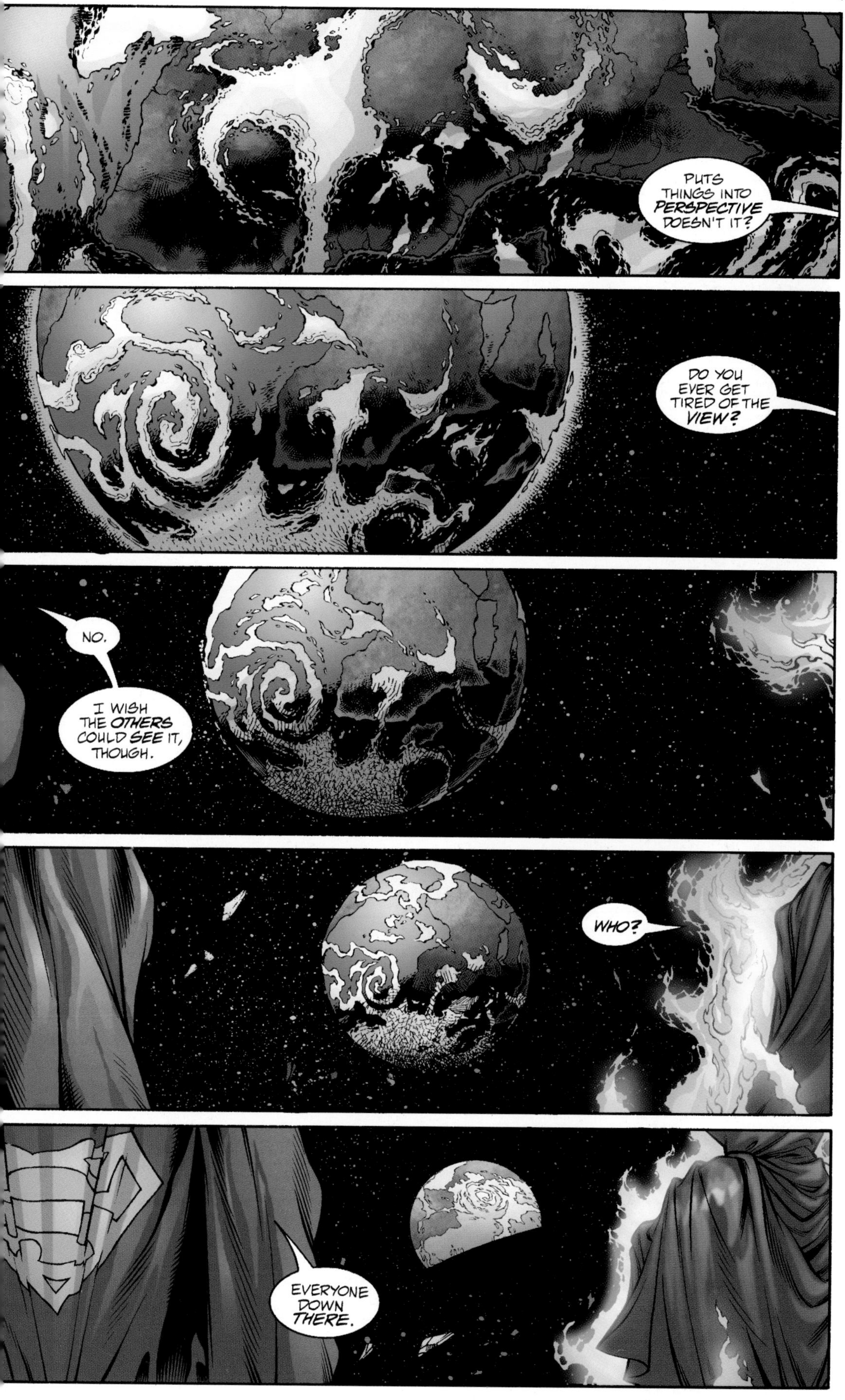
PUTS THINGS INTO PERSPECTIVE DOESN'T IT?
DO YOU EVER GET TIRED OF THE VIEW?
NO.
I WISH THE OTHERS COULD SEE IT, THOUGH.
WHO?
EVERYONE DOWN THERE.

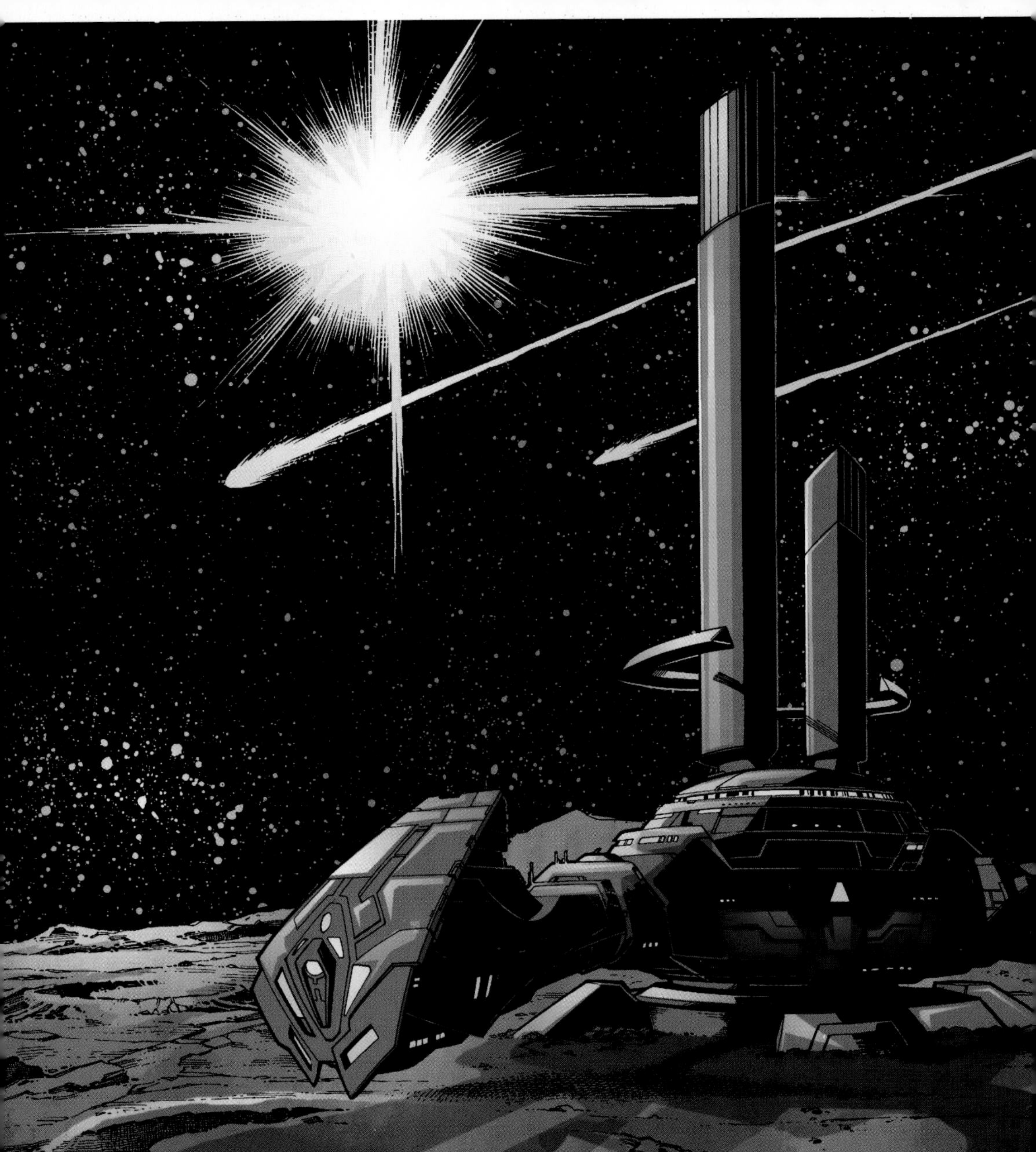

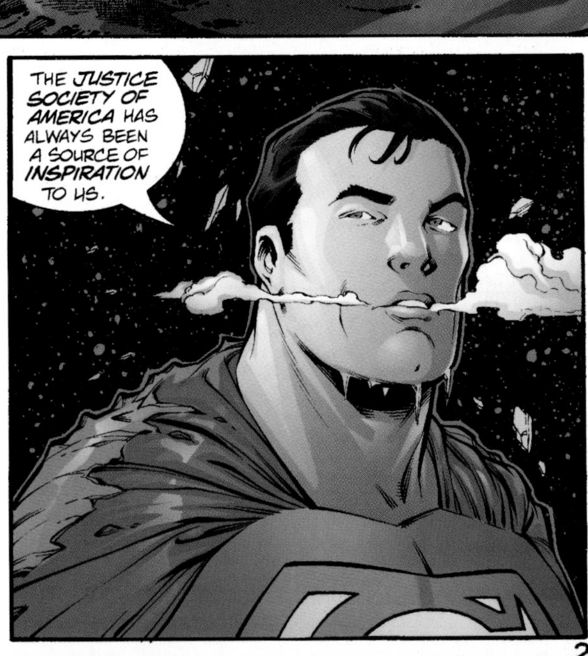
THE JUSTICE SOCIETY OF AMERICA HAS ALWAYS BEEN A SOURCE OF INSPIRATION TO US.

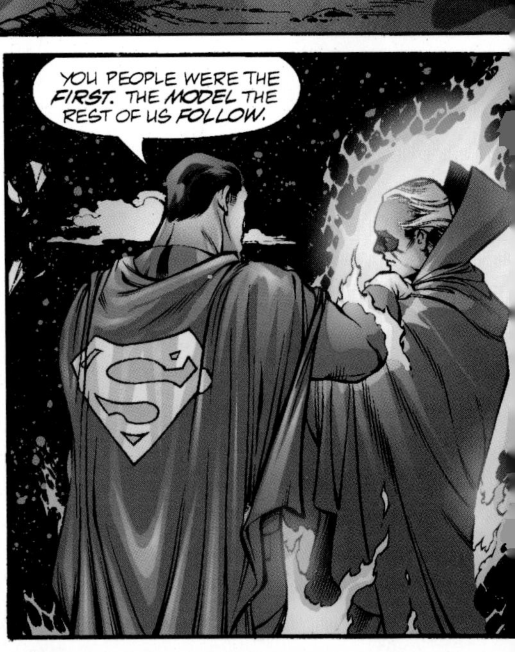
YOU PEOPLE WERE THE FIRST. THE MODEL THE REST OF US FOLLOW.

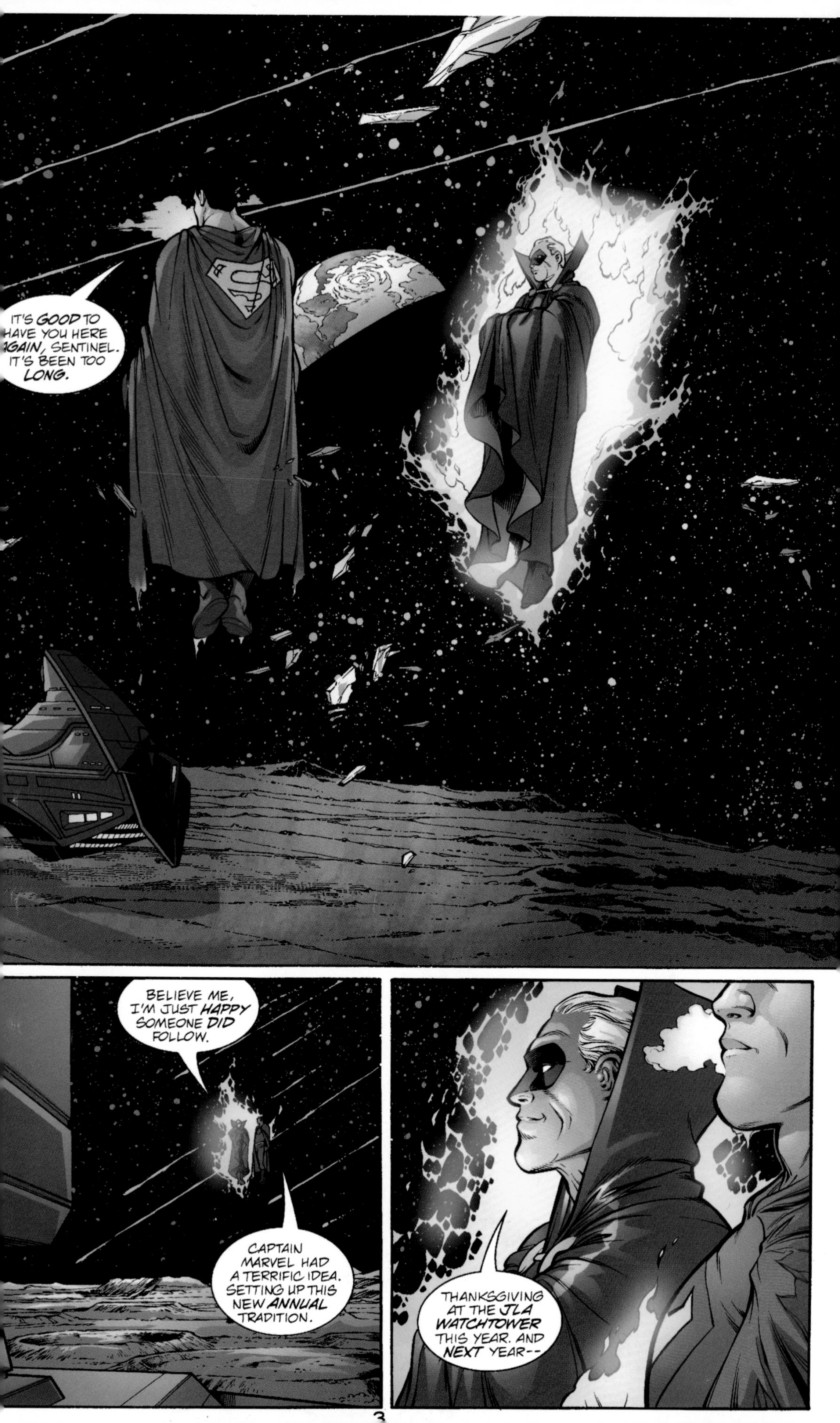
IT'S GOOD TO HAVE YOU HERE AGAIN, SENTINEL. IT'S BEEN TOO LONG.
BELIEVE ME, I'M JUST HAPPY SOMEONE DID FOLLOW.
CAPTAIN MARVEL HAD A TERRIFIC IDEA. SETTING UP THIS NEW ANNUAL TRADITION.
THANKSGIVING AT THE JLA WATCHTOWER THIS YEAR. AND NEXT YEAR--

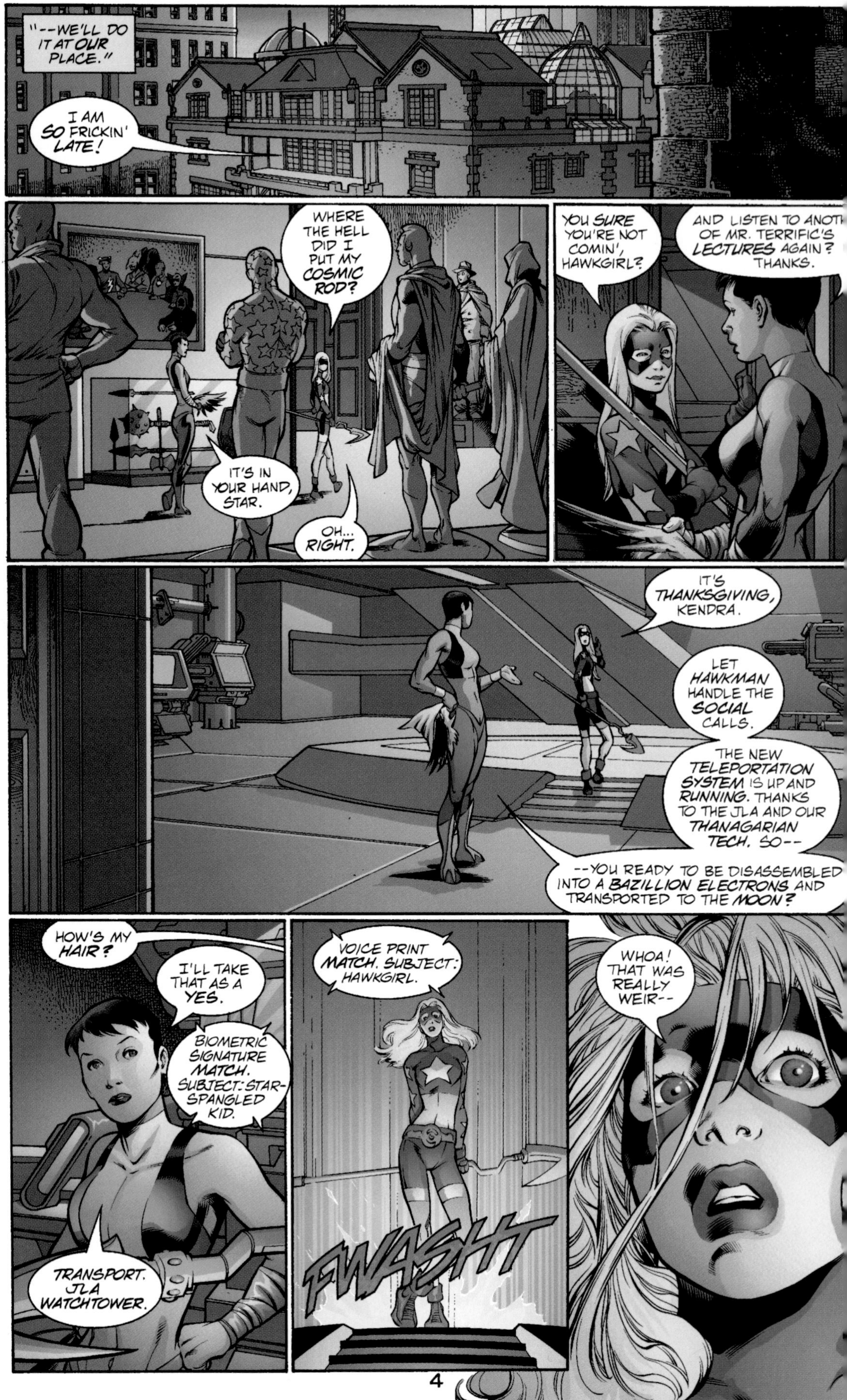
"--WE'LL DO IT AT OUR PLACE."
I AM SO FRICKIN' LATE!
WHERE THE HELL DID I PUT MY COSMIC ROD?
IT'S IN YOUR HAND, STAR.
OH... RIGHT.
YOU SURE YOU'RE NOT COMIN', HAWKGIRL?
AND LISTEN TO ANOTH OF MR. TERRIFIC'S LECTURES AGAIN? THANKS.
IT'S THANKSGIVING, KENDRA.
LET HAWKMAN HANDLE THE SOCIAL CALLS.
THE NEW TELEPORTATION SYSTEM IS UP AND RUNNING. THANKS TO THE JLA AND OUR THANAGARIAN TECH. SO--
--YOU READY TO BE DISASSEMBLED INTO A BAZILLION ELECTRONS AND TRANSPORTED TO THE MOON?
HOW'S MY HAIR?
I'LL TAKE THAT AS A YES.
BIOMETRIC SIGNATURE MATCH. SUBJECT: STAR-SPANGLED KID.
TRANSPORT. JLA WATCHTOWER.
VOICE PRINT MATCH. SUBJECT: HAWKGIRL.
FWASH
WHOA! THAT WAS REALLY WEIR--

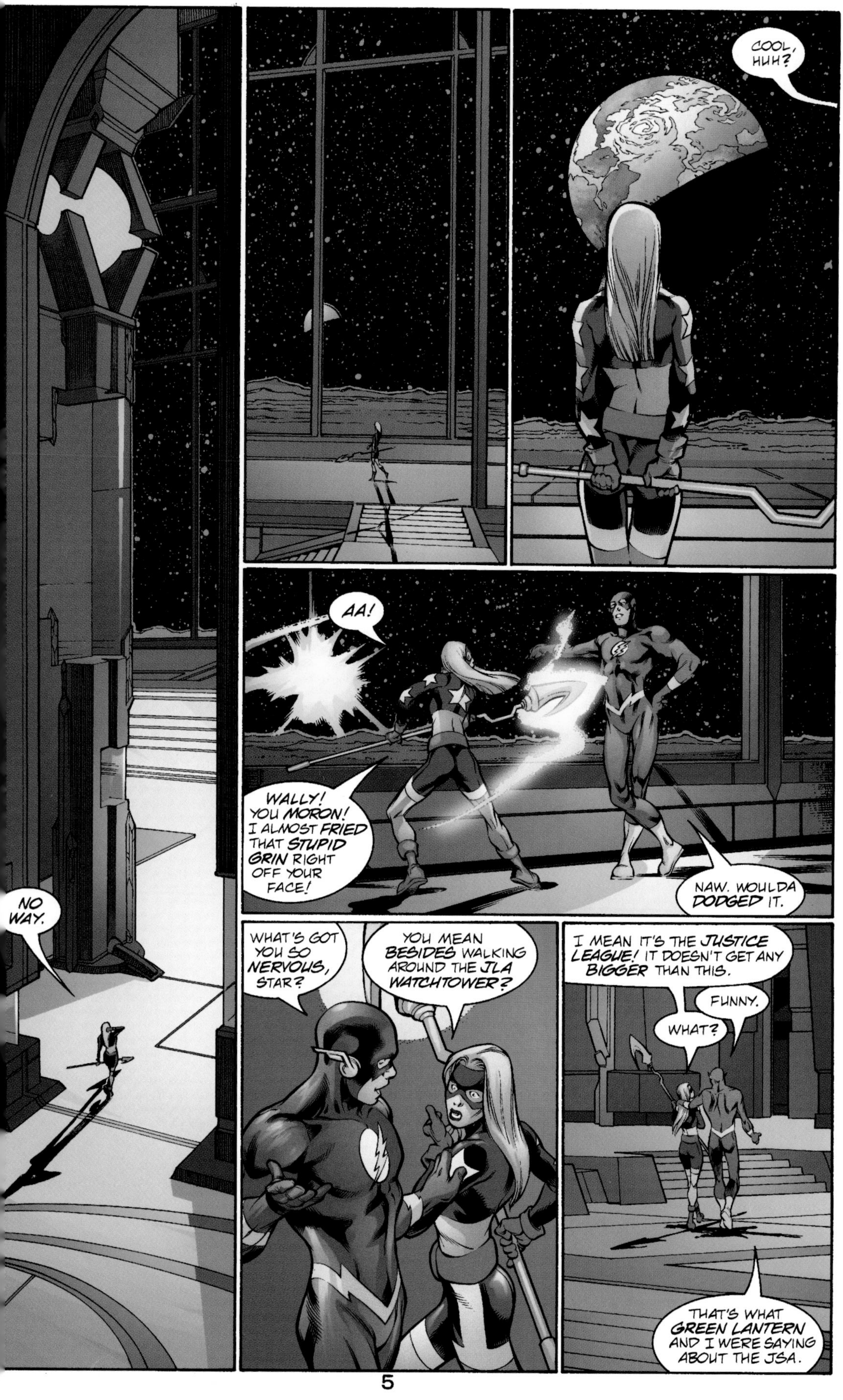
NO WAY.
COOL, HUH?
AA!
WALLY! YOU MORON! I ALMOST FRIED THAT STUPID GRIN RIGHT OFF YOUR FACE!
NAW. WOULDA DODGED IT.
WHAT'S GOT YOU SO NERVOUS, STAR?
YOU MEAN BESIDES WALKING AROUND THE JLA WATCHTOWER?
I MEAN IT'S THE JUSTICE LEAGUE! IT DOESN'T GET ANY BIGGER THAN THIS.
FUNNY.
WHAT?
THAT'S WHAT GREEN LANTERN AND I WERE SAYING ABOUT THE JSA.

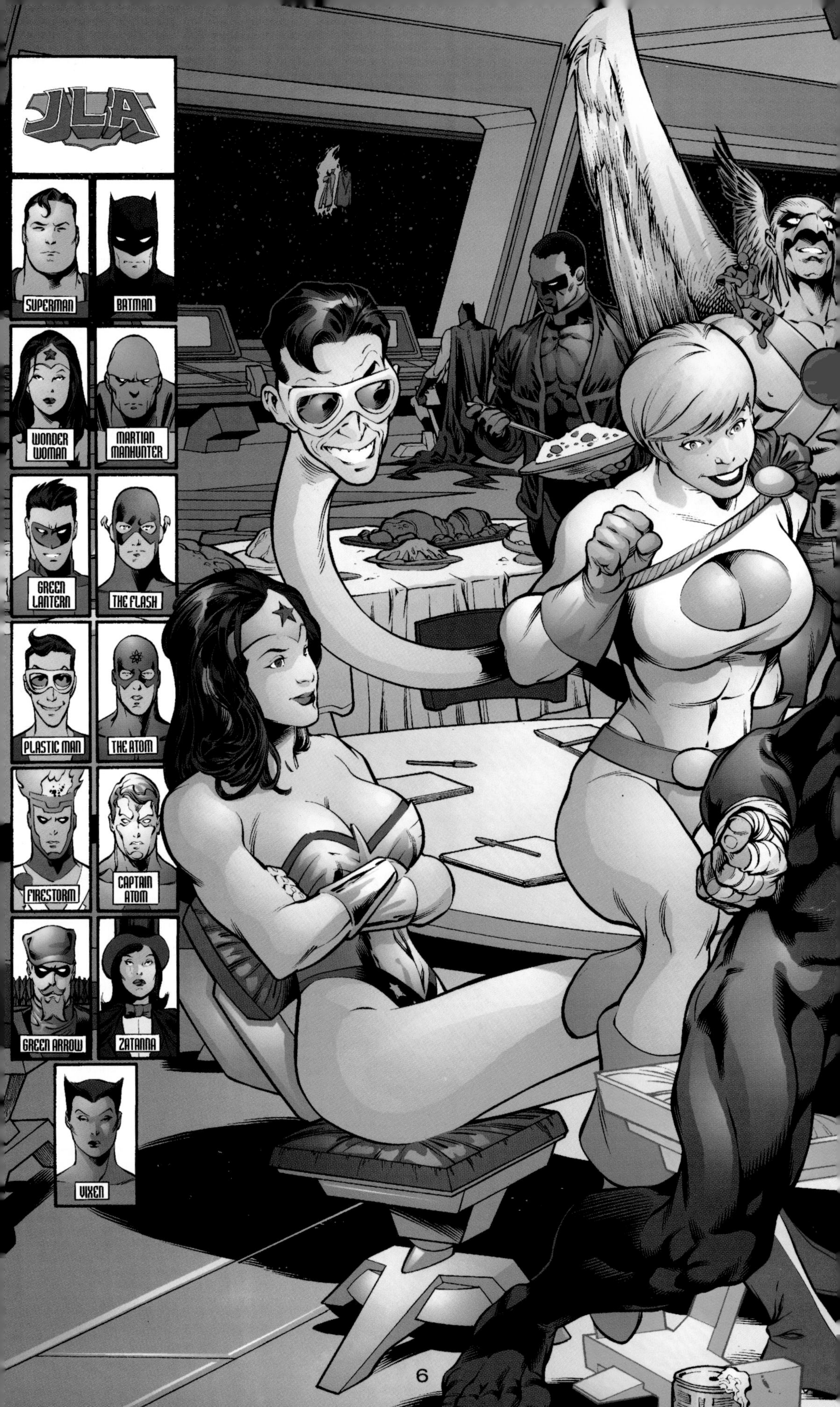
JLA
SUPERMAN
BATMAN
WONDER WOMAN
MARTIAN MANHUNTER
GREEN LANTERN
THE FLASH
PLASTIC MAN
THE ATOM
FIRESTORM
CAPTAIN ATOM
GREEN ARROW
ZATANNA
VIXEN

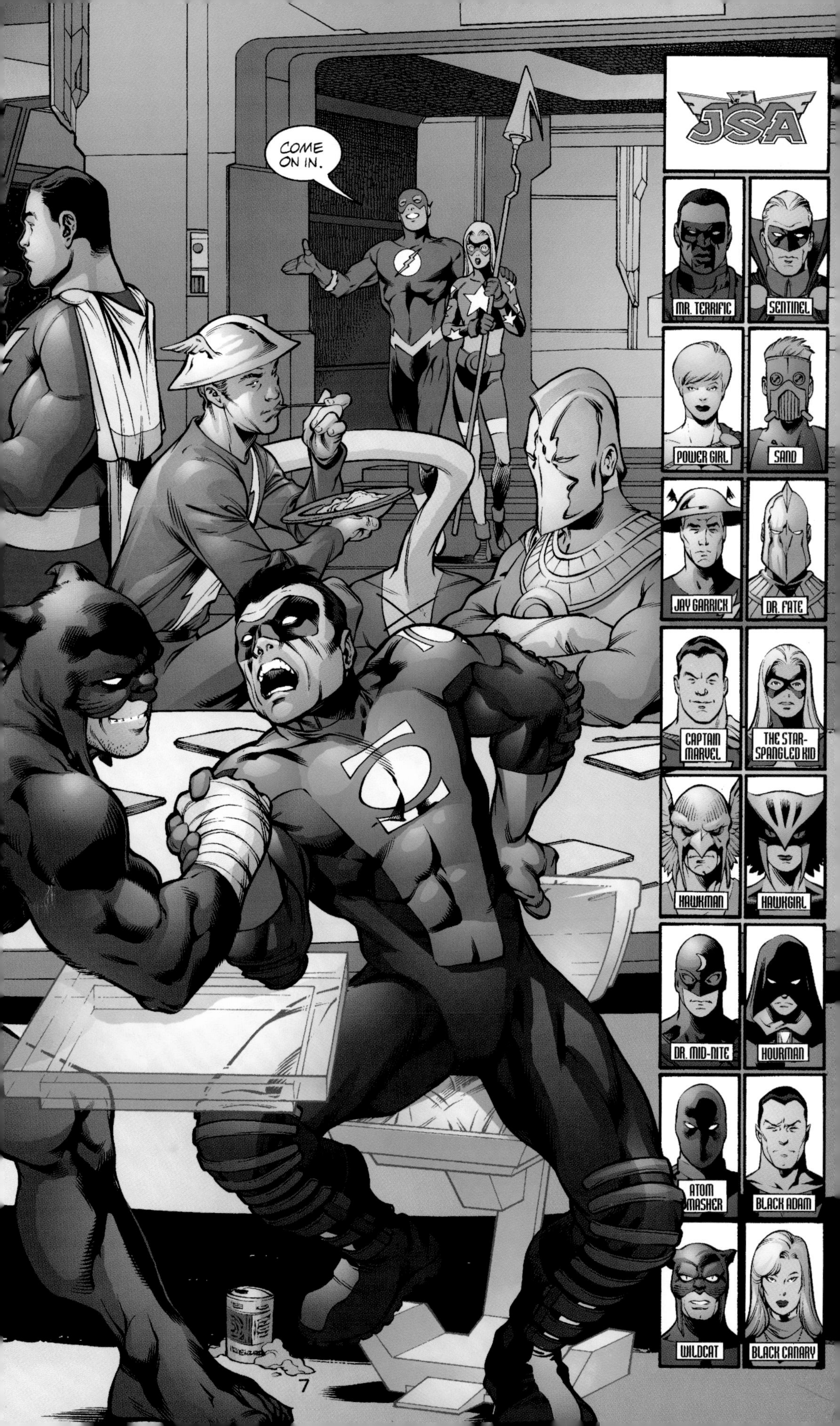
COME ON IN.
JSA
MR. TERRIFIC
SENTINEL
POWER GIRL
SAND
JAY GARRICK
DR. FATE
CAPTAIN MARVEL
THE STAR-SPANGLED KID
HAWKMAN
HAWKGIRL
DR. MID-NITE
HOURMAN
ATOM MASHER
BLACK ADAM
WILDCAT
BLACK CANARY

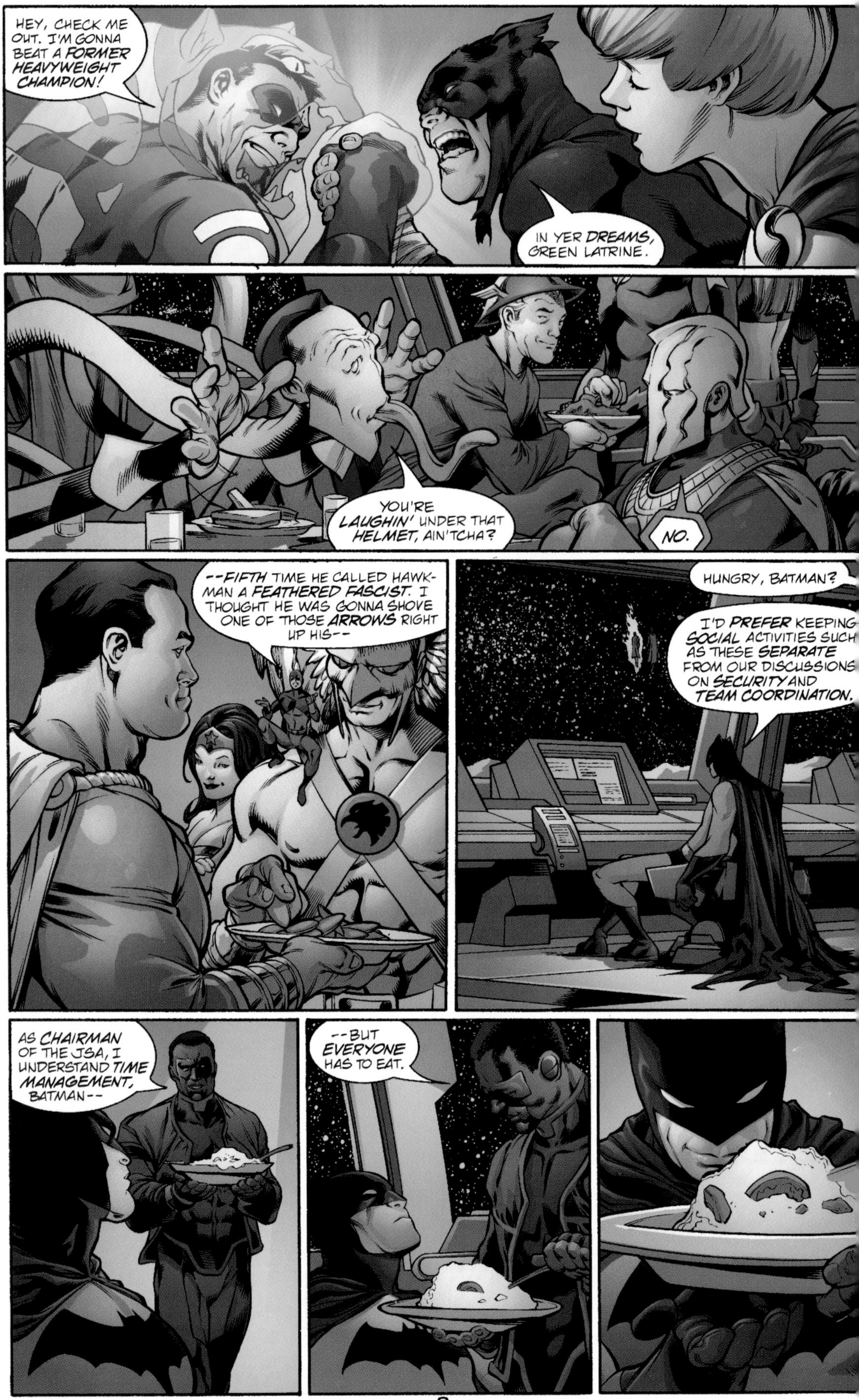
HEY, CHECK ME OUT. I'M GONNA BEAT A FORMER HEAVYWEIGHT CHAMPION!
IN YER DREAMS, GREEN LATRINE.
YOU'RE LAUGHIN' UNDER THAT HELMET, AIN'TCHA?
NO.
--FIFTH TIME HE CALLED HAWK-MAN A FEATHERED FASCIST. I THOUGHT HE WAS GONNA SHOVE ONE OF THOSE ARROWS RIGHT UP HIS--
HUNGRY, BATMAN?
I'D PREFER KEEPING SOCIAL ACTIVITIES SUCH AS THESE SEPARATE FROM OUR DISCUSSIONS ON SECURITY AND TEAM COORDINATION.
AS CHAIRMAN OF THE JSA, I UNDERSTAND TIME MANAGEMENT, BATMAN--
--BUT EVERYONE HAS TO EAT.

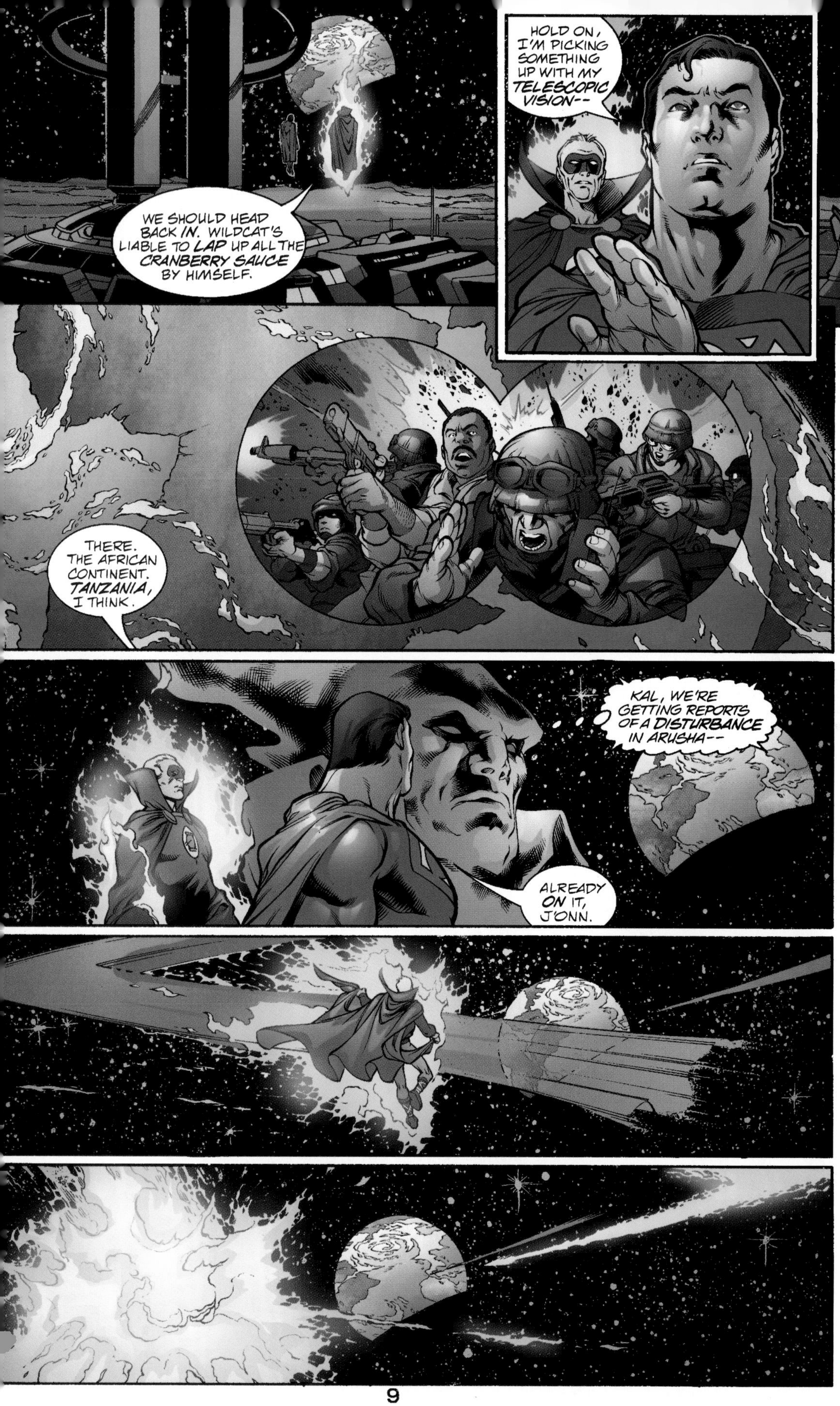
WE SHOULD HEAD BACK IN. WILDCAT'S LIABLE TO LAP UP ALL THE CRANBERRY SAUCE BY HIMSELF.
HOLD ON, I'M PICKING SOMETHING UP WITH MY TELESCOPIC VISION--
THERE. THE AFRICAN CONTINENT. TANZANIA, I THINK.
KAL, WE'RE GETTING REPORTS OF A DISTURBANCE IN ARUSHA--
ALREADY ON IT, J'ONN.

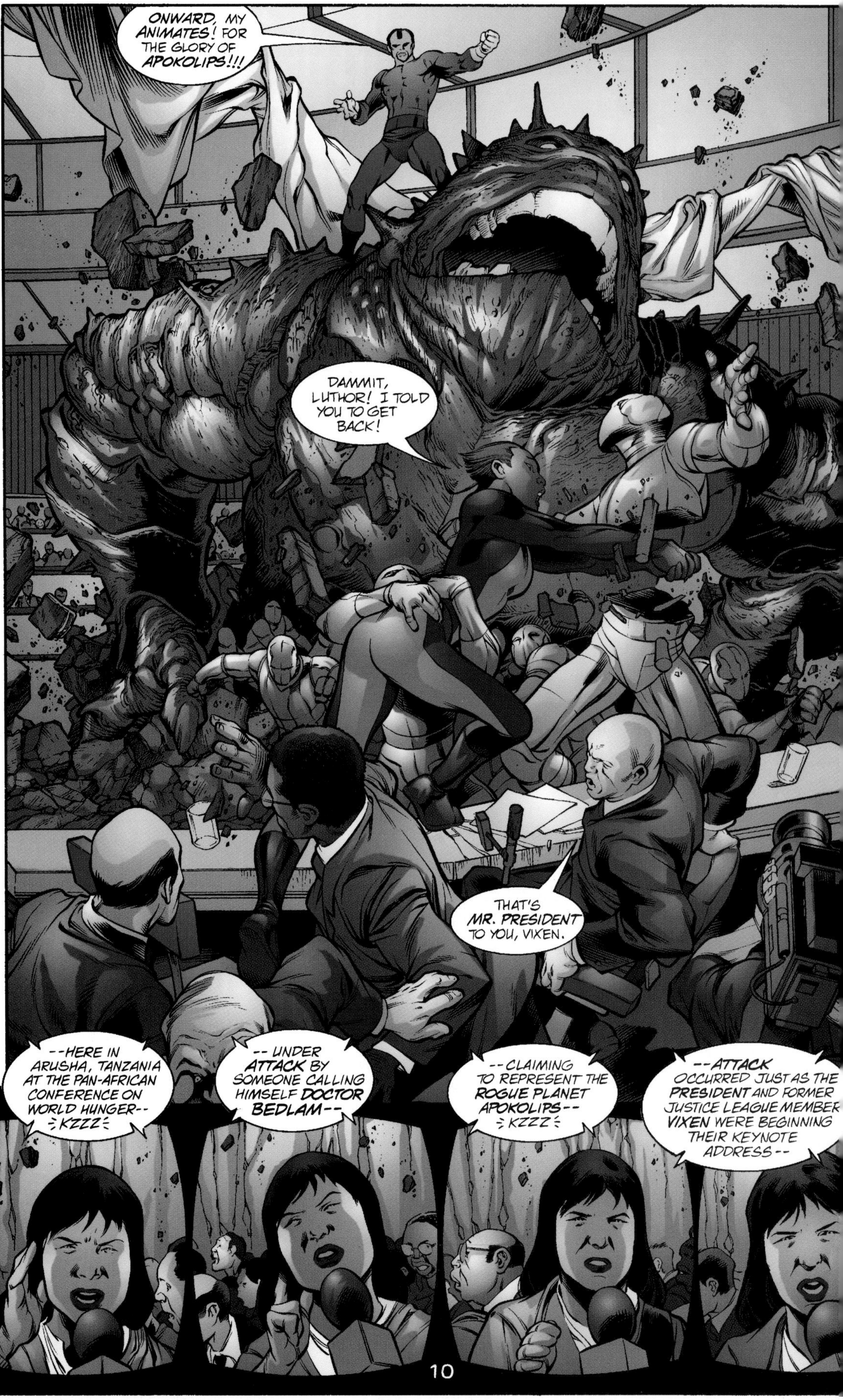
ONWARD, MY ANIMATES! FOR THE GLORY OF APOKOLIPS!!!
DAMMIT, LUTHOR! I TOLD YOU TO GET BACK!
THAT'S MR. PRESIDENT TO YOU, VIXEN.
--HERE IN ARUSHA, TANZANIA AT THE PAN-AFRICAN CONFERENCE ON WORLD HUNGER-- KZZZ
-- UNDER ATTACK BY SOMEONE CALLING HIMSELF DOCTOR BEDLAM--
--CLAIMING TO REPRESENT THE ROGUE PLANET APOKOLIPS-- KZZZ
--ATTACK OCCURRED JUST AS THE PRESIDENT AND FORMER JUSTICE LEAGUE MEMBER VIXEN WERE BEGINNING THEIR KEYNOTE ADDRESS--

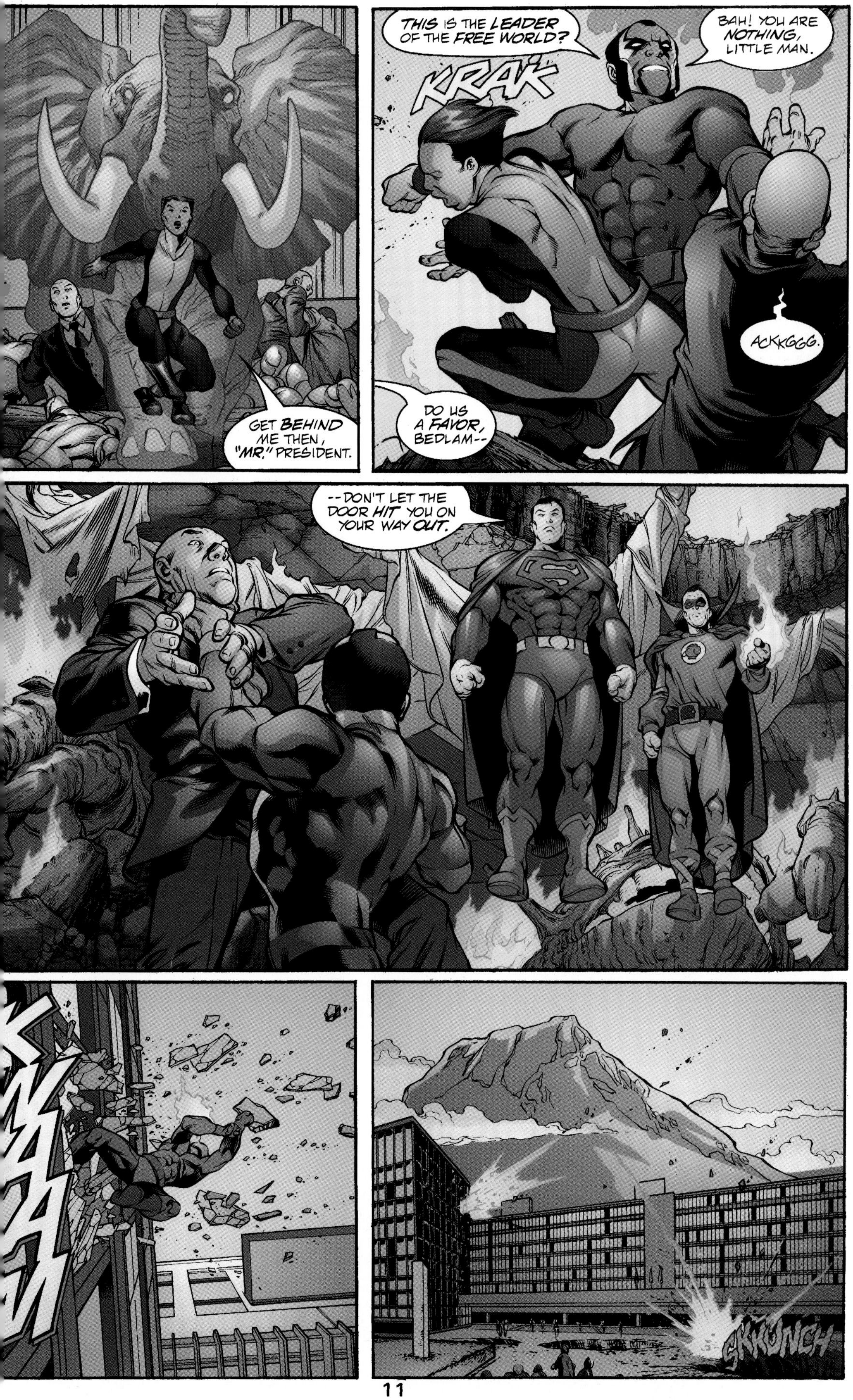
GET BEHIND ME THEN, "MR." PRESIDENT.
THIS IS THE LEADER OF THE FREE WORLD?
BAH! YOU ARE NOTHING, LITTLE MAN.
KRAK
ACKKGGG.
DO US A FAVOR, BEDLAM--
--DON'T LET THE DOOR HIT YOU ON YOUR WAY OUT.
SKKUNCH

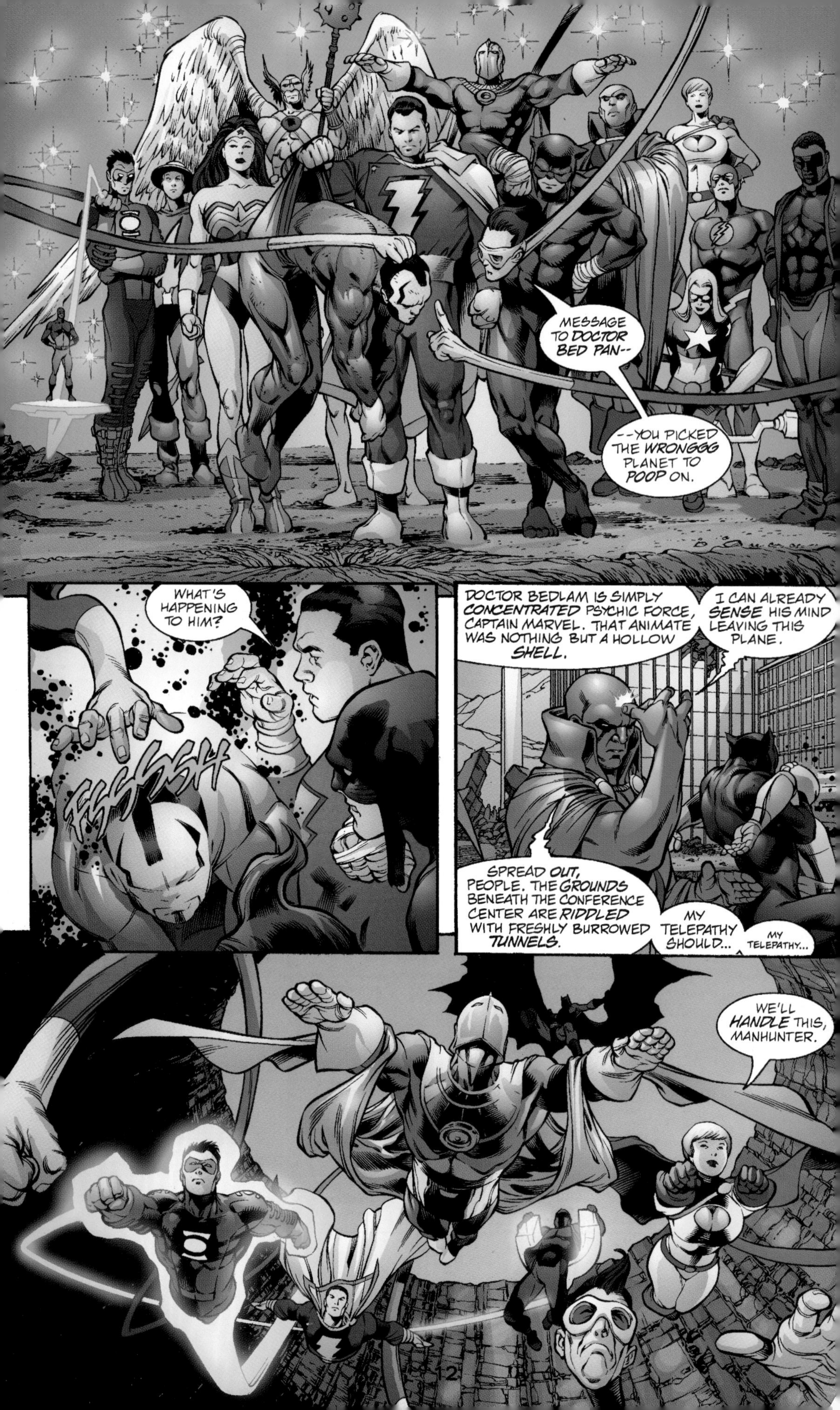
MESSAGE TO DOCTOR BED PAN--
--YOU PICKED THE WRONGGG PLANET TO POOP ON.
WHAT'S HAPPENING TO HIM?
FSSSSH
DOCTOR BEDLAM IS SIMPLY CONCENTRATED PSYCHIC FORCE, CAPTAIN MARVEL. THAT ANIMATE WAS NOTHING BUT A HOLLOW SHELL.
I CAN ALREADY SENSE HIS MIND LEAVING THIS PLANE.
SPREAD OUT, PEOPLE. THE GROUNDS BENEATH THE CONFERENCE CENTER ARE RIDDLED WITH FRESHLY BURROWED TUNNELS.
MY TELEPATHY SHOULD...
MY TELEPATHY...
WE'LL HANDLE THIS, MANHUNTER.

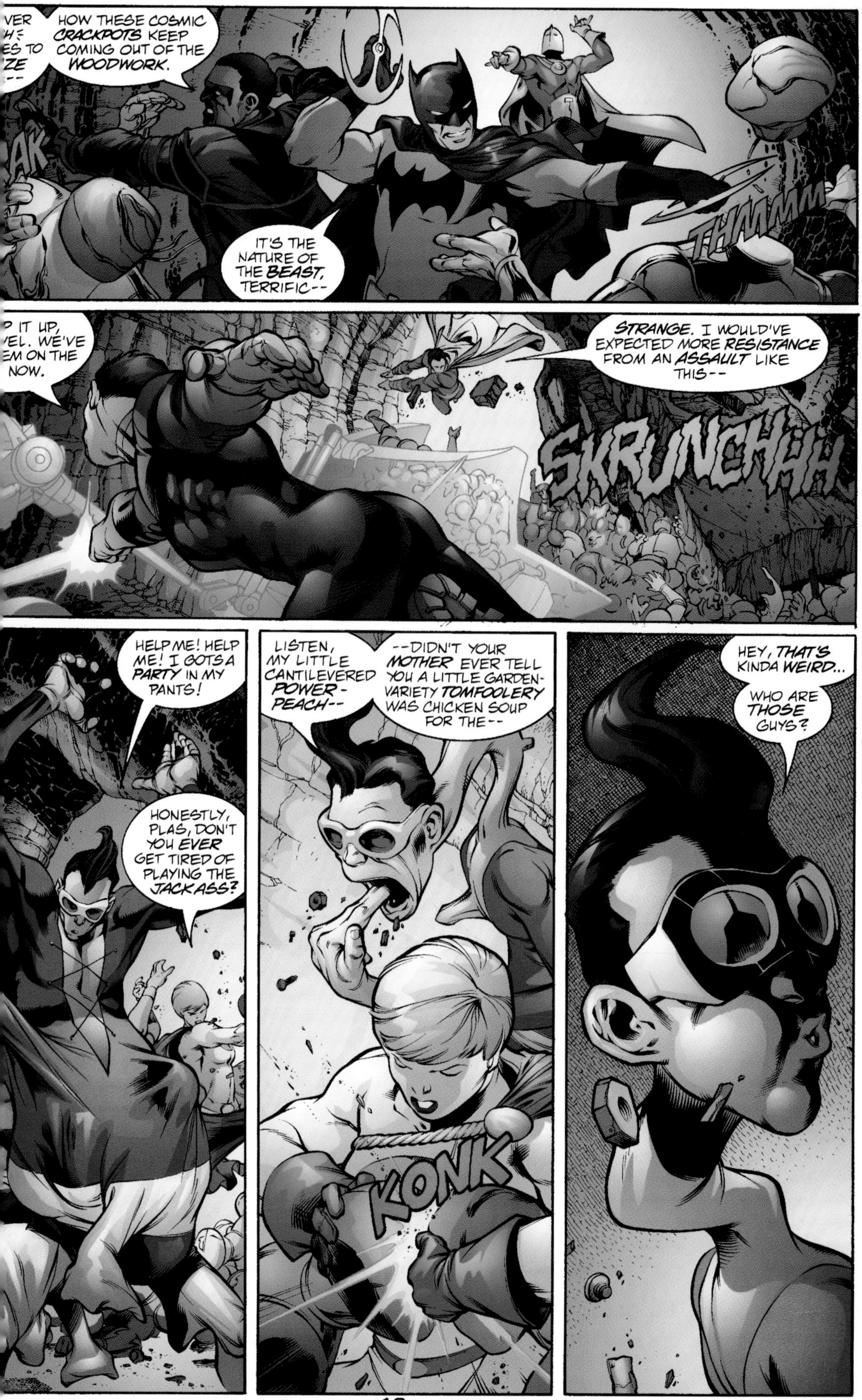
HOW THESE COSMIC CRACKPOTS KEEP COMING OUT OF THE WOODWORK.
IT'S THE NATURE OF THE BEAST, TERRIFIC--
THMMM
STRANGE. I WOULD'VE EXPECTED MORE RESISTANCE FROM AN ASSAULT LIKE THIS--
SKRUNCHHH
HELP ME! HELP ME! I GOTS A PARTY IN MY PANTS!
HONESTLY, PLAS, DON'T YOU EVER GET TIRED OF PLAYING THE JACKASS?
LISTEN, MY LITTLE CANTILEVERED POWER-PEACH--
--DIDN'T YOUR MOTHER EVER TELL YOU A LITTLE GARDEN-VARIETY TOMFOOLERY WAS CHICKEN SOUP FOR THE--
KONK
HEY, THAT'S KINDA WEIRD...
WHO ARE THOSE GUYS?

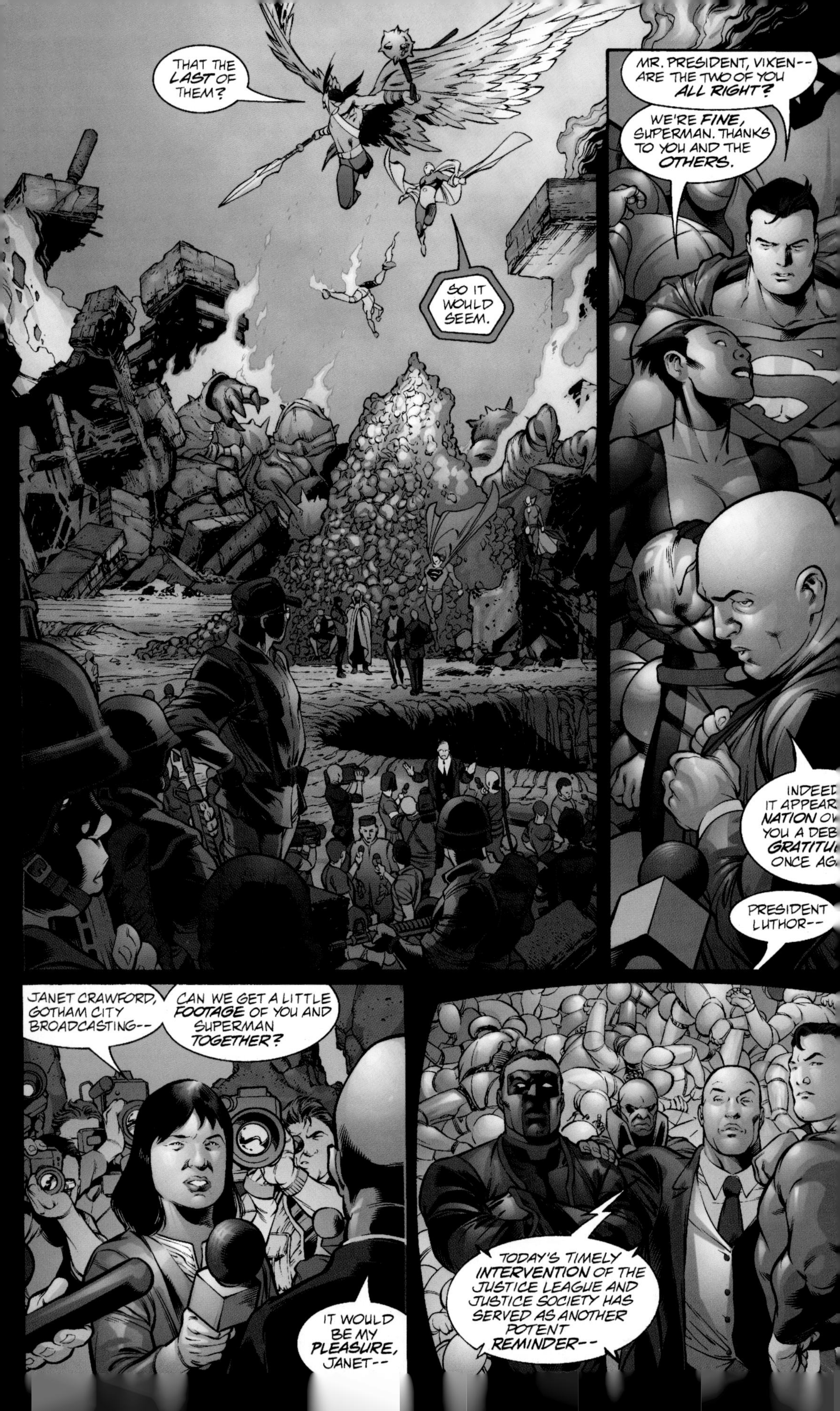
THAT THE LAST OF THEM?
SO IT WOULD SEEM.
MR. PRESIDENT, VIXEN-- ARE THE TWO OF YOU ALL RIGHT?
WE'RE FINE, SUPERMAN. THANKS TO YOU AND THE OTHERS.
INDEED IT APPEAR NATION O YOU A DEB GRATITU ONCE AG
PRESIDENT LUTHOR--
JANET CRAWFORD, GOTHAM CITY BROADCASTING--
CAN WE GET A LITTLE FOOTAGE OF YOU AND SUPERMAN TOGETHER?
IT WOULD BE MY PLEASURE, JANET--
TODAY'S TIMELY INTERVENTION OF THE JUSTICE LEAGUE AND JUSTICE SOCIETY HAS SERVED AS ANOTHER POTENT REMINDER--

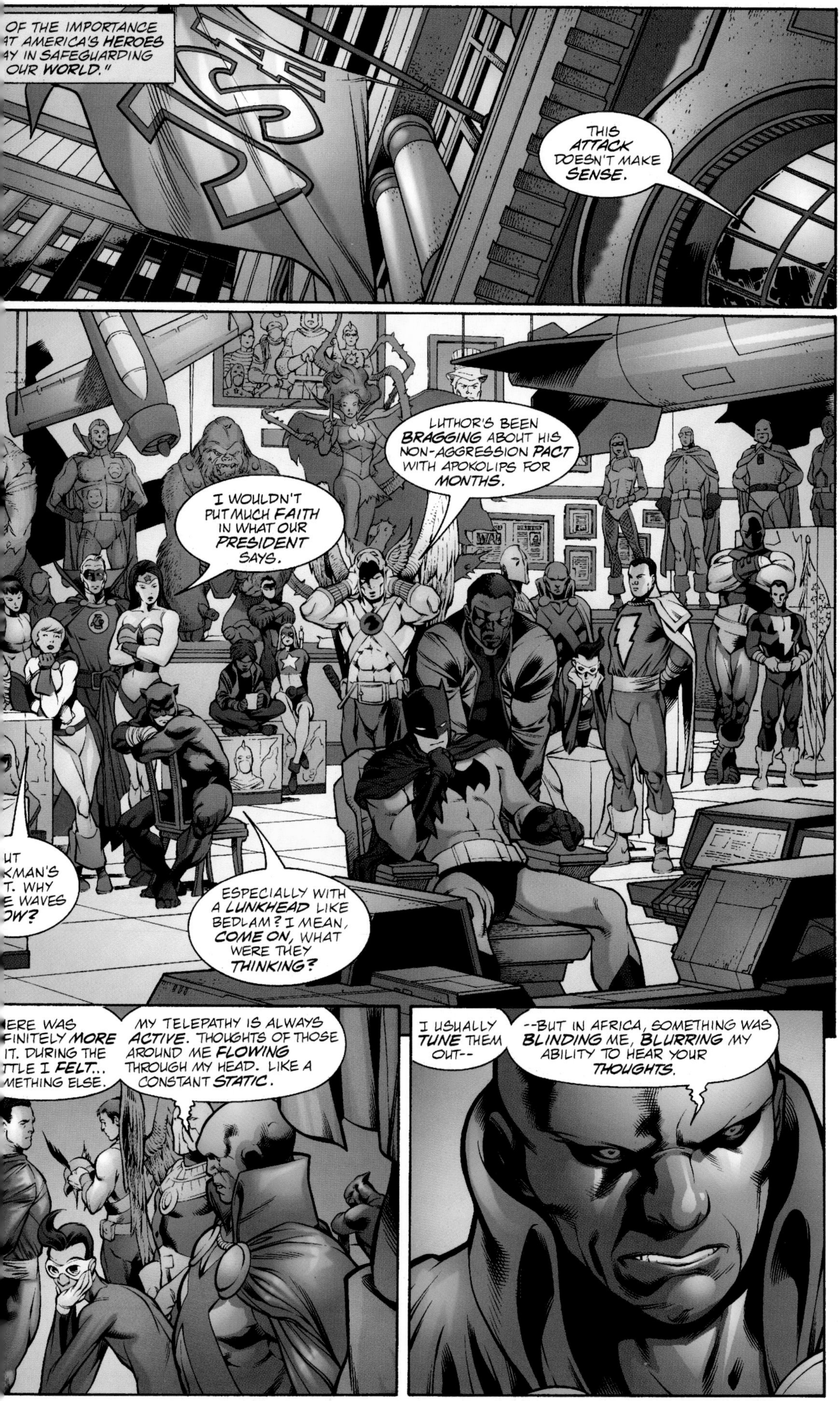

OF THE IMPORTANCE AT AMERICA'S HEROES AY IN SAFEGUARDING OUR WORLD."
THIS ATTACK DOESN'T MAKE SENSE.
I WOULDN'T PUT MUCH FAITH IN WHAT OUR PRESIDENT SAYS.
LUTHOR'S BEEN BRAGGING ABOUT HIS NON-AGGRESSION PACT WITH APOKOLIPS FOR MONTHS.
UT KMAN'S T. WHY E WAVES OW?
ESPECIALLY WITH A LUNKHEAD LIKE BEDLAM? I MEAN, COME ON, WHAT WERE THEY THINKING?
ERE WAS FINITELY MORE IT. DURING THE TTLE I FELT... METHING ELSE.
MY TELEPATHY IS ALWAYS ACTIVE. THOUGHTS OF THOSE AROUND ME FLOWING THROUGH MY HEAD. LIKE A CONSTANT STATIC.
I USUALLY TUNE THEM OUT--
--BUT IN AFRICA, SOMETHING WAS BLINDING ME, BLURRING MY ABILITY TO HEAR YOUR THOUGHTS.

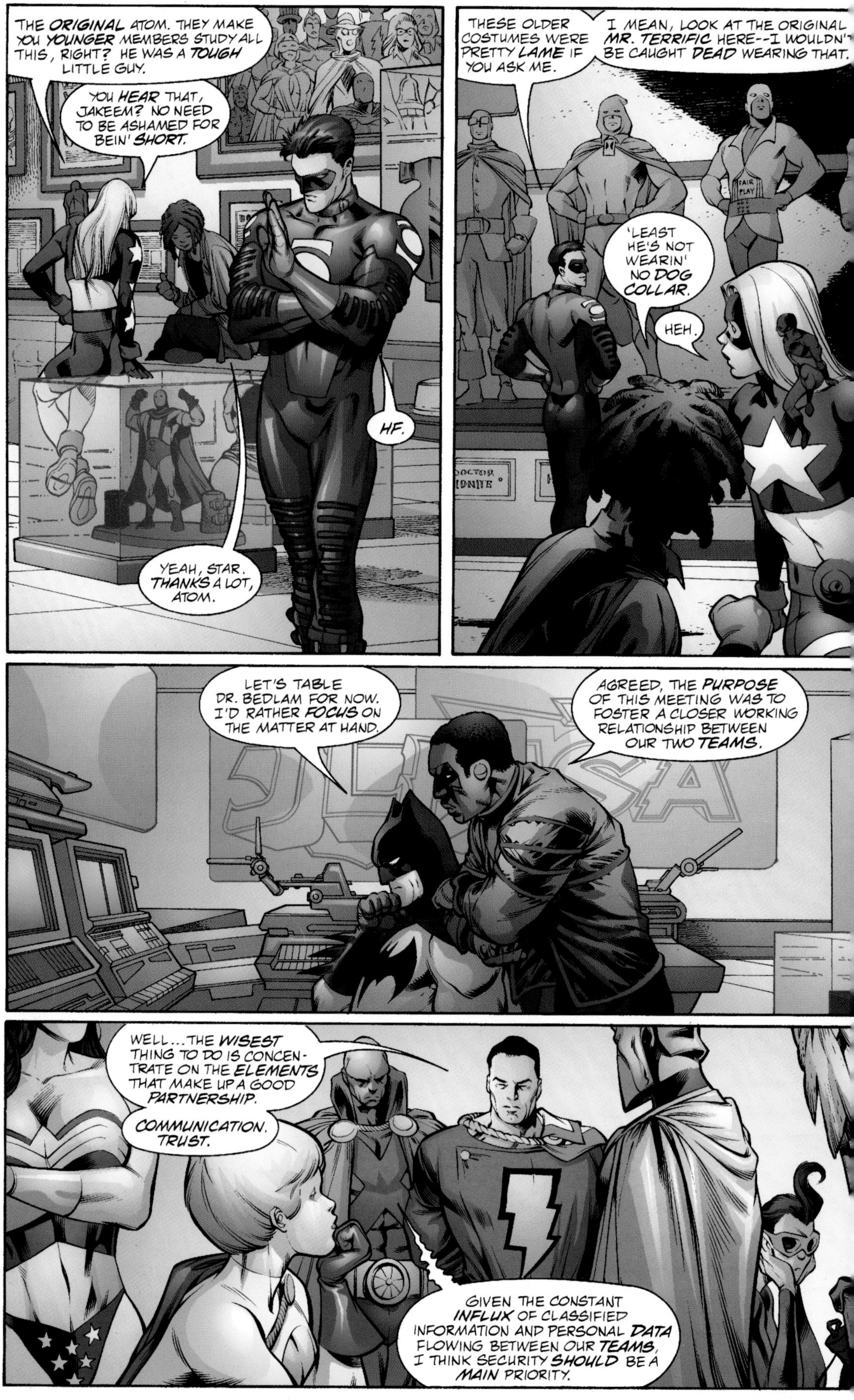
THE ORIGINAL ATOM. THEY MAKE YOU YOUNGER MEMBERS STUDY ALL THIS, RIGHT? HE WAS A TOUGH LITTLE GUY.
YOU HEAR THAT, JAKEEM? NO NEED TO BE ASHAMED FOR BEIN' SHORT.
HF.
YEAH, STAR. THANKS A LOT, ATOM.
THESE OLDER COSTUMES WERE PRETTY LAME IF YOU ASK ME.
I MEAN, LOOK AT THE ORIGINAL MR. TERRIFIC HERE--I WOULDN'T BE CAUGHT DEAD WEARING THAT.
'LEAST HE'S NOT WEARIN' NO DOG COLLAR.
HEH.
FAIR PLAY
DOCTOR MIDNITE
LET'S TABLE DR. BEDLAM FOR NOW. I'D RATHER FOCUS ON THE MATTER AT HAND.
AGREED, THE PURPOSE OF THIS MEETING WAS TO FOSTER A CLOSER WORKING RELATIONSHIP BETWEEN OUR TWO TEAMS.
WELL... THE WISEST THING TO DO IS CONCENTRATE ON THE ELEMENTS THAT MAKE UP A GOOD PARTNERSHIP.
COMMUNICATION. TRUST.
GIVEN THE CONSTANT INFLUX OF CLASSIFIED INFORMATION AND PERSONAL DATA FLOWING BETWEEN OUR TEAMS, I THINK SECURITY SHOULD BE A MAIN PRIORITY.

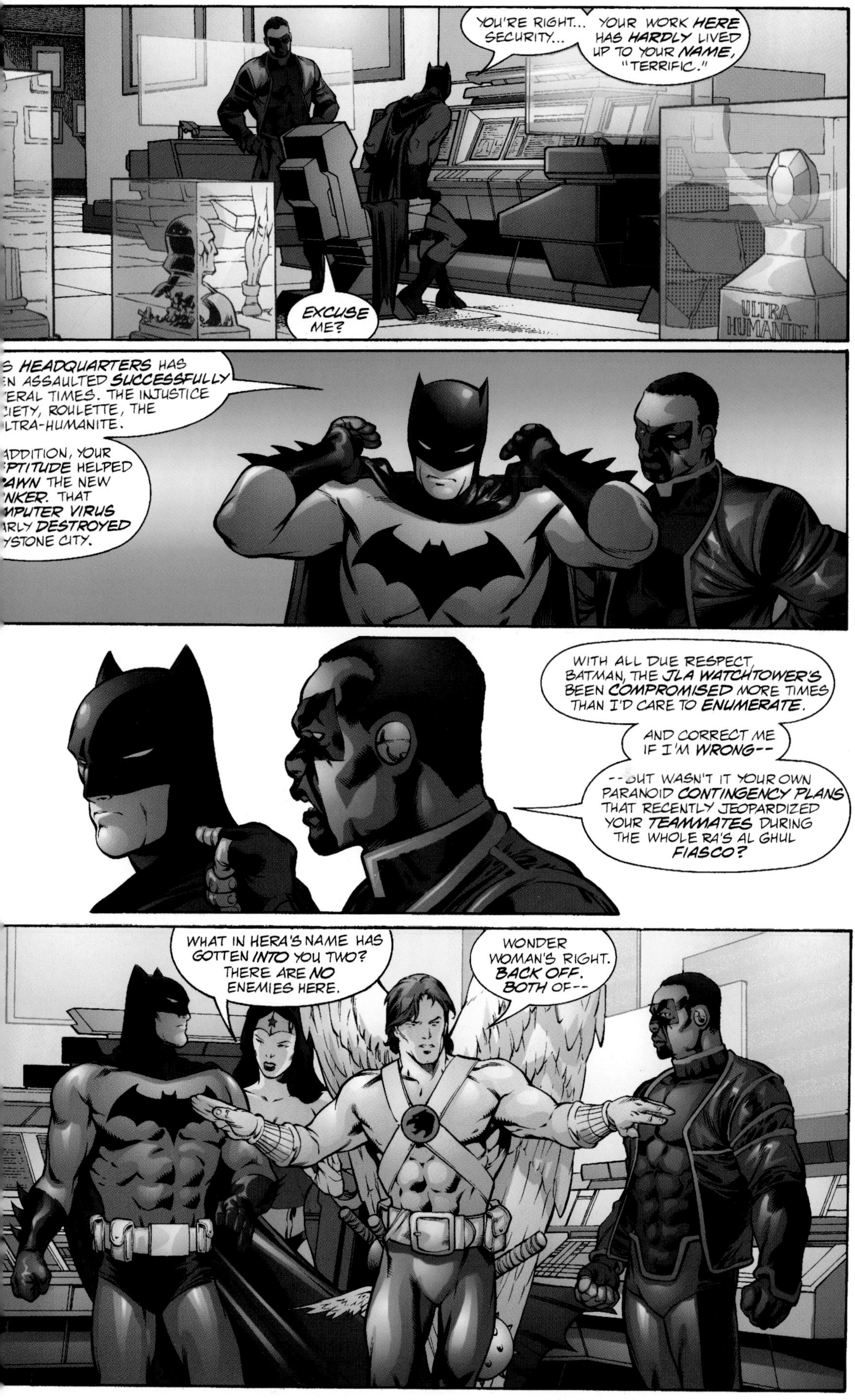

YOU'RE RIGHT... SECURITY...
YOUR WORK HERE HAS HARDLY LIVED UP TO YOUR NAME, "TERRIFIC."
EXCUSE ME?
ULTRA HUMANITE
S HEADQUARTERS HAS EN ASSAULTED SUCCESSFULLY ERAL TIMES. THE INJUSTICE CIETY, ROULETTE, THE LTRA-HUMANITE.
ADDITION, YOUR PTITUDE HELPED AWN THE NEW NKER. THAT MPUTER VIRUS ARLY DESTROYED YSTONE CITY.
WITH ALL DUE RESPECT, BATMAN, THE JLA WATCHTOWER'S BEEN COMPROMISED MORE TIMES THAN I'D CARE TO ENUMERATE.
AND CORRECT ME IF I'M WRONG--
--BUT WASN'T IT YOUR OWN PARANOID CONTINGENCY PLANS THAT RECENTLY JEOPARDIZED YOUR TEAMMATES DURING THE WHOLE RA'S AL GHUL FIASCO?
WHAT IN HERA'S NAME HAS GOTTEN INTO YOU TWO? THERE ARE NO ENEMIES HERE.
WONDER WOMAN'S RIGHT. BACK OFF. BOTH OF--

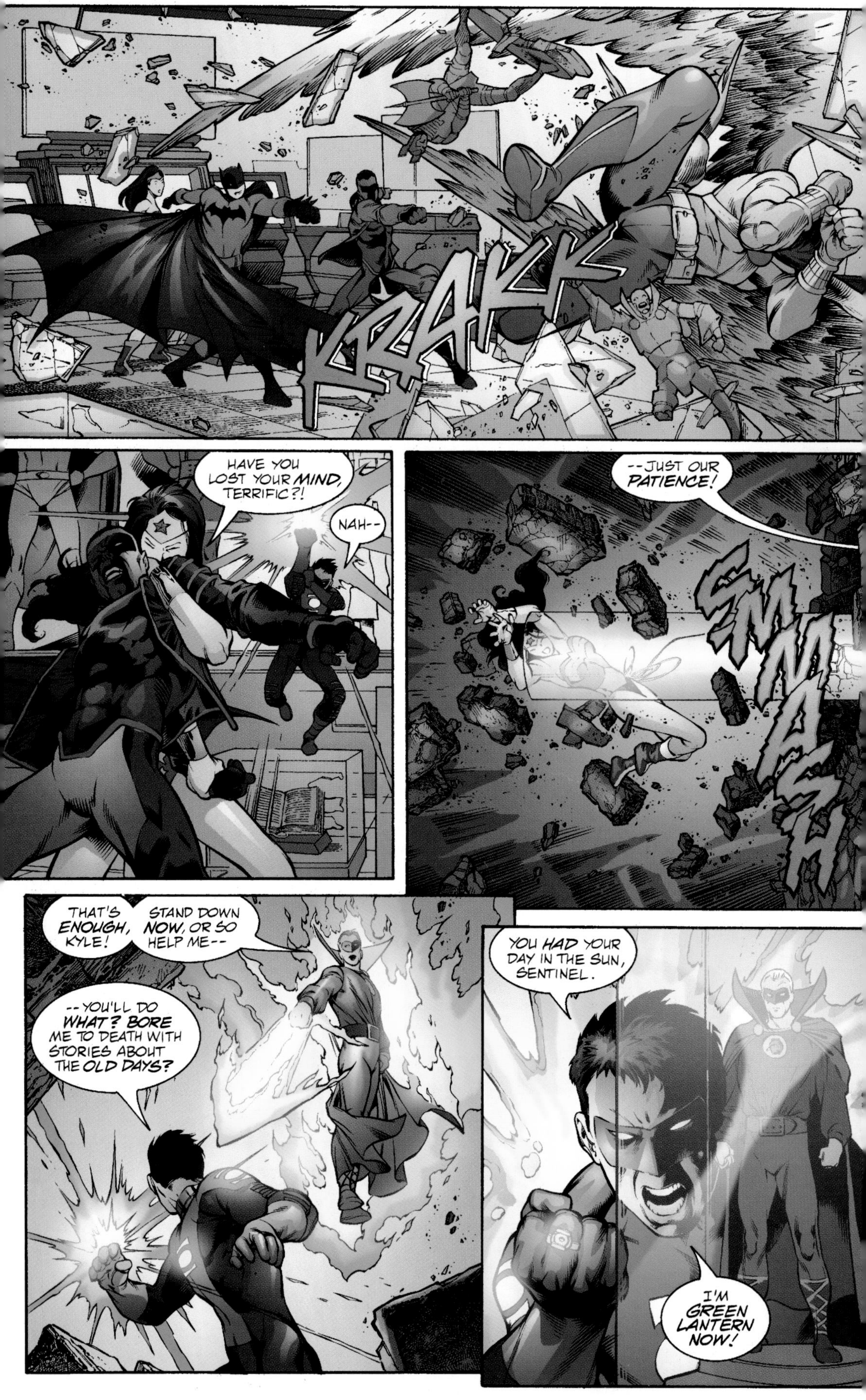
KRAKK
HAVE YOU LOST YOUR MIND, TERRIFIC?!
NAH--
--JUST OUR PATIENCE!
SMMASH
THAT'S ENOUGH, KYLE!
STAND DOWN NOW, OR SO HELP ME--
--YOU'LL DO WHAT? BORE ME TO DEATH WITH STORIES ABOUT THE OLD DAYS?
YOU HAD YOUR DAY IN THE SUN, SENTINEL.
I'M GREEN LANTERN NOW!

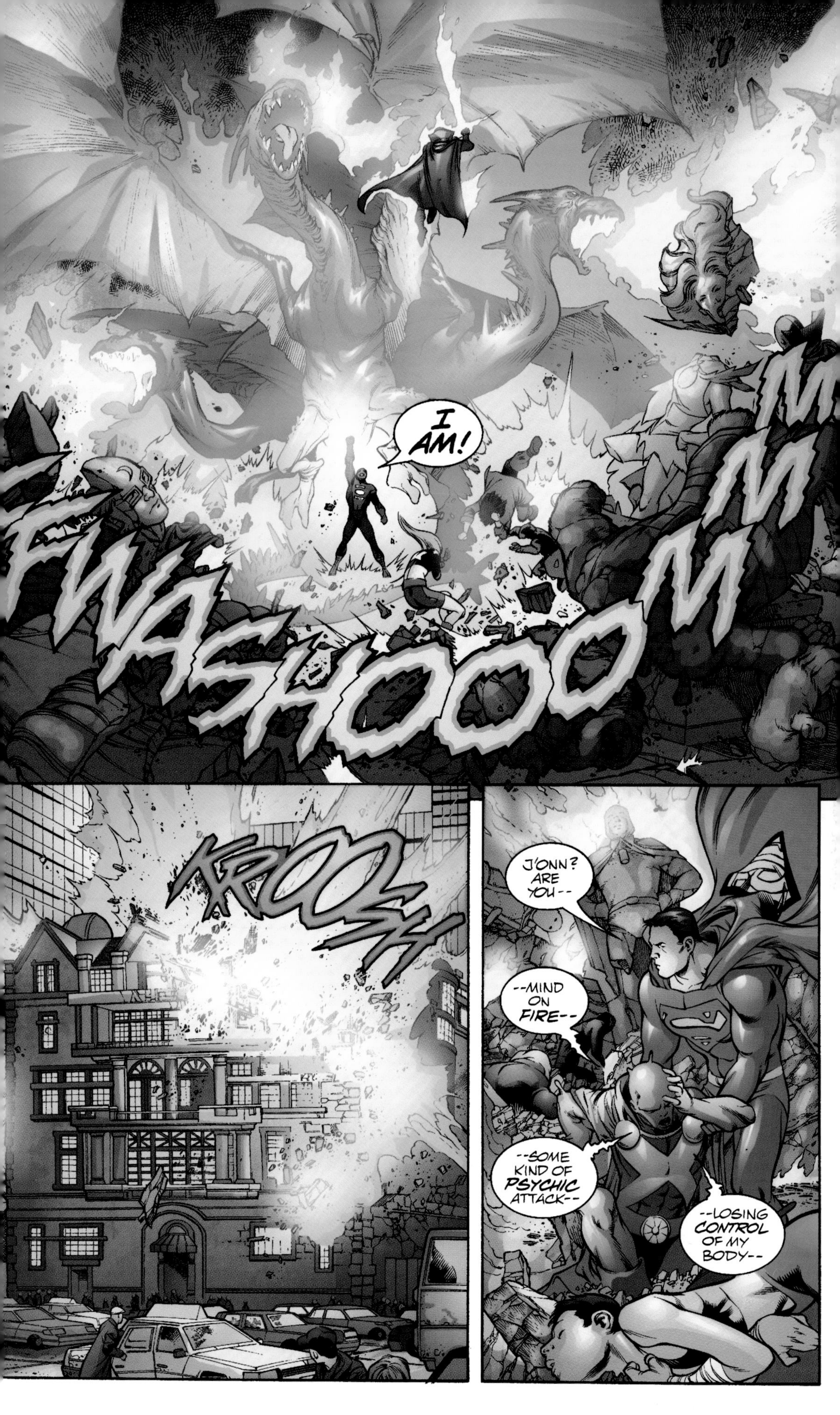
I AM!
FWASHOOOMMMM
KROOSH
J'ONN? ARE YOU--
--MIND ON FIRE--
--SOME KIND OF PSYCHIC ATTACK--
--LOSING CONTROL OF MY BODY--

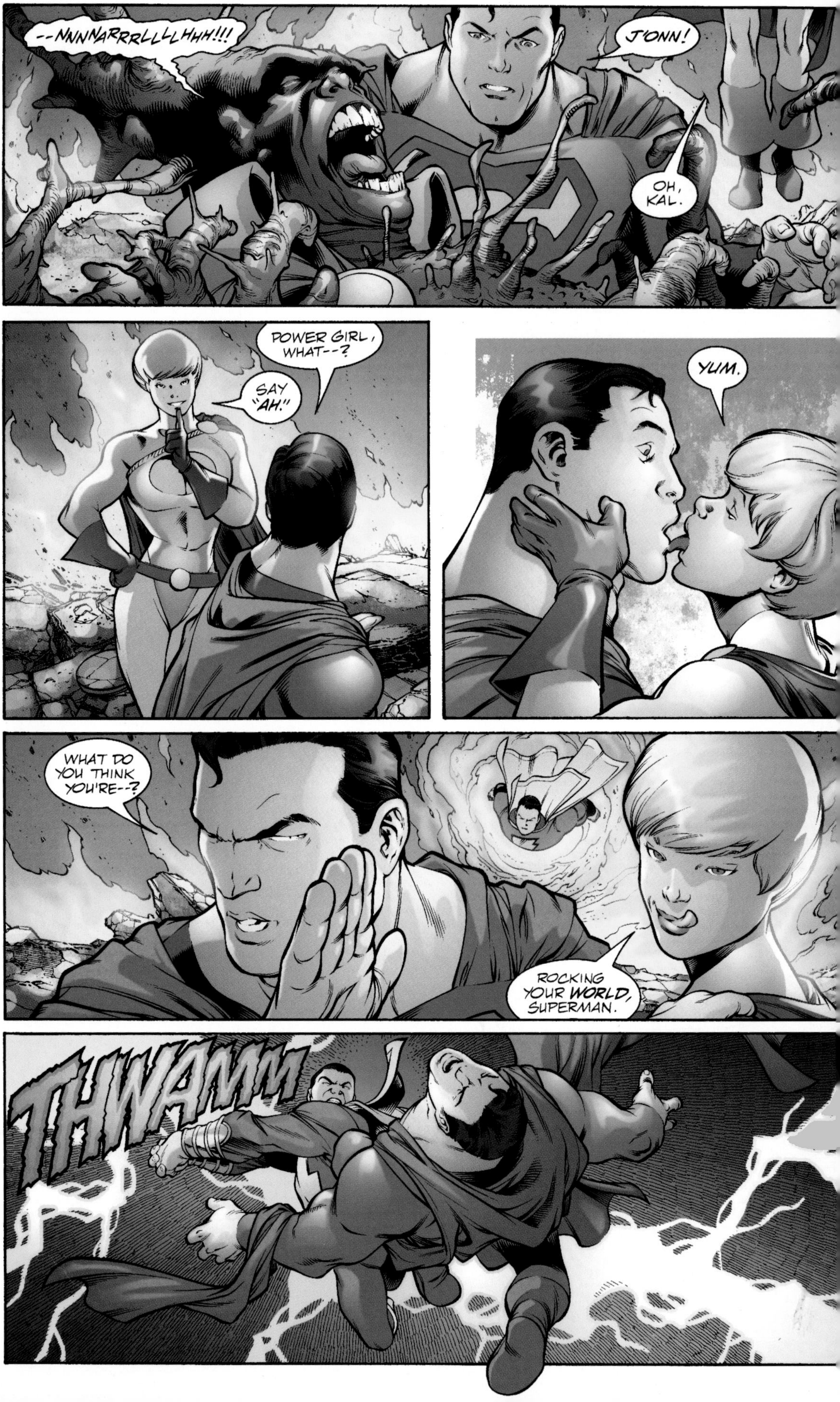
--NNNNARRRLLLLHHH!!!
J'ONN!
OH, KAL.
POWER GIRL, WHAT--?
SAY "AH."
YUM.
WHAT DO YOU THINK YOU'RE--?
ROCKING YOUR WORLD, SUPERMAN.
THWAMM

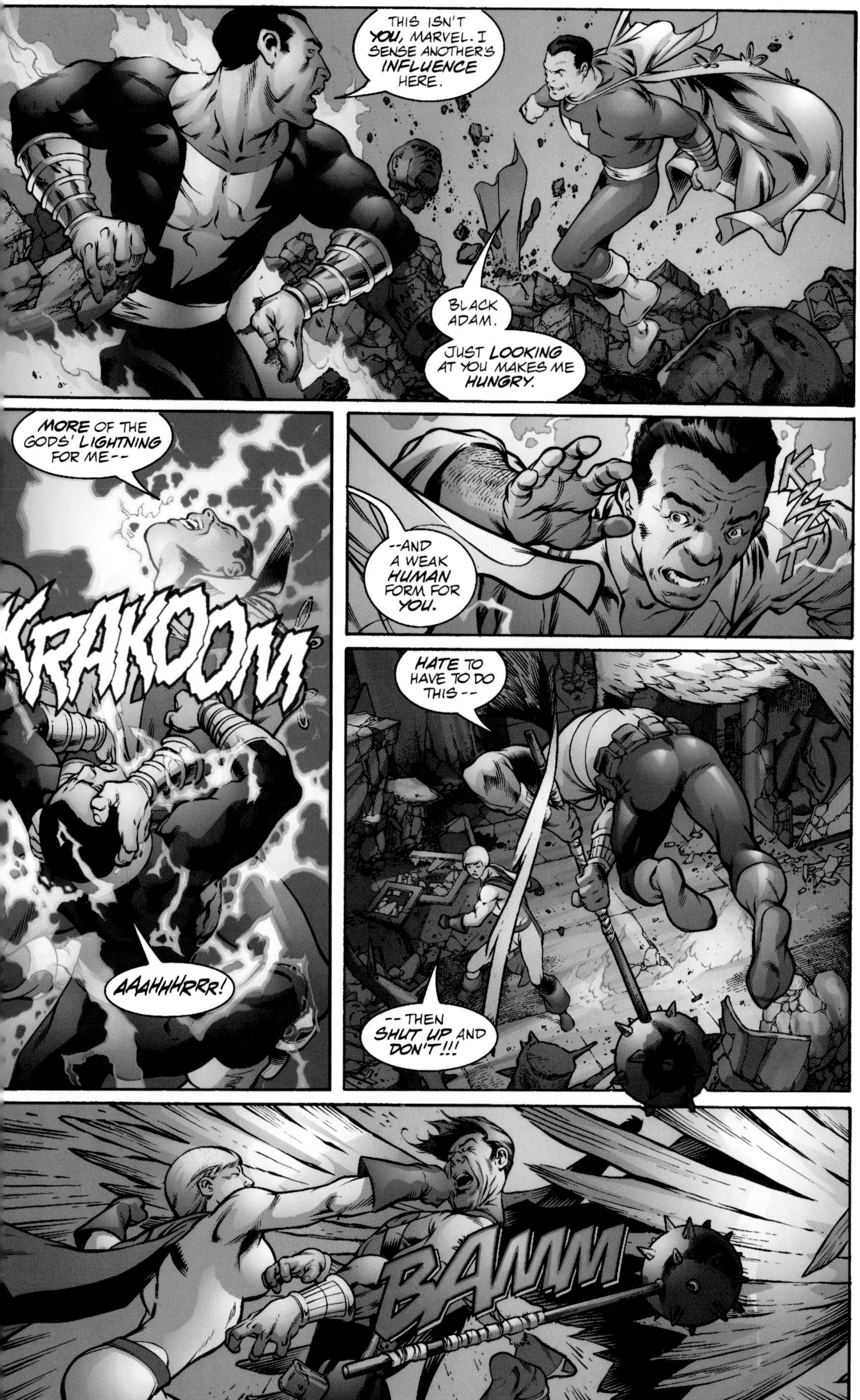
THIS ISN'T YOU, MARVEL. I SENSE ANOTHER'S INFLUENCE HERE.
BLACK ADAM.
JUST LOOKING AT YOU MAKES ME HUNGRY.
MORE OF THE GODS' LIGHTNING FOR ME--
KRAKOOM
AAAHHHRRR!
--AND A WEAK HUMAN FORM FOR YOU.
KWAT
HATE TO HAVE TO DO THIS--
--THEN SHUT UP AND DON'T!!!
BAMM

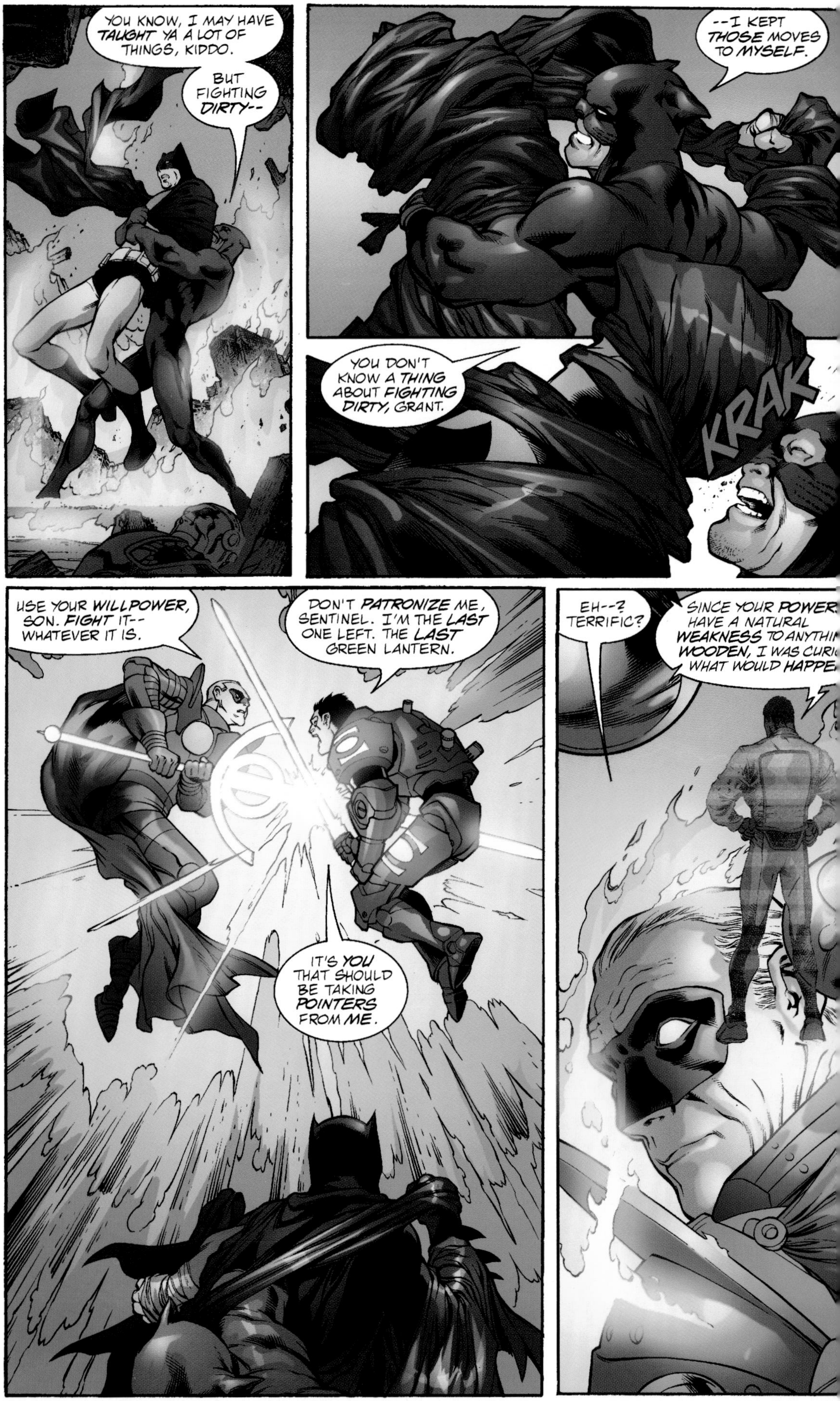
YOU KNOW, I MAY HAVE TAUGHT YA A LOT OF THINGS, KIDDO.
BUT FIGHTING DIRTY--
--I KEPT THOSE MOVES TO MYSELF.
YOU DON'T KNOW A THING ABOUT FIGHTING DIRTY, GRANT.
KRAK
USE YOUR WILLPOWER, SON. FIGHT IT--WHATEVER IT IS.
DON'T PATRONIZE ME, SENTINEL. I'M THE LAST ONE LEFT. THE LAST GREEN LANTERN.
IT'S YOU THAT SHOULD BE TAKING POINTERS FROM ME.
EH--? TERRIFIC?

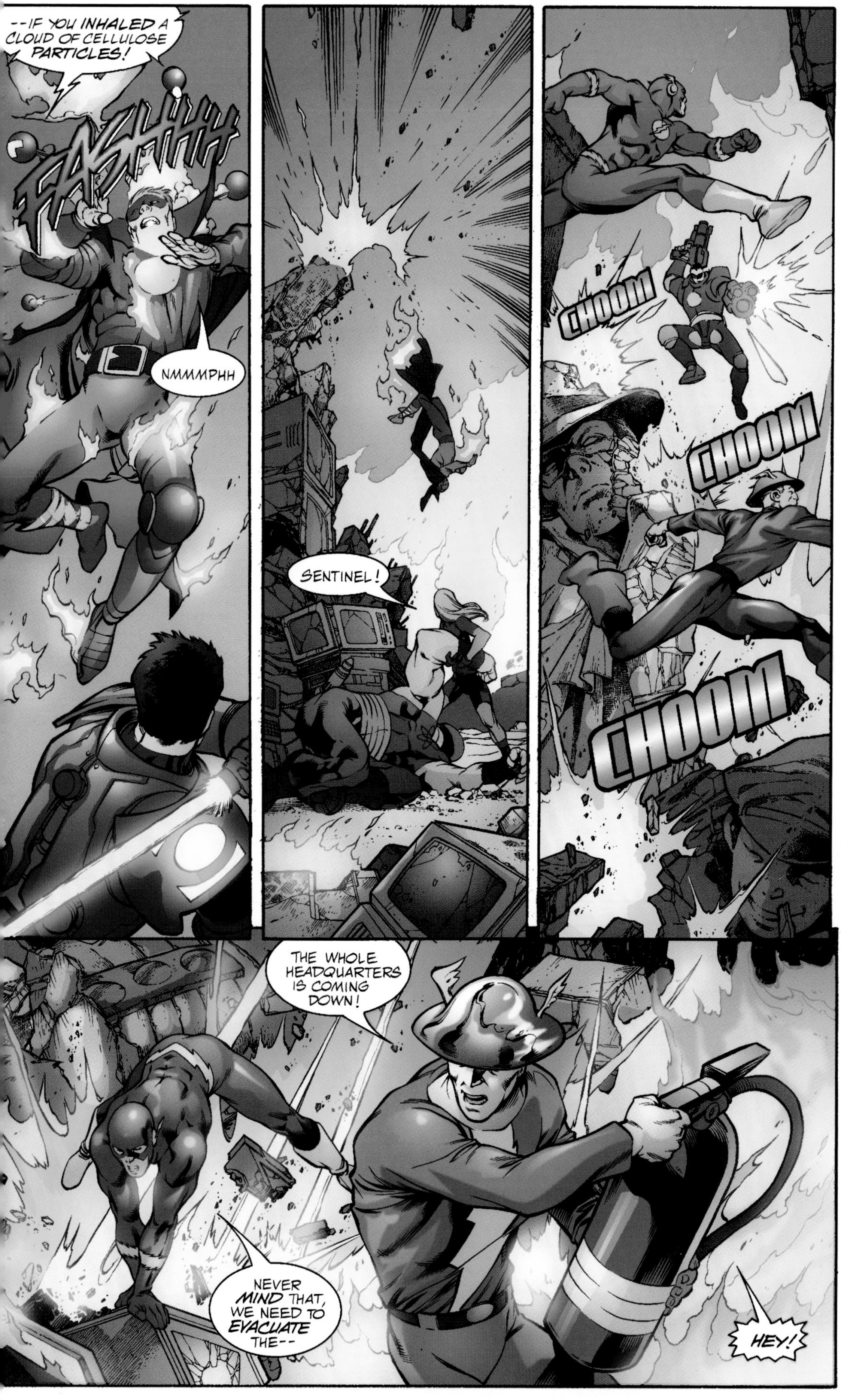
--IF YOU INHALED A CLOUD OF CELLULOSE PARTICLES!
FASHHH
NMMMPHH
SENTINEL!
CHOOM
CHOOM
CHOOM
THE WHOLE HEADQUARTERS IS COMING DOWN!
NEVER MIND THAT, WE NEED TO EVACUATE THE--
HEY!

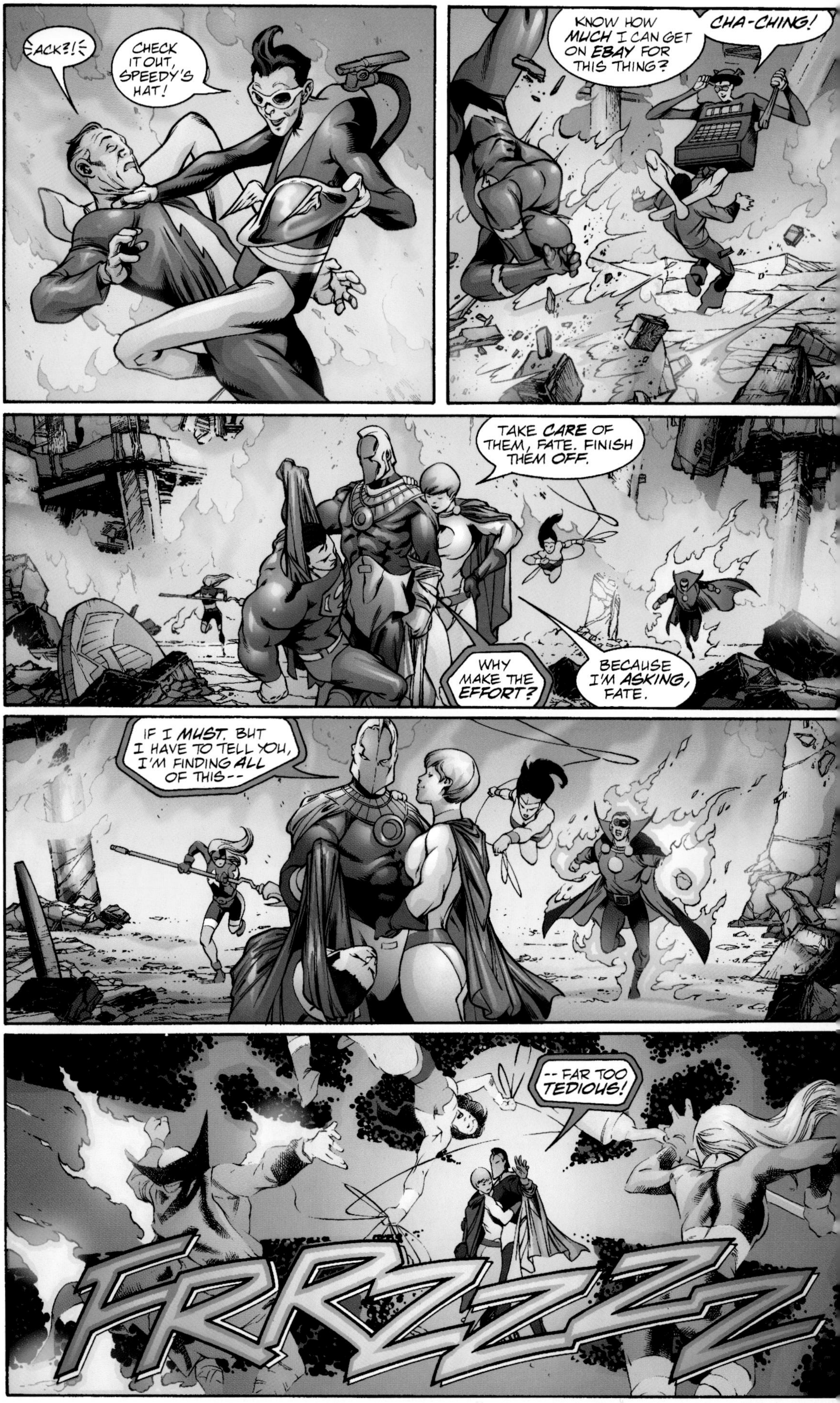
ACK?!
CHECK IT OUT, SPEEDY'S HAT!
KNOW HOW MUCH I CAN GET ON EBAY FOR THIS THING?
CHA-CHING!
TAKE CARE OF THEM, FATE. FINISH THEM OFF.
WHY MAKE THE EFFORT?
BECAUSE I'M ASKING, FATE.
IF I MUST. BUT I HAVE TO TELL YOU, I'M FINDING ALL OF THIS--
--FAR TOO TEDIOUS!
FRRZZZZ

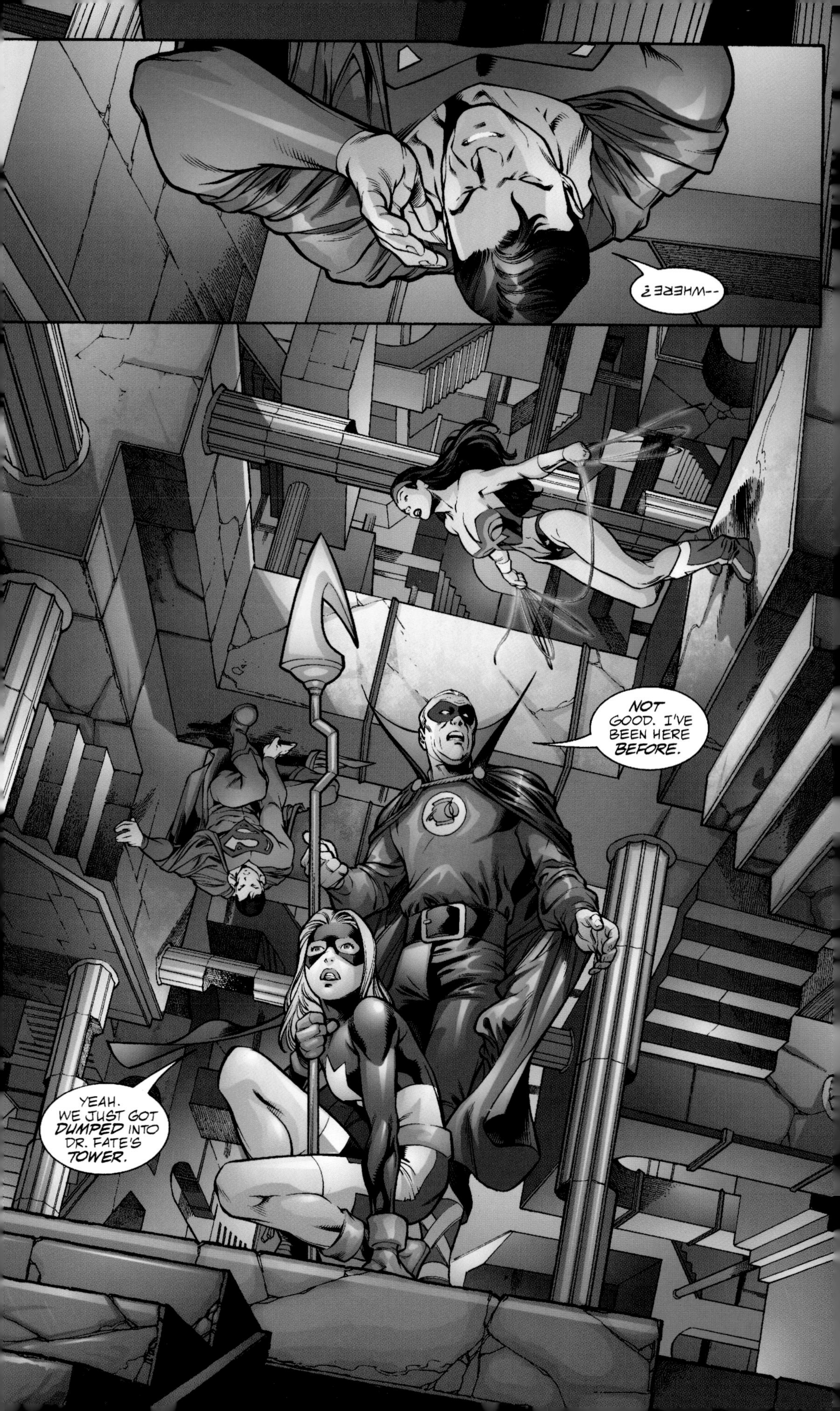
--WHERE?
NOT GOOD. I'VE BEEN HERE BEFORE.
YEAH. WE JUST GOT DUMPED INTO DR. FATE'S TOWER.

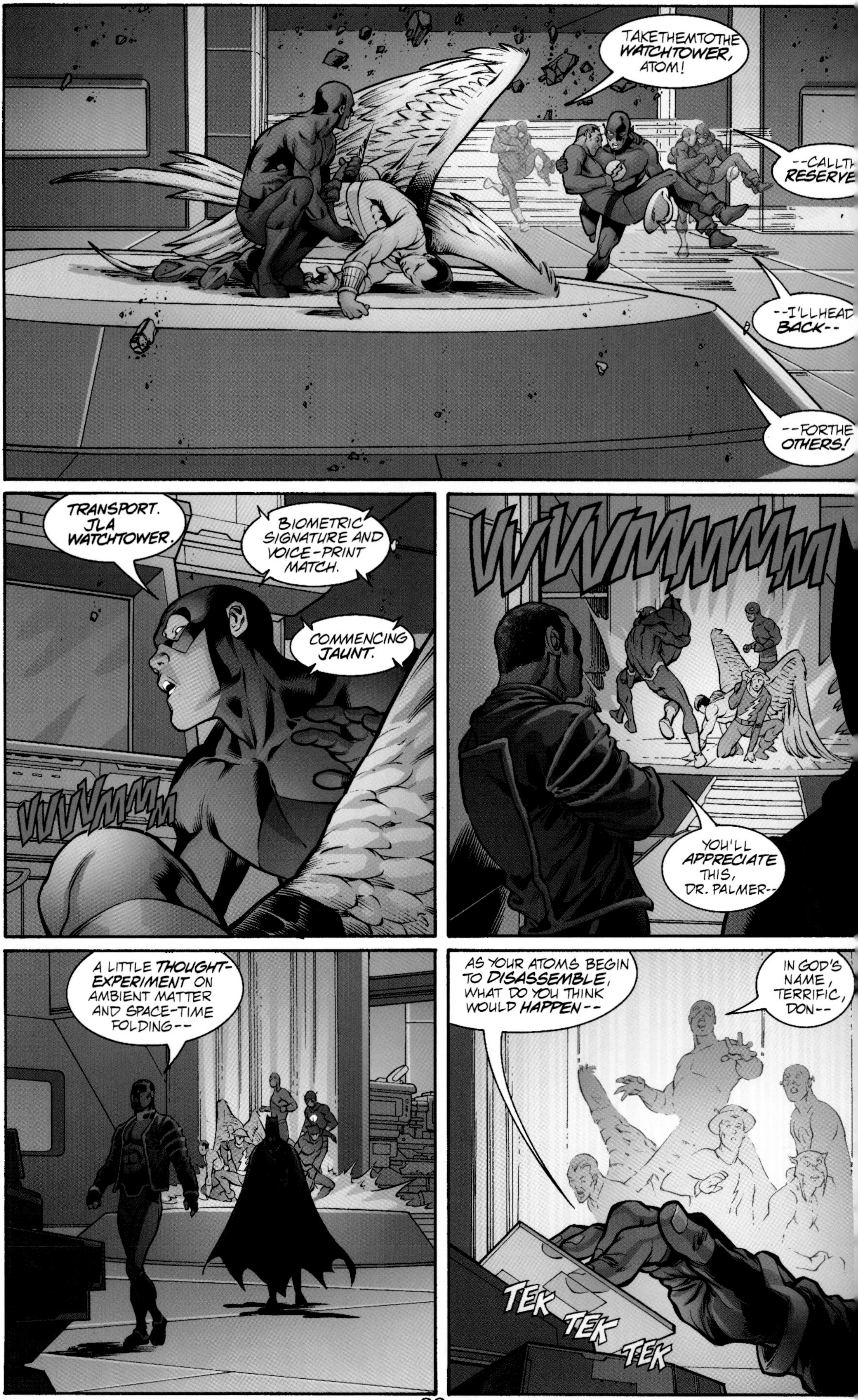
TAKE THEM TO THE WATCHTOWER, ATOM!
--CALL TH RESERVE
--I'LL HEAD BACK--
--FOR THE OTHERS!
TRANSPORT. JLA WATCHTOWER.
BIOMETRIC SIGNATURE AND VOICE-PRINT MATCH.
COMMENCING JAUNT.
VVVVMMM
VVVVMMMMM
YOU'LL APPRECIATE THIS, DR. PALMER--
A LITTLE THOUGHT-EXPERIMENT ON AMBIENT MATTER AND SPACE-TIME FOLDING--
AS YOUR ATOMS BEGIN TO DISASSEMBLE, WHAT DO YOU THINK WOULD HAPPEN--
IN GOD'S NAME, TERRIFIC, DON--
TEK
TEK
TEK

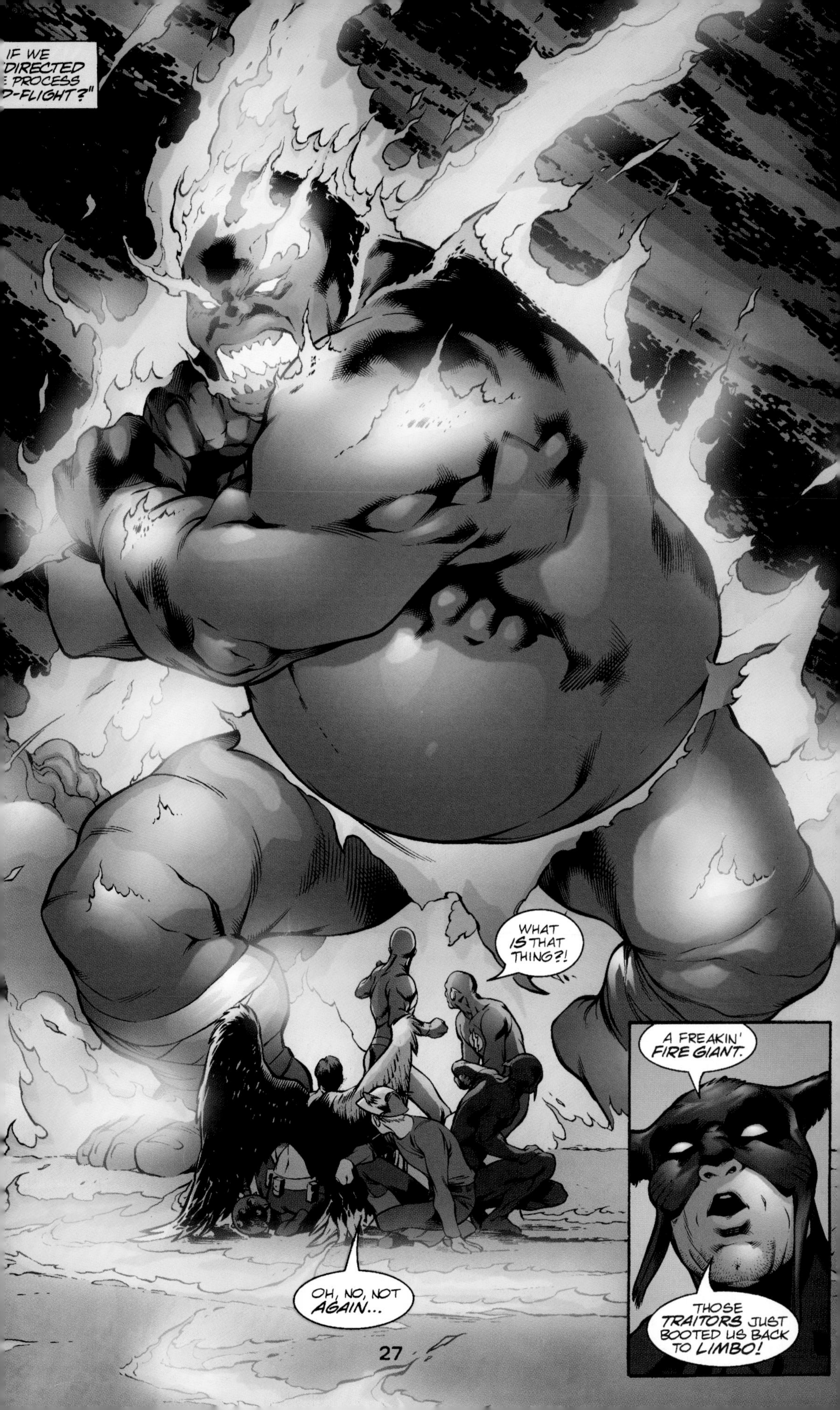
IF WE DIRECTED E PROCESS D-FLIGHT?"
WHAT IS THAT THING?!
A FREAKIN' FIRE GIANT.
OH, NO, NOT AGAIN...
THOSE TRAITORS JUST BOOTED US BACK TO LIMBO!

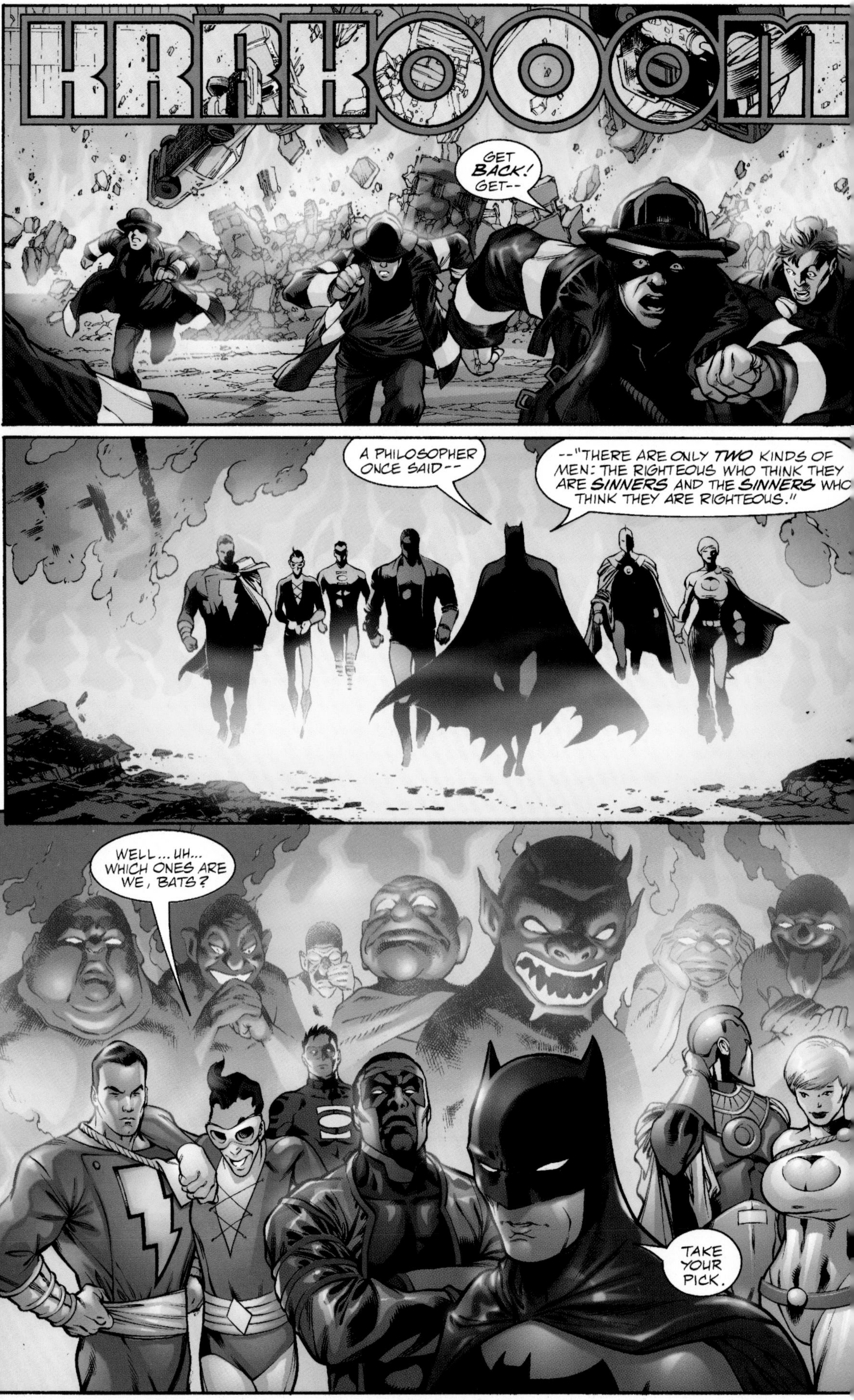
KRAKOOOM
GET BACK! GET--
A PHILOSOPHER ONCE SAID--
--"THERE ARE ONLY TWO KINDS OF MEN: THE RIGHTEOUS WHO THINK THEY ARE SINNERS AND THE SINNERS WHO THINK THEY ARE RIGHTEOUS."
WELL... UH... WHICH ONES ARE WE, BATS?
TAKE YOUR PICK.

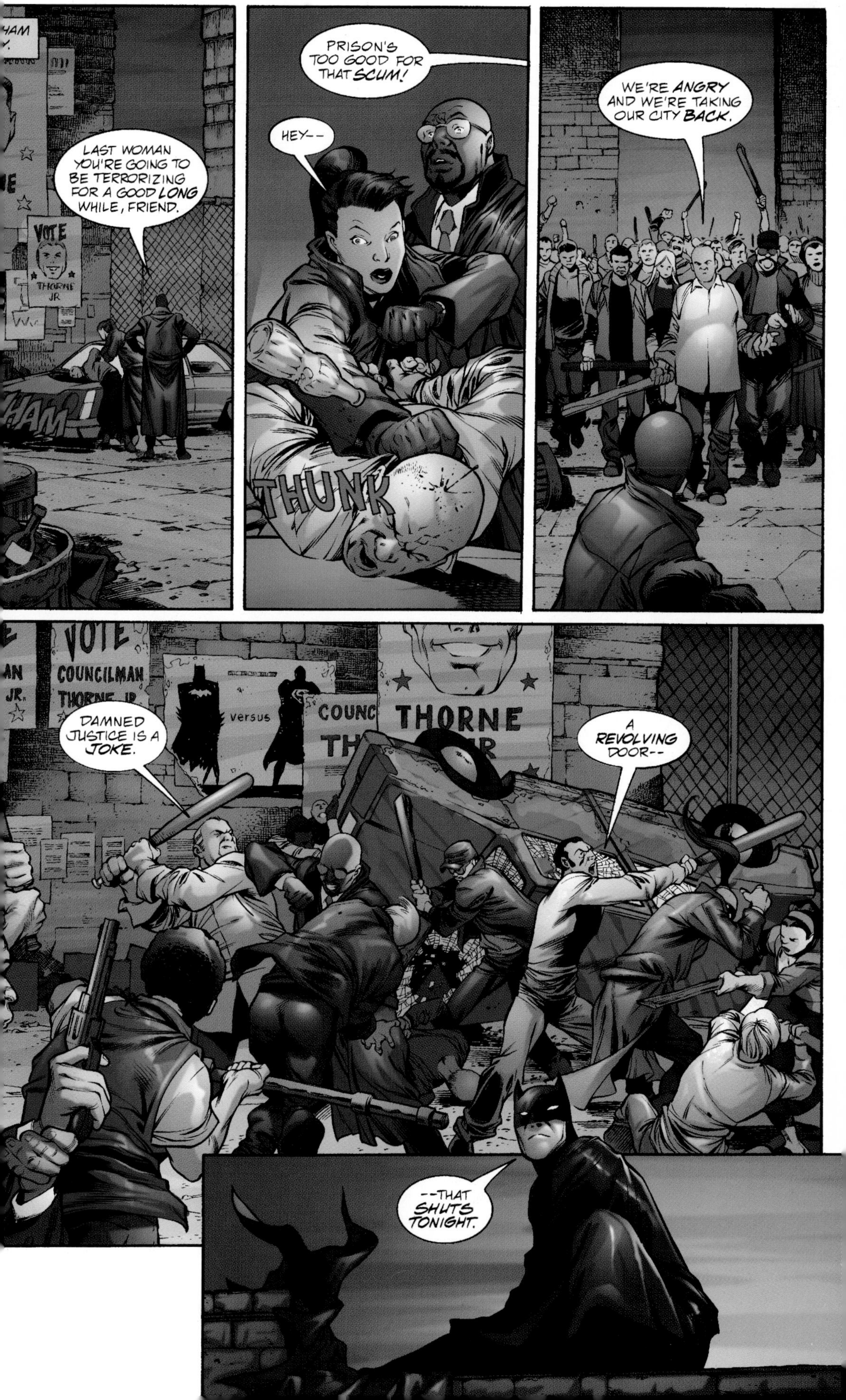
LAST WOMAN YOU'RE GOING TO BE TERRORIZING FOR A GOOD LONG WHILE, FRIEND.
VOTE
THORNE JR
PRISON'S TOO GOOD FOR THAT SCUM!
HEY--
THUNK
WE'RE ANGRY AND WE'RE TAKING OUR CITY BACK.
VOTE COUNCILMAN THORNE JR
versus
THORNE
DAMNED JUSTICE IS A JOKE.
A REVOLVING DOOR--
--THAT SHUTS TONIGHT.

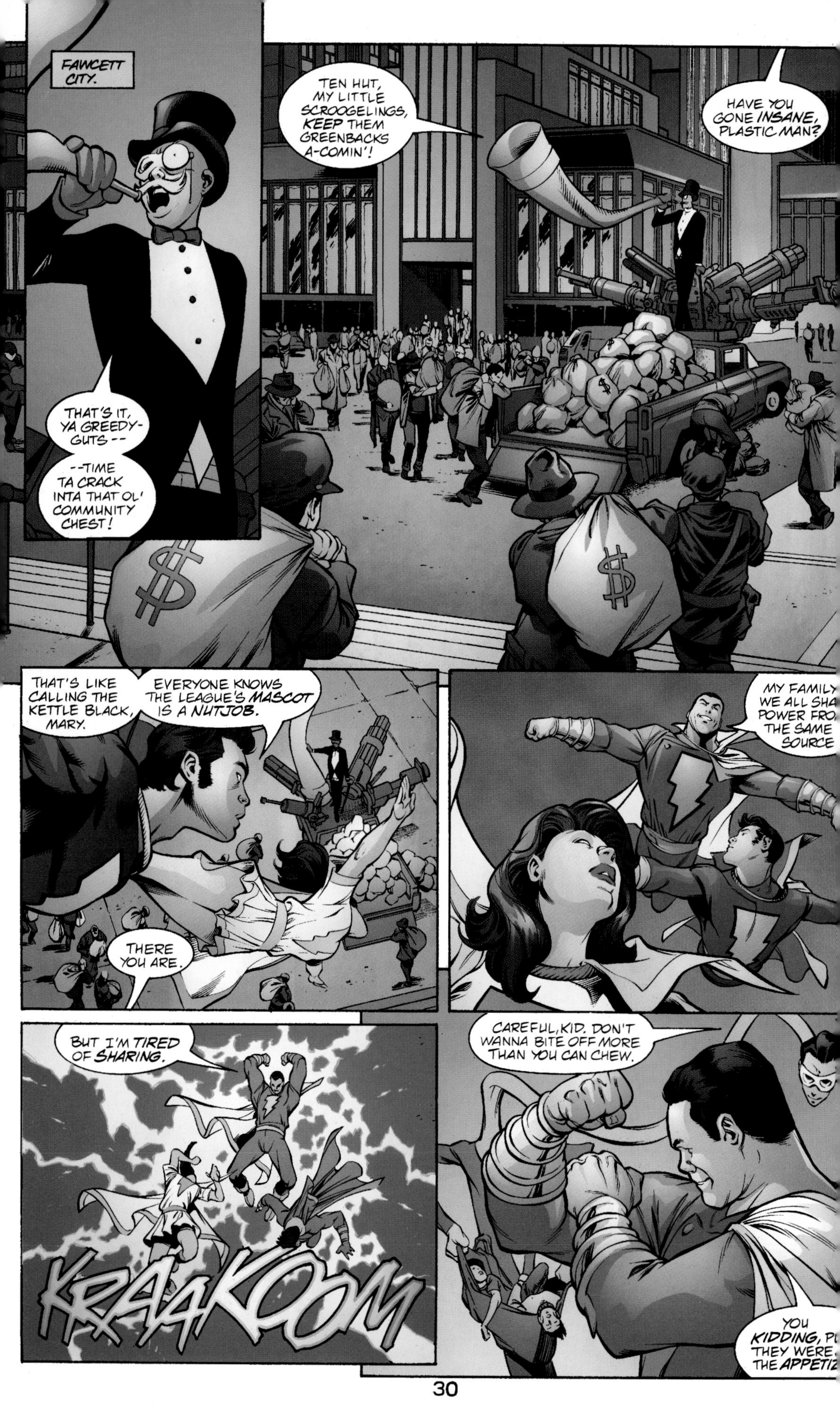
FAWCETT CITY.
TEN HUT, MY LITTLE SCROOGELINGS, KEEP THEM GREENBACKS A-COMIN'!
HAVE YOU GONE INSANE, PLASTIC MAN?
THAT'S IT, YA GREEDY-GUTS --
--TIME TA CRACK INTA THAT OL' COMMUNITY CHEST!
THAT'S LIKE CALLING THE KETTLE BLACK, MARY.
EVERYONE KNOWS THE LEAGUE'S MASCOT IS A NUTJOB.
THERE YOU ARE.
MY FAMILY WE ALL SHA POWER FRO THE SAME SOURCE
BUT I'M TIRED OF SHARING.
KRAAKOOM
CAREFUL, KID. DON'T WANNA BITE OFF MORE THAN YOU CAN CHEW.
YOU KIDDING, P THEY WERE THE APPETIZ

JLA WATCHTOWER INFIRMARY:

PROGRESS REPORT. THIS IS DR. MID-NITE, ATTENDING PHYSICIAN.

HAWKGIRL, JAKEEM THUNDER AND ATOM SMASHER CONTINUE TO *IMPROVE.*

IN THE WAKE OF CAPTAIN MARVEL'S *ATTACK,* BLACK ADAM HAS *REVERTED* TO THEO ADAM, THE HUMAN *HOST* HE SHARES A *SYMBIOTIC RELATIONSHIP* WITH.

FOR THE *MOMENT,* HE'S BEEN *STABILIZED.*

IT'S THE *MARTIAN MANHUNTER* THAT I'M *MOST WORRIED* ABOUT.

DUE TO *SEVERE* THIRD DEGREE BURNS HIS *XENO-MORPHIC SYSTEM* HAS GONE INTO *SHOCK* AND SUBSEQUENTLY LOST ALL *PHYSICAL INTEGRITY.*

--WARN YOU-- HKKKKKK-- DOCTOR--

EASY, J'ONN. DON'T TRY TO *SPEAK--*

--TELEPATHY, THEN--

--FADING, HAVE TO BE QUICK--

WATCH THOR-- *AAARRR!*

MANHUNTER! I...I WISH I KNEW HOW TO TAKE THE PAIN AWAY BUT--

UOY LLIW WON PEELS, RETNUHNAM.

WHAT--?

-- NNNNNNN

31

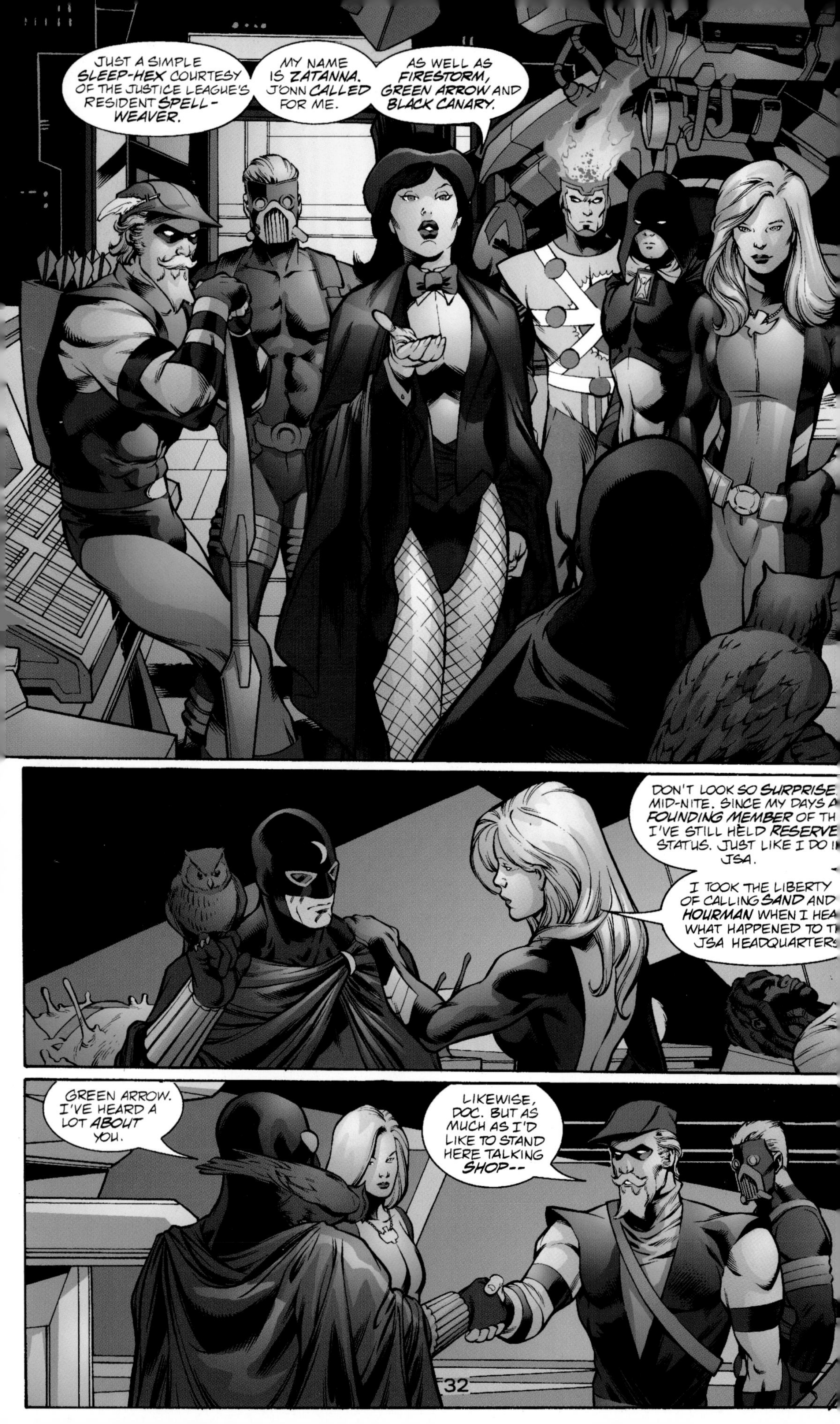

JUST A SIMPLE SLEEP-HEX COURTESY OF THE JUSTICE LEAGUE'S RESIDENT SPELL-WEAVER.
MY NAME IS ZATANNA. J'ONN CALLED FOR ME.
AS WELL AS FIRESTORM, GREEN ARROW AND BLACK CANARY.
DON'T LOOK SO SURPRISE MID-NITE. SINCE MY DAYS A FOUNDING MEMBER OF TH I'VE STILL HELD RESERVE STATUS. JUST LIKE I DO I JSA.
I TOOK THE LIBERTY OF CALLING SAND AND HOURMAN WHEN I HEA WHAT HAPPENED TO T JSA HEADQUARTER
GREEN ARROW. I'VE HEARD A LOT ABOUT YOU.
LIKEWISE, DOC. BUT AS MUCH AS I'D LIKE TO STAND HERE TALKING SHOP--

MOSCOW

ANGKOR WAT

HONG KONG

TIMES SQUARE

THE CONGO

"I THINK WE'VE GOT A **WORLD** THAT NEEDS **SAVING.**"

FROM WHAT I **KNOW,** *NINE* OF OUR TEAMMATES ARE **MISSING.**

AND ACCORDING TO J'ONN, **SEVEN** APPEAR TO HAVE GONE **INSANE.**

AND THE REST OF THE WORLD'S **HEROES** ARE SUDDENLY UP TO THEIR EARS DEALING WITH SOME KIND OF WIDESPREAD PSYCHOTIC **OUTBREAK.**

SOMEONE'S **HIT** US. AND HIT US **HARD.**

LET'S BACK UP. WHAT DO WE *KNOW* ABOUT BEDLAM? *MR. MIRACLE* TUSSLED WITH HIM A FEW TIMES.

ACCORDING TO D.E.O. INTELLIGENCE, DOCTOR BEDLAM IS AN ASTRAL BEING FROM THE FAR PLANET OF APOKOLIPS. BEDLAM PROJECTS HIS **THOUGHTS** INTO OTHER PEOPLE'S **BODIES**--USES THEM LIKE **PUPPETS.**

MAYBE. SAY THE **GOAL** WAS SIMPLY TO GET IN CLOSE *PROXIMITY* TO LUTHOR?

J'ONN **DID** TELL ME TO **WATCH** LUTHOR--

ATTACKING THE PRESIDENT OF THE UNITED STATES DOESN'T REALLY FIT HIS M.O. HE'S USUALLY MORE LOW-KEY. LIKES TO STAY OUT OF THE SPOTLIGHT.

WELL, UM, WHAT IF SOMEONE **ELSE** WERE USING BEDLAM?

TO WHAT **END?** WISH I *CONTROLLED* MY PROPHETIC **TIME-VISIONS.** SEE WHAT'S IN STORE FOR LUTHOR AND THE REST OF US.

WHAT ARE YOU STARING AT?

WHA'? OH. **SORRY,** MAN. I JUST... I CAN **SEE** MOLECULAR STRUCTURES AND...YOU'RE A **SILICON**-BASED LIFEFORM.

A **SAND-MAN,** YES. I'M **AWARE** OF THAT.

SILICON.

FOURTEENTH ELEMENT IN THE **PERIODIC TABLE.** ATOMIC WEIGHT **TWENTY-EIGHT** POINT **ZERO. EIGHT. FIVE. FIVE...** INTERESTING.

WHAT THE HELL IS **THAT?!**

IT'S CALLED THE **ROCK OF ETERNITY.**

ROCK OF **WHAT?**

I'LL EXPLAIN WHEN WE GET THERE. BUT IF ITS APPEARANCE MEANS WHAT I **THINK** IT DOES, OUR SITUATION JUST TOOK A **DEFINITE** TURN FOR THE **WORSE.**

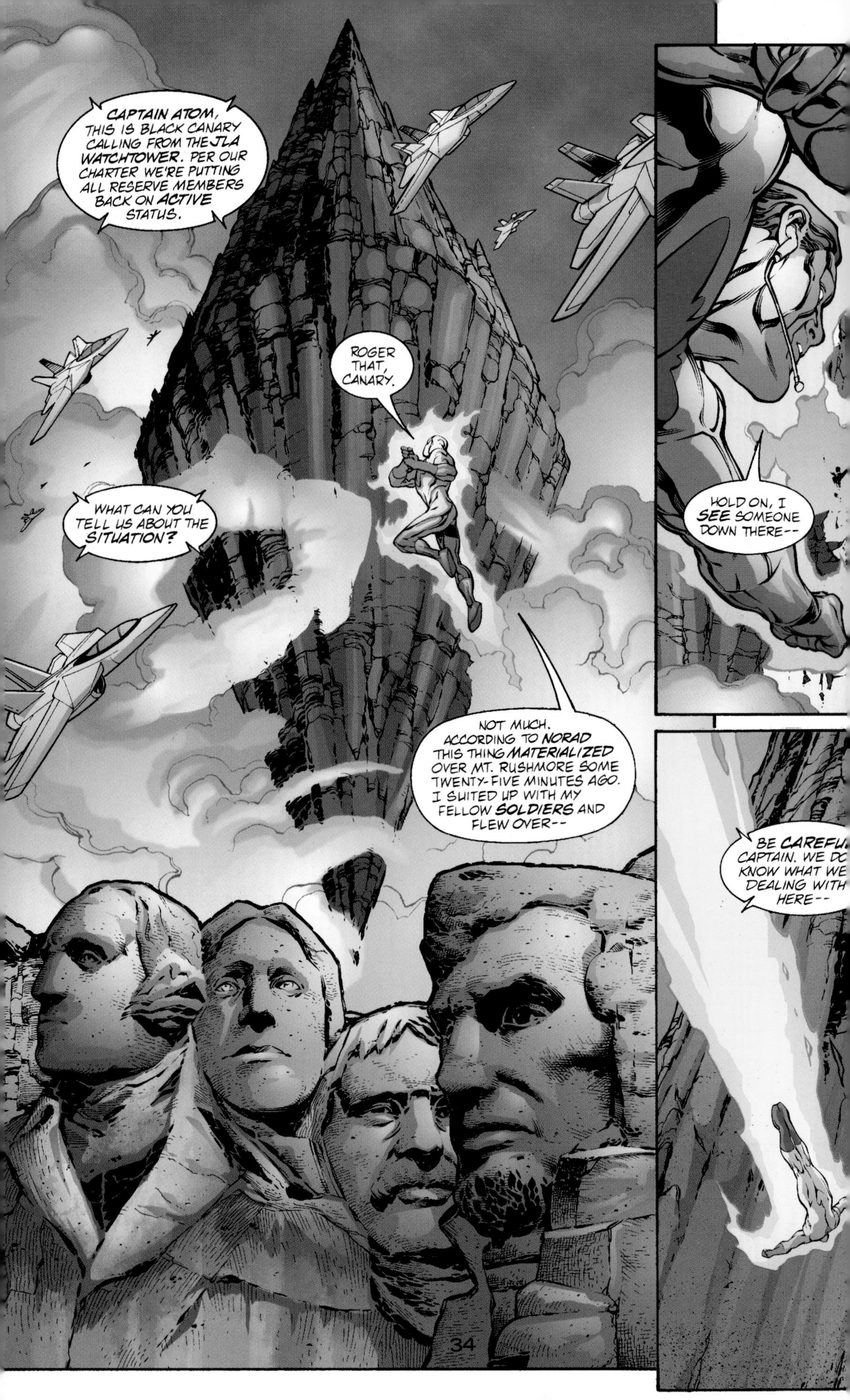

CAPTAIN ATOM, THIS IS BLACK CANARY CALLING FROM THE JLA WATCHTOWER. PER OUR CHARTER WE'RE PUTTING ALL RESERVE MEMBERS BACK ON ACTIVE STATUS.
ROGER THAT, CANARY.
WHAT CAN YOU TELL US ABOUT THE SITUATION?
NOT MUCH. ACCORDING TO NORAD THIS THING MATERIALIZED OVER MT. RUSHMORE SOME TWENTY-FIVE MINUTES AGO. I SUITED UP WITH MY FELLOW SOLDIERS AND FLEW OVER--
HOLD ON, I SEE SOMEONE DOWN THERE--

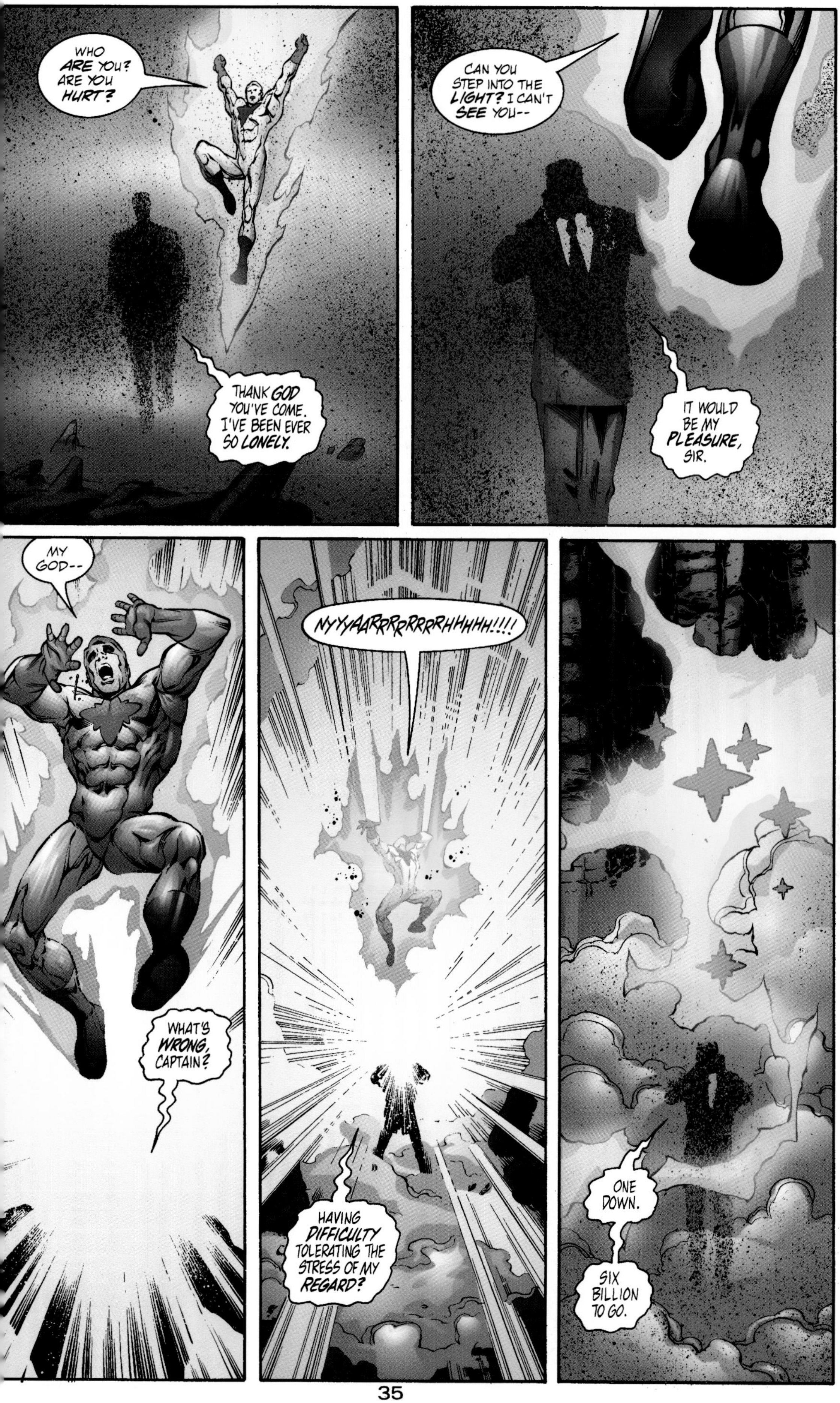
WHO ARE YOU? ARE YOU HURT?
THANK GOD YOU'VE COME. I'VE BEEN EVER SO LONELY.
CAN YOU STEP INTO THE LIGHT? I CAN'T SEE YOU--
IT WOULD BE MY PLEASURE, SIR.
MY GOD--
WHAT'S WRONG, CAPTAIN?
NYYYAARRRRRRRRHHHHH!!!!
HAVING DIFFICULTY TOLERATING THE STRESS OF MY REGARD?
ONE DOWN.
SIX BILLION TO GO.

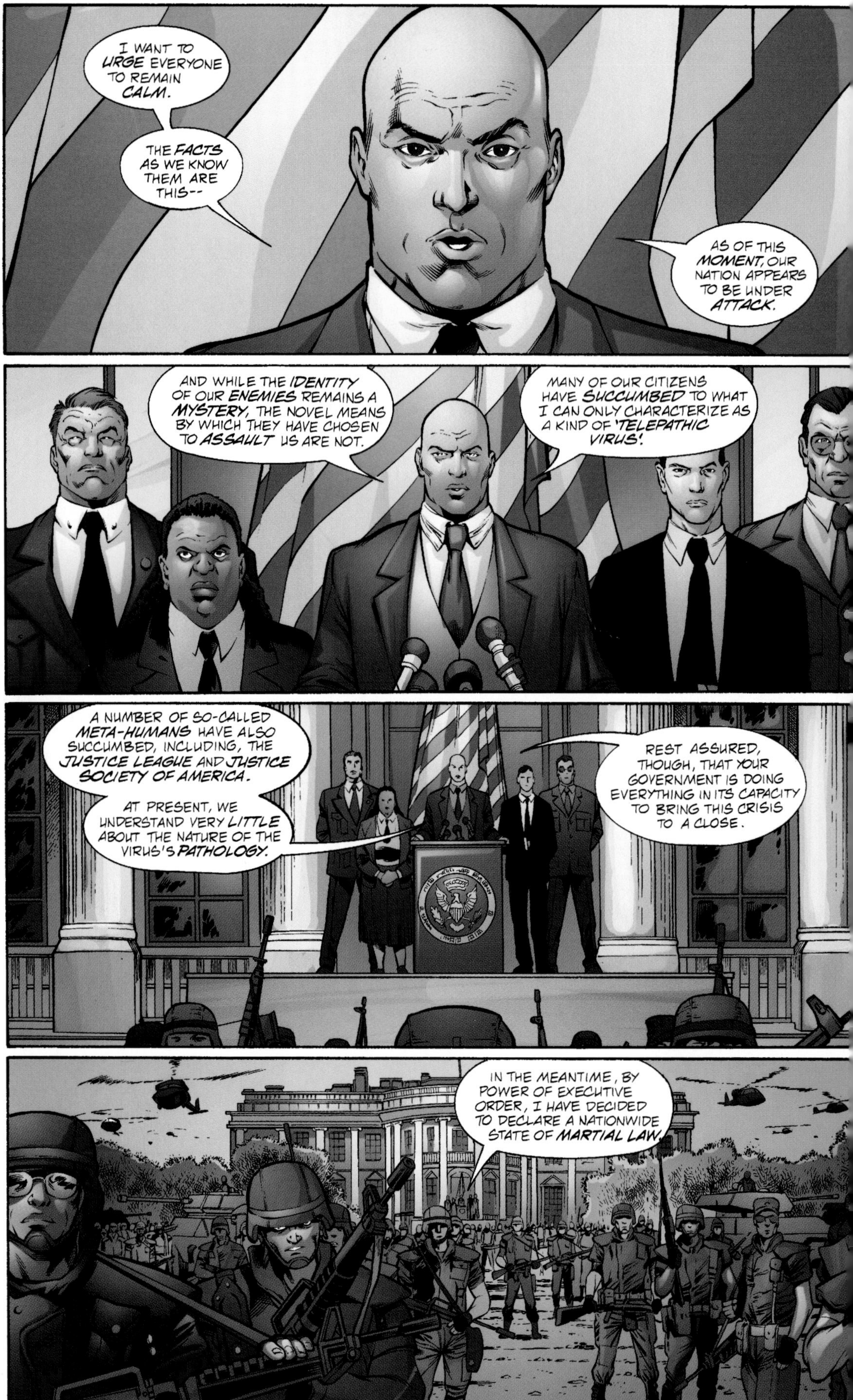
I WANT TO URGE EVERYONE TO REMAIN CALM.
THE FACTS AS WE KNOW THEM ARE THIS--
AS OF THIS MOMENT, OUR NATION APPEARS TO BE UNDER ATTACK.
AND WHILE THE IDENTITY OF OUR ENEMIES REMAINS A MYSTERY, THE NOVEL MEANS BY WHICH THEY HAVE CHOSEN TO ASSAULT US ARE NOT.
MANY OF OUR CITIZENS HAVE SUCCUMBED TO WHAT I CAN ONLY CHARACTERIZE AS A KIND OF 'TELEPATHIC VIRUS'.
A NUMBER OF SO-CALLED META-HUMANS HAVE ALSO SUCCUMBED, INCLUDING, THE JUSTICE LEAGUE AND JUSTICE SOCIETY OF AMERICA.
AT PRESENT, WE UNDERSTAND VERY LITTLE ABOUT THE NATURE OF THE VIRUS'S PATHOLOGY.
REST ASSURED, THOUGH, THAT YOUR GOVERNMENT IS DOING EVERYTHING IN ITS CAPACITY TO BRING THIS CRISIS TO A CLOSE.
IN THE MEANTIME, BY POWER OF EXECUTIVE ORDER, I HAVE DECIDED TO DECLARE A NATIONWIDE STATE OF MARTIAL LAW.

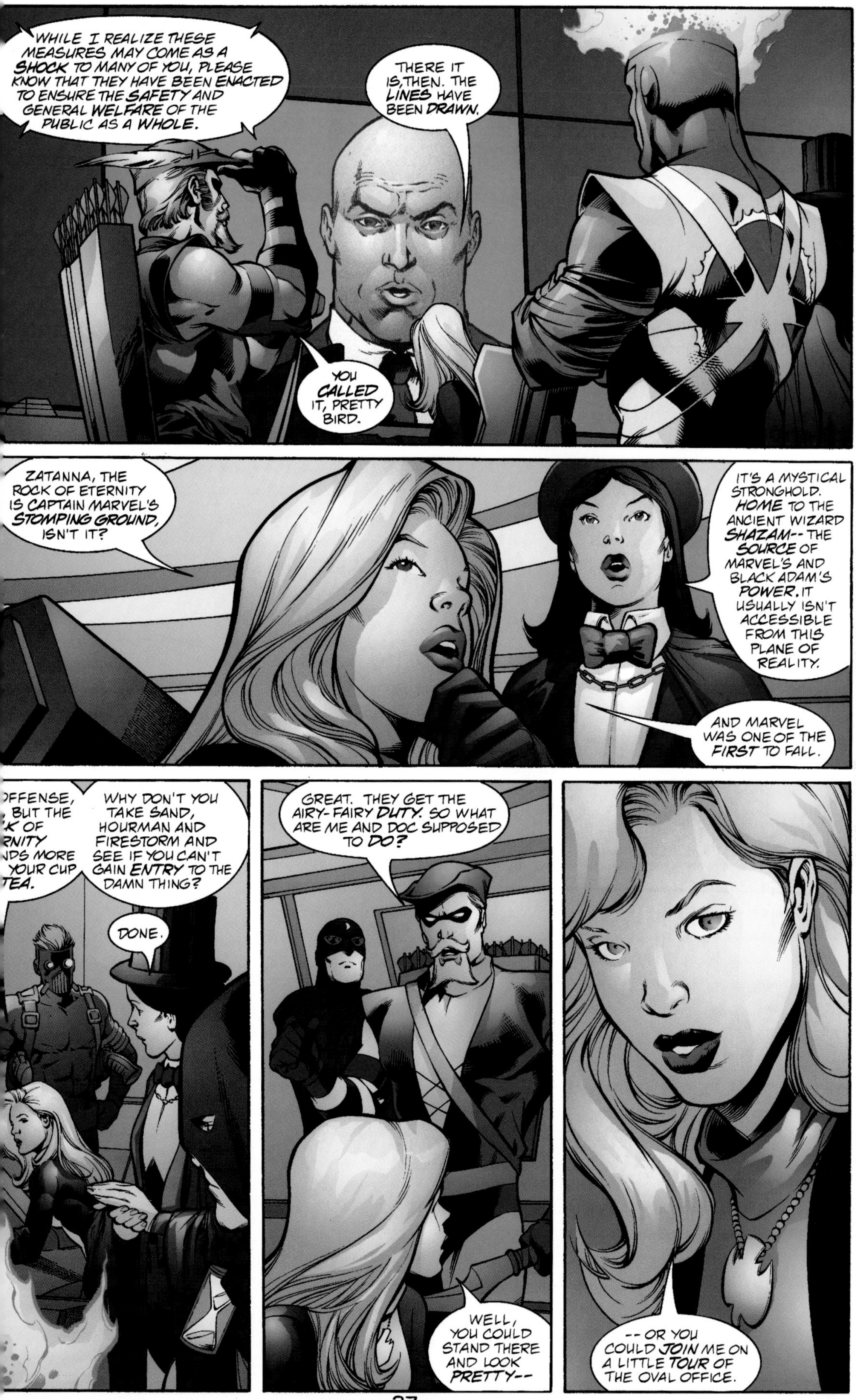
WHILE I REALIZE THESE MEASURES MAY COME AS A SHOCK TO MANY OF YOU, PLEASE KNOW THAT THEY HAVE BEEN ENACTED TO ENSURE THE SAFETY AND GENERAL WELFARE OF THE PUBLIC AS A WHOLE.
THERE IT IS, THEN. THE LINES HAVE BEEN DRAWN.
YOU CALLED IT, PRETTY BIRD.
ZATANNA, THE ROCK OF ETERNITY IS CAPTAIN MARVEL'S STOMPING GROUND, ISN'T IT?
IT'S A MYSTICAL STRONGHOLD. HOME TO THE ANCIENT WIZARD SHAZAM-- THE SOURCE OF MARVEL'S AND BLACK ADAM'S POWER. IT USUALLY ISN'T ACCESSIBLE FROM THIS PLANE OF REALITY.
AND MARVEL WAS ONE OF THE FIRST TO FALL.
FFENSE, BUT THE K OF RNITY NDS MORE YOUR CUP TEA.
WHY DON'T YOU TAKE SAND, HOURMAN AND FIRESTORM AND SEE IF YOU CAN'T GAIN ENTRY TO THE DAMN THING?
DONE.
GREAT. THEY GET THE AIRY-FAIRY DUTY. SO WHAT ARE ME AND DOC SUPPOSED TO DO?
WELL, YOU COULD STAND THERE AND LOOK PRETTY--
--OR YOU COULD JOIN ME ON A LITTLE TOUR OF THE OVAL OFFICE.

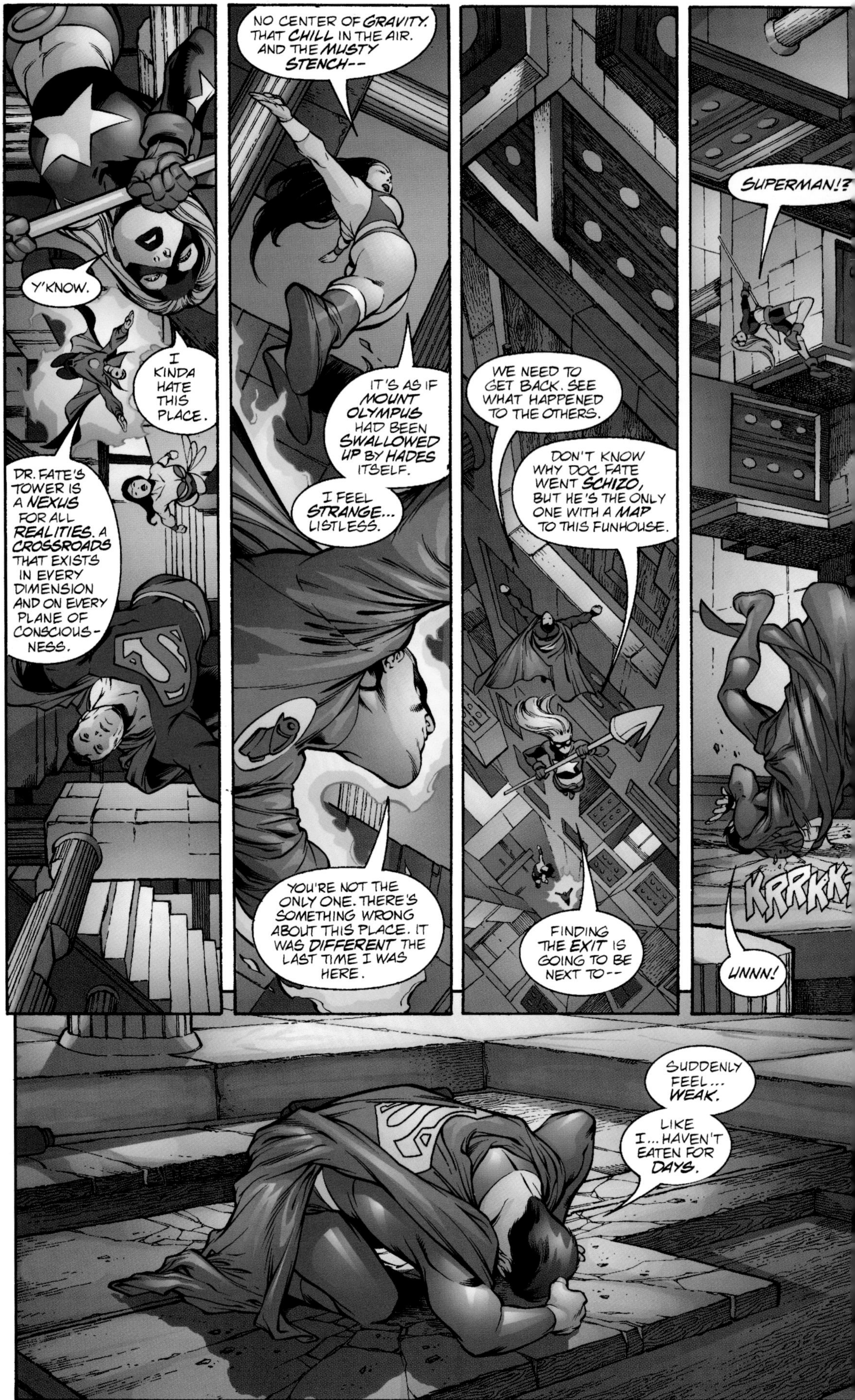
Y'KNOW.
I KINDA HATE THIS PLACE.
DR. FATE'S TOWER IS A NEXUS FOR ALL REALITIES. A CROSSROADS THAT EXISTS IN EVERY DIMENSION AND ON EVERY PLANE OF CONSCIOUS-NESS.
NO CENTER OF GRAVITY. THAT CHILL IN THE AIR. AND THE MUSTY STENCH--
IT'S AS IF MOUNT OLYMPUS HAD BEEN SWALLOWED UP BY HADES ITSELF.
I FEEL STRANGE... LISTLESS.
YOU'RE NOT THE ONLY ONE. THERE'S SOMETHING WRONG ABOUT THIS PLACE. IT WAS DIFFERENT THE LAST TIME I WAS HERE.
WE NEED TO GET BACK. SEE WHAT HAPPENED TO THE OTHERS.
DON'T KNOW WHY DOC FATE WENT SCHIZO, BUT HE'S THE ONLY ONE WITH A MAP TO THIS FUNHOUSE.
FINDING THE EXIT IS GOING TO BE NEXT TO--
SUPERMAN!?
KRRKK
UNNN!
SUDDENLY FEEL... WEAK.
LIKE I... HAVEN'T EATEN FOR DAYS.

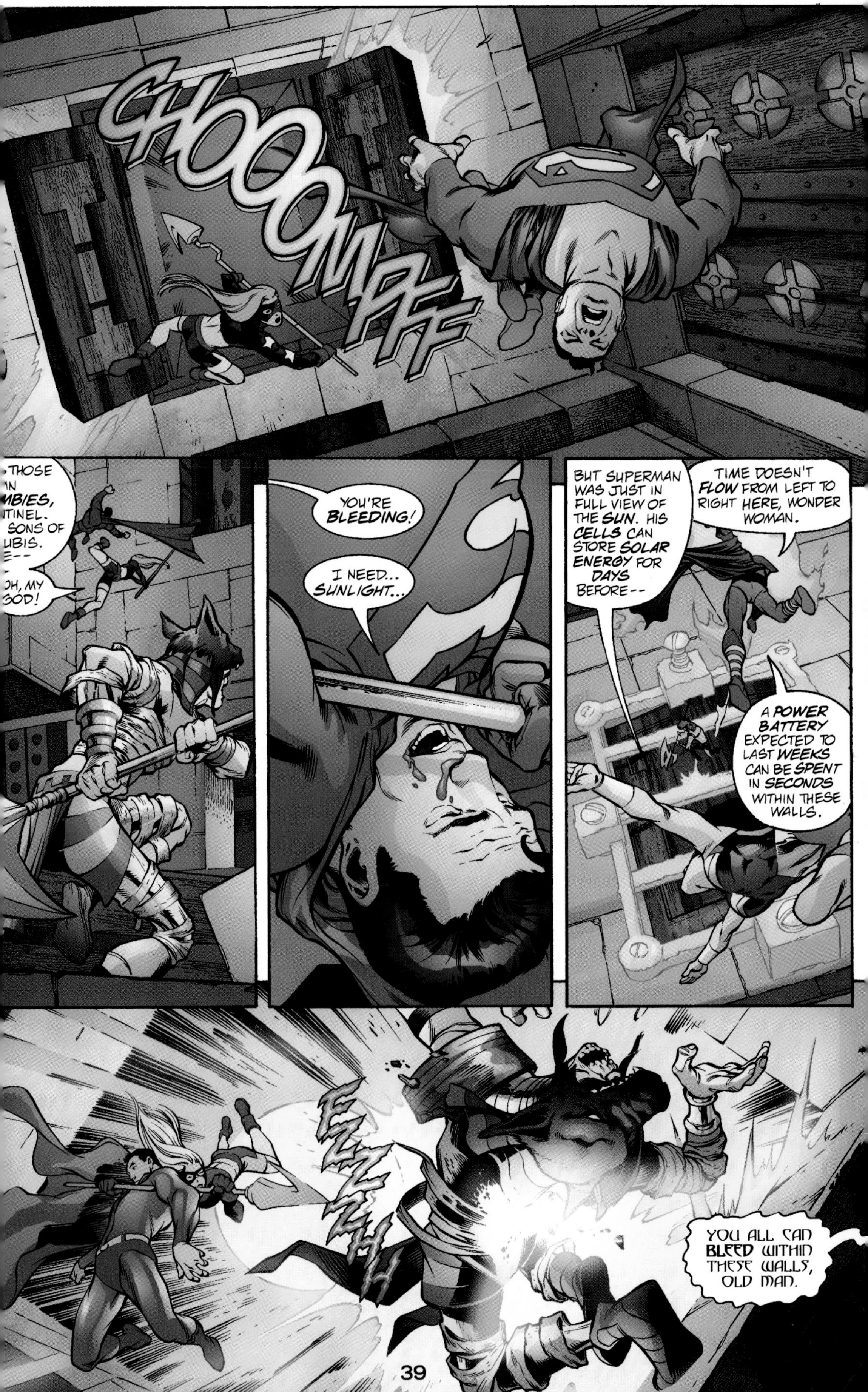
CHOOOMPFF
YOU'RE BLEEDING!
I NEED... SUNLIGHT...
BUT SUPERMAN WAS JUST IN FULL VIEW OF THE SUN. HIS CELLS CAN STORE SOLAR ENERGY FOR DAYS BEFORE--
TIME DOESN'T FLOW FROM LEFT TO RIGHT HERE, WONDER WOMAN.
A POWER BATTERY EXPECTED TO LAST WEEKS CAN BE SPENT IN SECONDS WITHIN THESE WALLS.
YOU ALL CAN BLEED WITHIN THESE WALLS, OLD MAN.

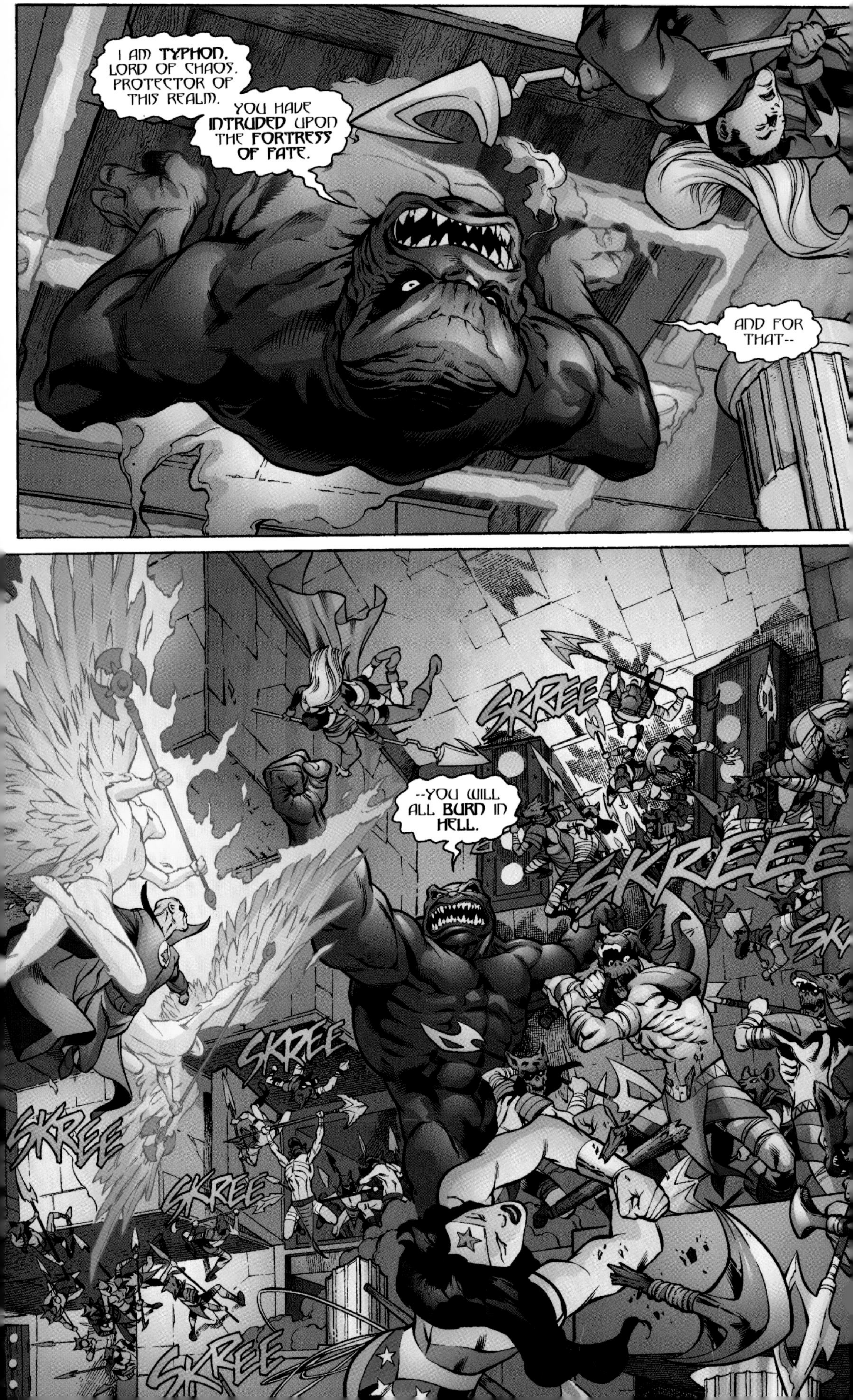
I AM **TYPHON**, LORD OF CHAOS. PROTECTOR OF THIS REALM.
YOU HAVE **INTRUDED** UPON THE **FORTRESS OF FATE**.
AND FOR THAT--
--YOU WILL ALL **BURN** IN **HELL**.
SKREE
SKREEE
SKREE
SKREE
SKREE
SKREE

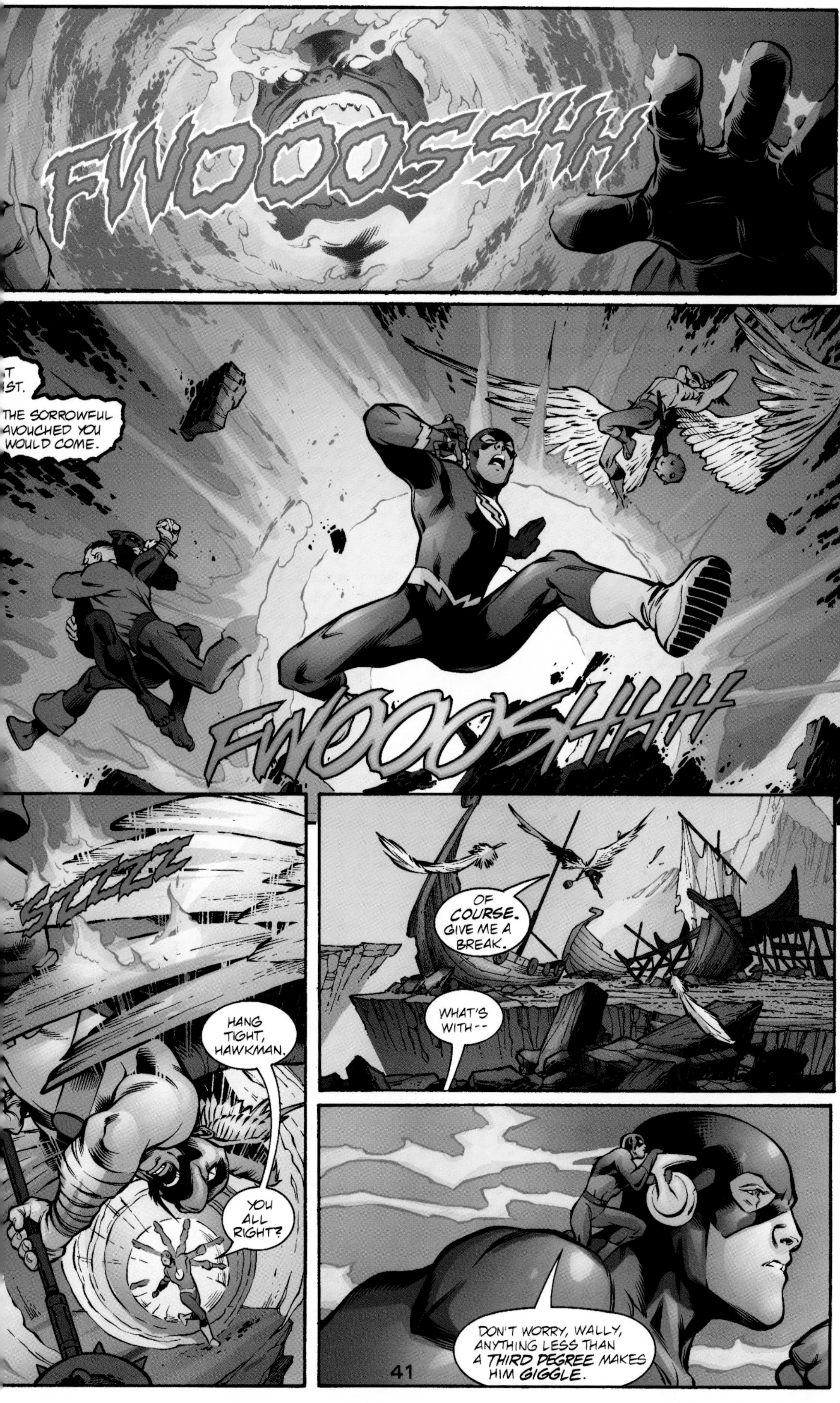
FWOOOSHH
THE SORROWFUL AVOUCHED YOU WOULD COME.
FWOOOSHHH
SZZZZZ
HANG TIGHT, HAWKMAN.
YOU ALL RIGHT?
OF COURSE. GIVE ME A BREAK.
WHAT'S WITH--
DON'T WORRY, WALLY, ANYTHING LESS THAN A THIRD DEGREE MAKES HIM GIGGLE.

GOD, NO. NOT AGAIN...

THERE *ARE* THINGS WORSE THAN DEATH, TED. *MUCH* WORSE

WE'RE IN LIMBO?

THE ORIGINAL JSA WERE *IMPRISONED* HERE FOR *YEARS*, WALLY. FORCED TO FIGHT A *BATTLE* NEITHER SIDE COULD EVER WIN. NO MATTER HOW *FAST* WE STRUCK, THIS DEMON... SURTUR... TOOK WHAT WE THREW AT HIM AND CAME BACK FOR MORE.

THE TIME WE SPENT HE THE PAIN W ABOUT TO THROUGH.. SORRY, WA

IT IS CALLED *RAGNAROK.* THE *TWILIGHT* OF THE *GODS.*

THE HEROES OF *NORSE* LEGEND FOUGHT THEIR FINAL WAR HERE. THAT BEHEMOTH GETS *OUT,* THE WORLD *ENDS.*

DOCTOR BEDLAM. OUR TEAMMATES TURNING AGAINST US. SURTUR. THIS IS CONNECTED, I'M SURE OF THAT. I JUST CAN'T BEGIN TO GUESS HOW.

SO WHICH DO WE RU OUT A' HER

WE *DON'T,* FLASH JUNIOR.

DON'T MEAN NO OFFENSE TO ANYONE HERE. I MEAN, THIS IS A GOOD *GROUP* OF JOES. BUT THE *LAST* TIME WE FOUGHT THIS *HOT SHOT* TO A *STANDSTILL* --

--IT TOOK THE ENTIRE *JUSTICE SOCIETY OF AMERICA* TO DO IT.

FSSHHH

WE AIN'T GONNA LAST *TWO* ROUNDS.

42

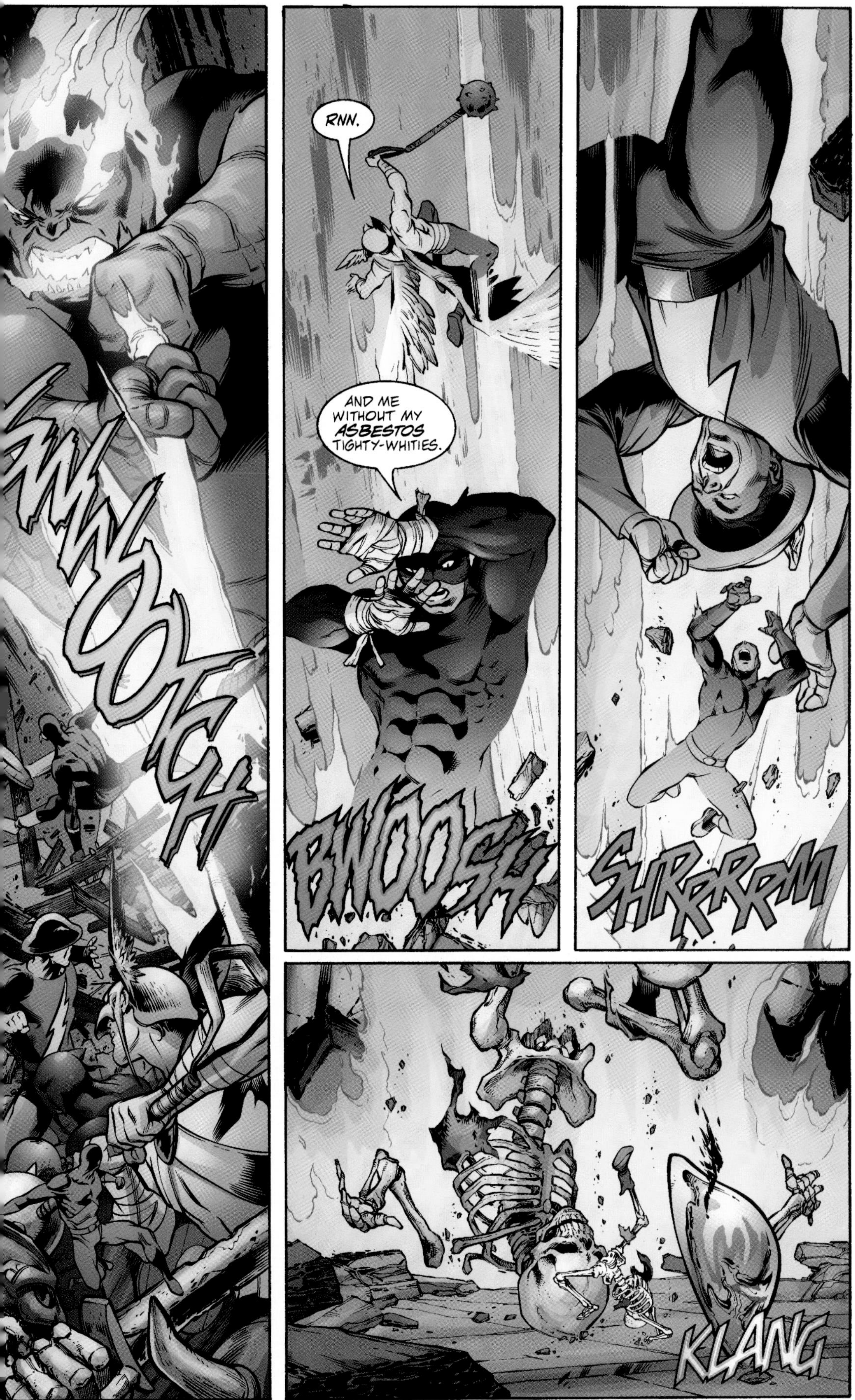
WHOOOSH
RNN.
AND ME WITHOUT MY ASBESTOS TIGHTY-WHITIES.
BWOOSH
SHRRRRM
KLANG

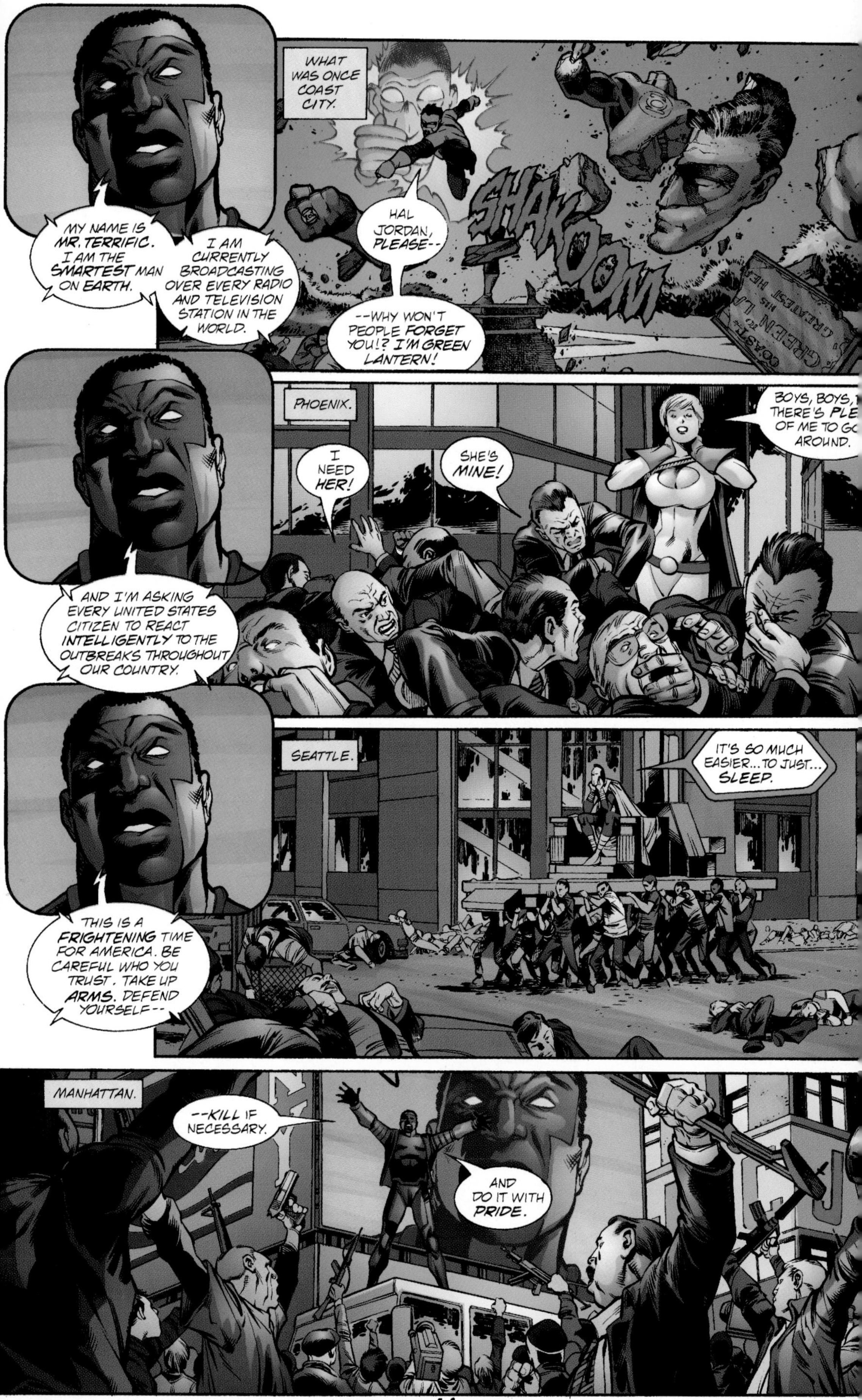

WHAT WAS ONCE COAST CITY.
MY NAME IS MR. TERRIFIC. I AM THE SMARTEST MAN ON EARTH.
I AM CURRENTLY BROADCASTING OVER EVERY RADIO AND TELEVISION STATION IN THE WORLD.
HAL JORDAN, PLEASE--
--WHY WON'T PEOPLE FORGET YOU!? I'M GREEN LANTERN!
SHAKOOM
PHOENIX.
BOYS, BOYS, THERE'S PLE OF ME TO GO AROUND.
I NEED HER!
SHE'S MINE!
AND I'M ASKING EVERY UNITED STATES CITIZEN TO REACT INTELLIGENTLY TO THE OUTBREAKS THROUGHOUT OUR COUNTRY.
SEATTLE.
IT'S SO MUCH EASIER... TO JUST... SLEEP.
THIS IS A FRIGHTENING TIME FOR AMERICA. BE CAREFUL WHO YOU TRUST. TAKE UP ARMS. DEFEND YOURSELF--
MANHATTAN.
--KILL IF NECESSARY.
AND DO IT WITH PRIDE.

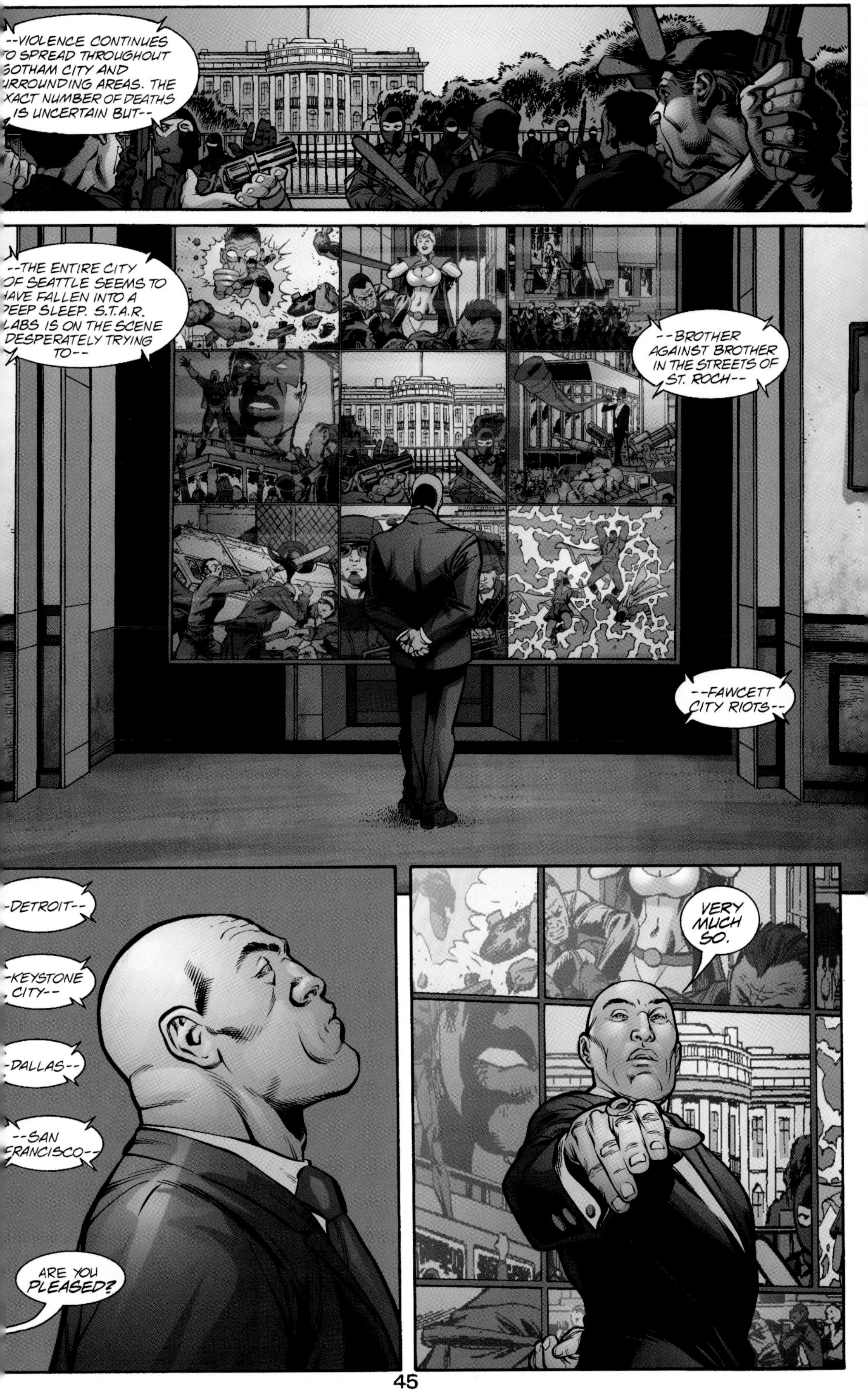
--VIOLENCE CONTINUES TO SPREAD THROUGHOUT GOTHAM CITY AND SURROUNDING AREAS. THE EXACT NUMBER OF DEATHS IS UNCERTAIN BUT--
--THE ENTIRE CITY OF SEATTLE SEEMS TO HAVE FALLEN INTO A DEEP SLEEP. S.T.A.R. LABS IS ON THE SCENE DESPERATELY TRYING TO--
--BROTHER AGAINST BROTHER IN THE STREETS OF ST. ROCH--
--FAWCETT CITY RIOTS--
-DETROIT--
-KEYSTONE CITY--
-DALLAS--
--SAN FRANCISCO--
ARE YOU PLEASED?
VERY MUCH SO.

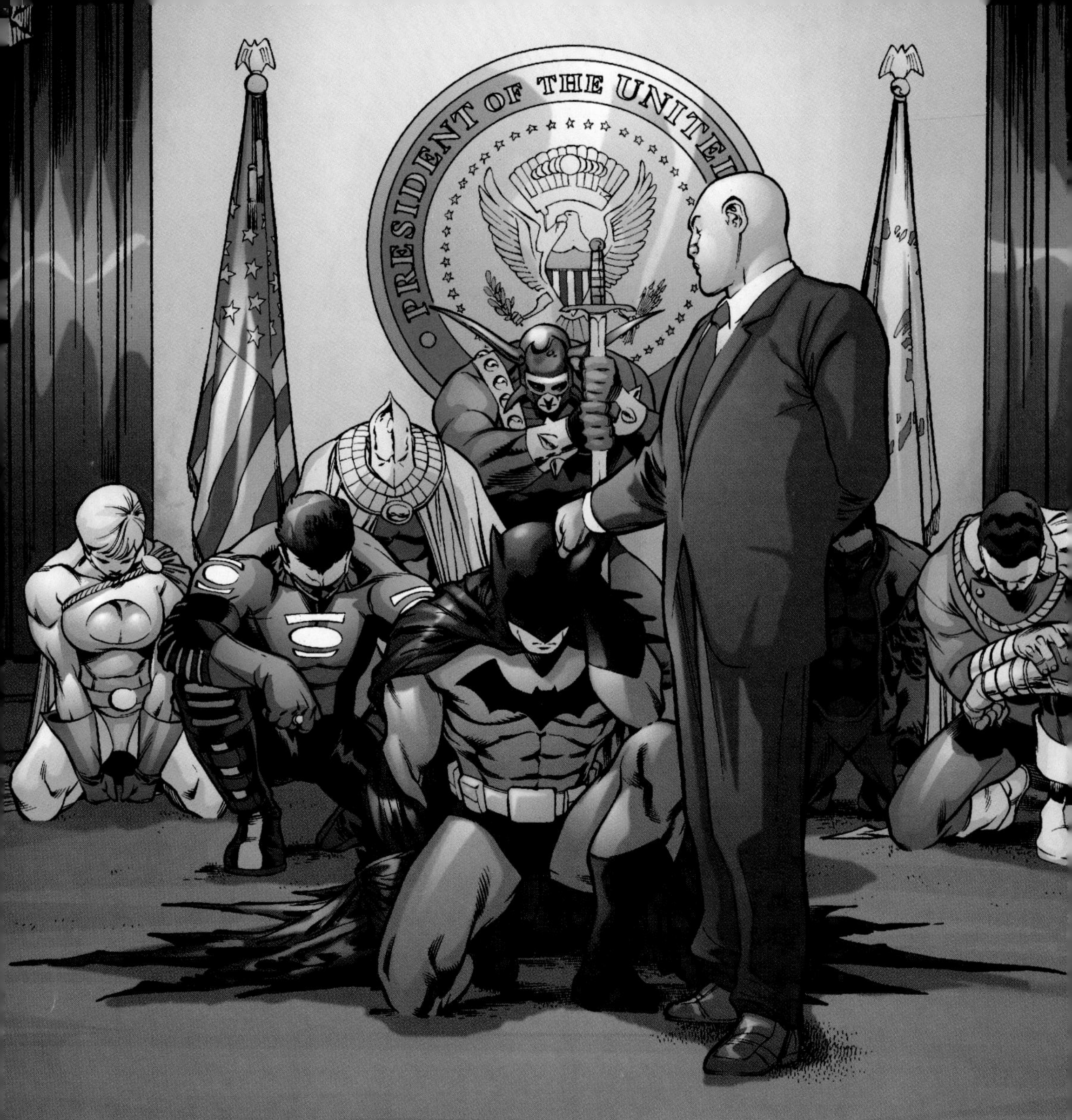
PRESIDENT OF THE UNITED

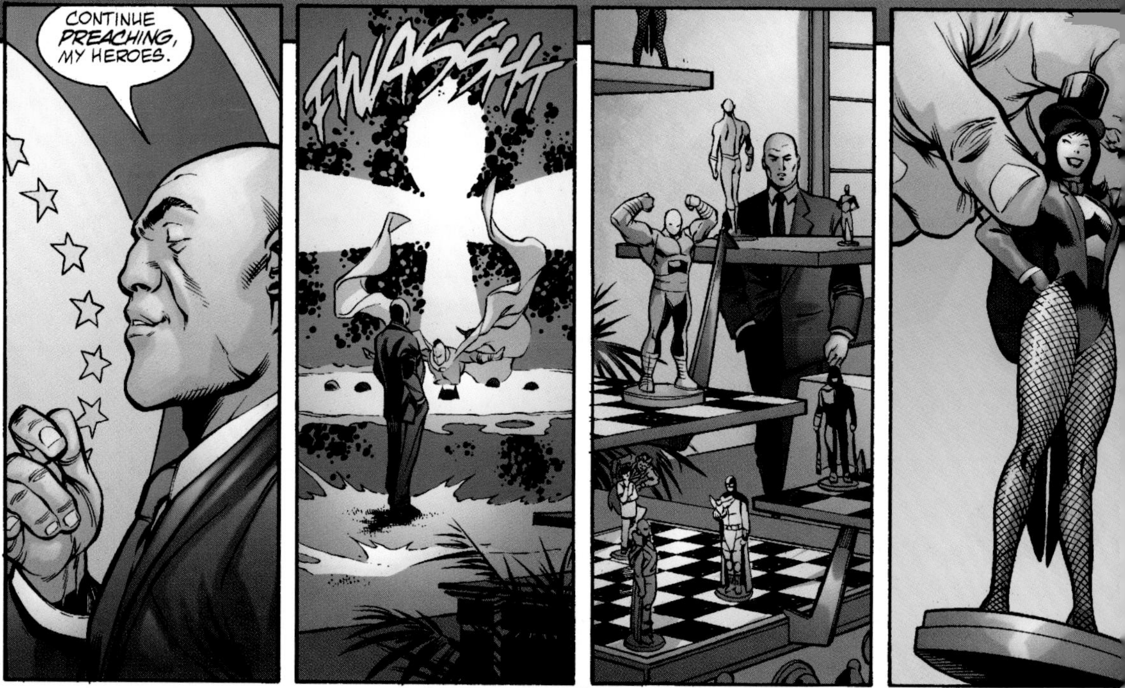
CONTINUE PREACHING, MY HEROES.
FWASHH

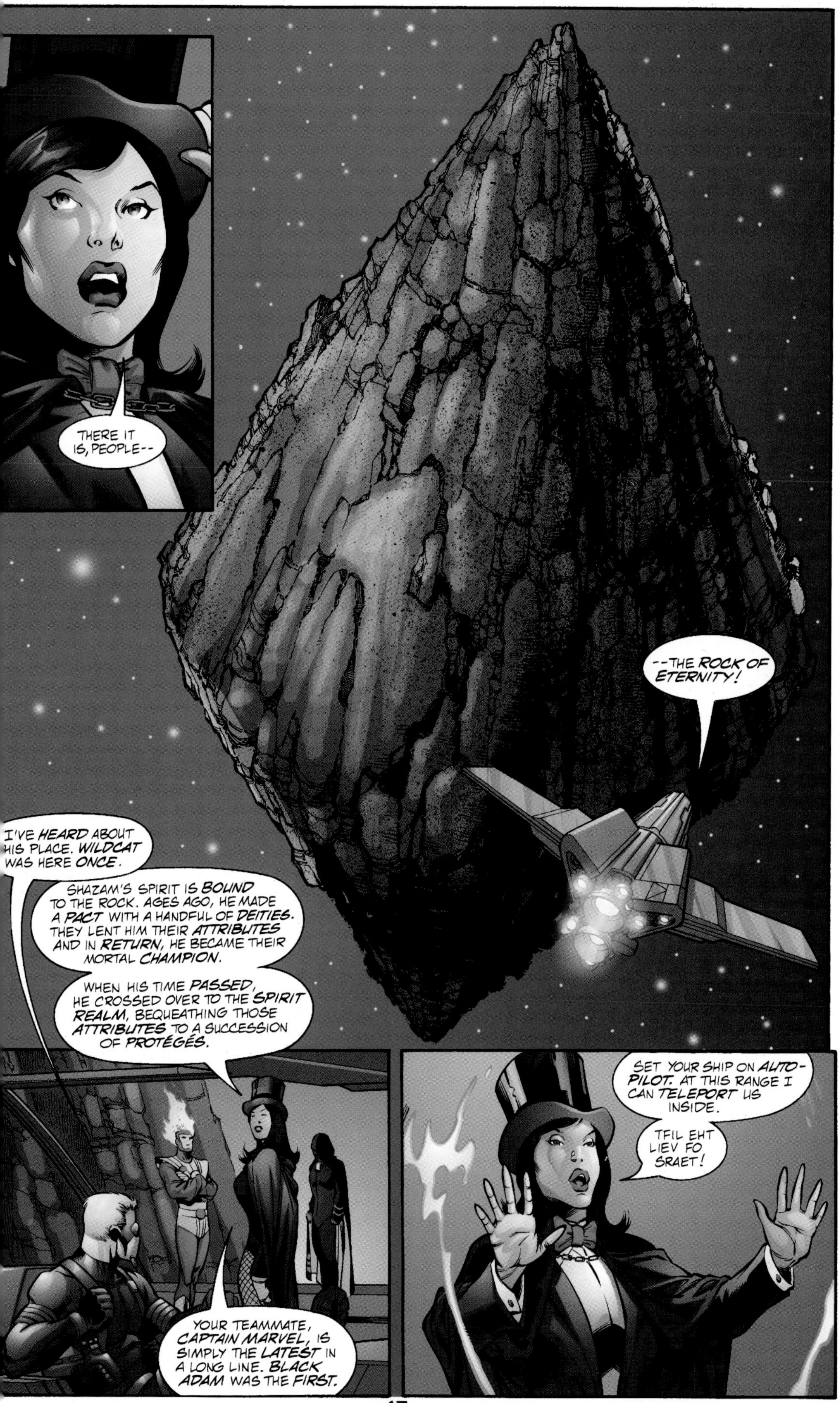
THERE IT IS, PEOPLE--
--THE ROCK OF ETERNITY!
I'VE HEARD ABOUT HIS PLACE. WILDCAT WAS HERE ONCE.
SHAZAM'S SPIRIT IS BOUND TO THE ROCK. AGES AGO, HE MADE A PACT WITH A HANDFUL OF DEITIES. THEY LENT HIM THEIR ATTRIBUTES AND IN RETURN, HE BECAME THEIR MORTAL CHAMPION.
WHEN HIS TIME PASSED, HE CROSSED OVER TO THE SPIRIT REALM, BEQUEATHING THOSE ATTRIBUTES TO A SUCCESSION OF PROTÉGÉS.
YOUR TEAMMATE, CAPTAIN MARVEL, IS SIMPLY THE LATEST IN A LONG LINE. BLACK ADAM WAS THE FIRST.
SET YOUR SHIP ON AUTO-PILOT. AT THIS RANGE I CAN TELEPORT US INSIDE.
TFIL EHT LIEV FO SRAET!

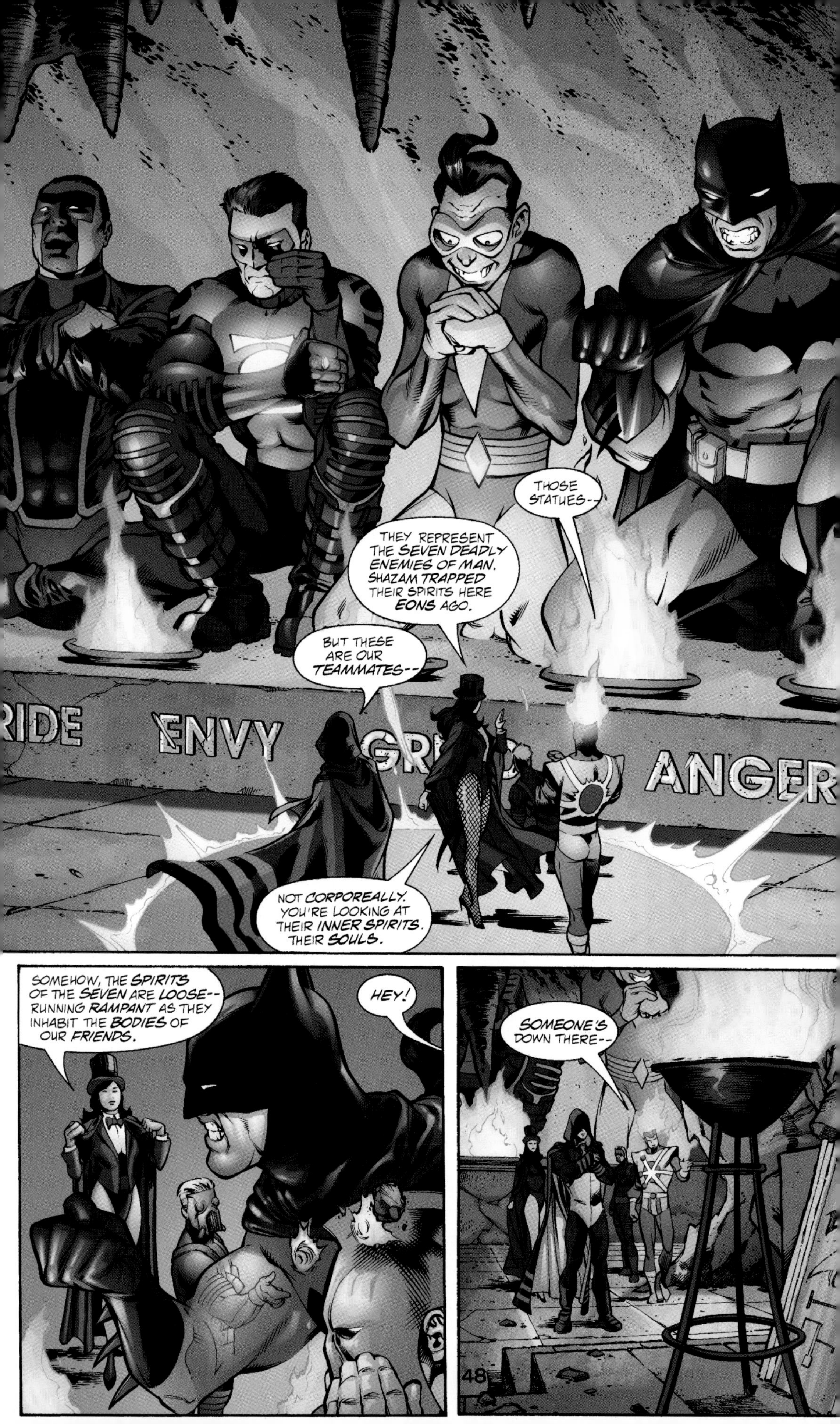
THOSE STATUES--
THEY REPRESENT THE SEVEN DEADLY ENEMIES OF MAN. SHAZAM TRAPPED THEIR SPIRITS HERE EONS AGO.
BUT THESE ARE OUR TEAMMATES--
ENVY
ANGER
NOT CORPOREALLY. YOU'RE LOOKING AT THEIR INNER SPIRITS. THEIR SOULS.
SOMEHOW, THE SPIRITS OF THE SEVEN ARE LOOSE-- RUNNING RAMPANT AS THEY INHABIT THE BODIES OF OUR FRIENDS.
HEY!
SOMEONE'S DOWN THERE--

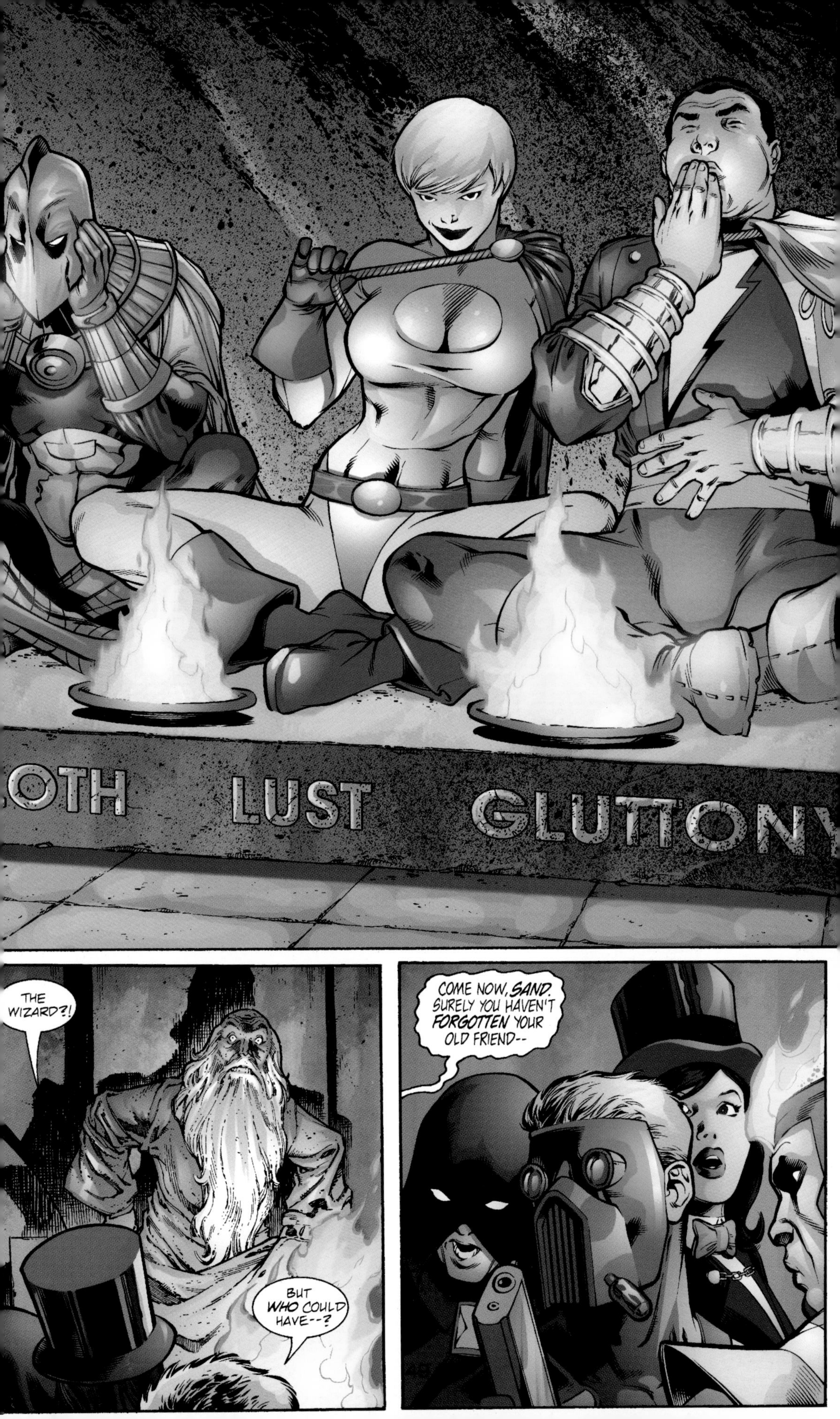

LOTH
LUST
GLUTTONY
THE WIZARD?!
BUT WHO COULD HAVE--?
COME NOW, SAND. SURELY YOU HAVEN'T FORGOTTEN YOUR OLD FRIEND--

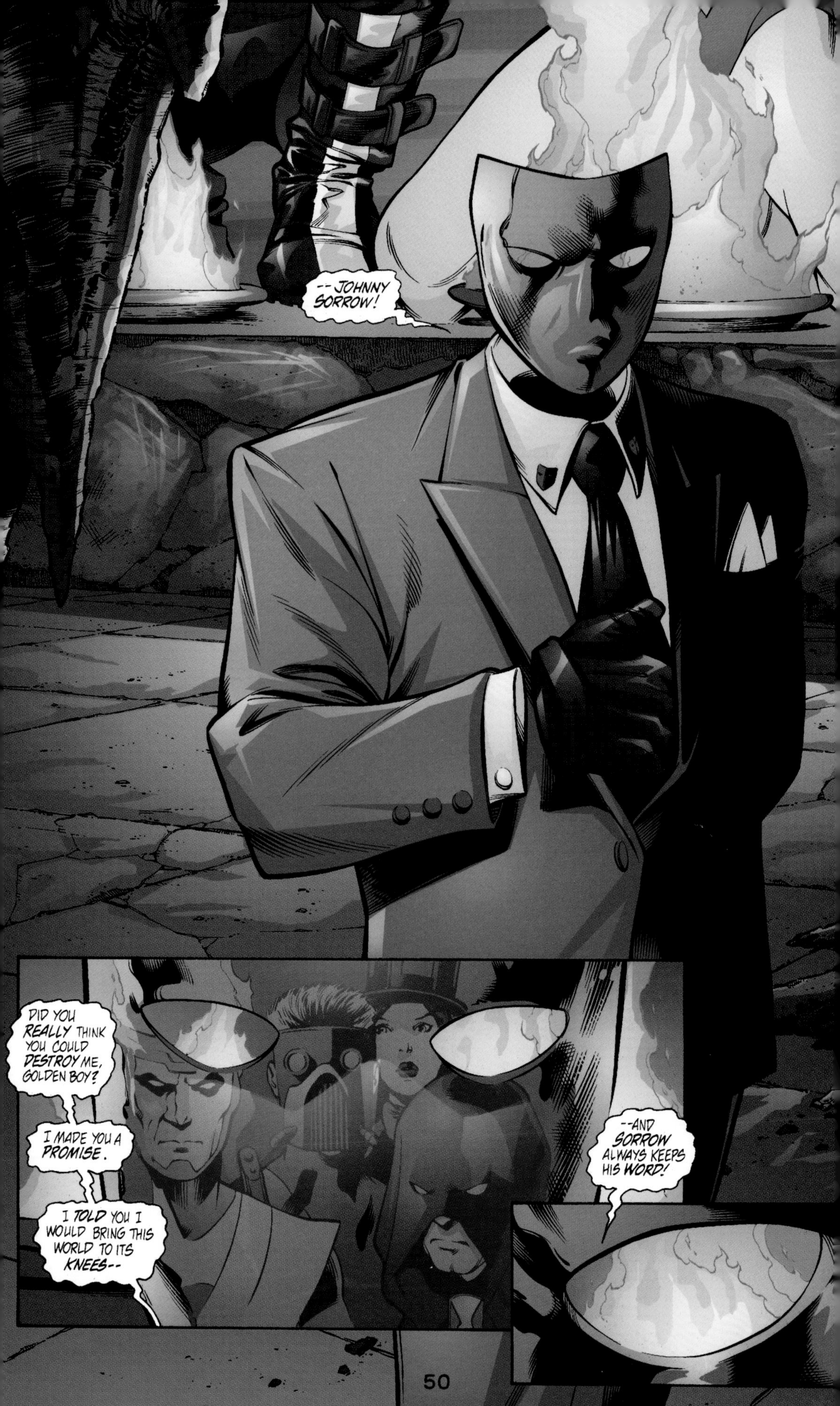
--JOHNNY SORROW!
DID YOU REALLY THINK YOU COULD DESTROY ME, GOLDEN BOY?
I MADE YOU A PROMISE.
I TOLD YOU I WOULD BRING THIS WORLD TO ITS KNEES--
--AND SORROW ALWAYS KEEPS HIS WORD!

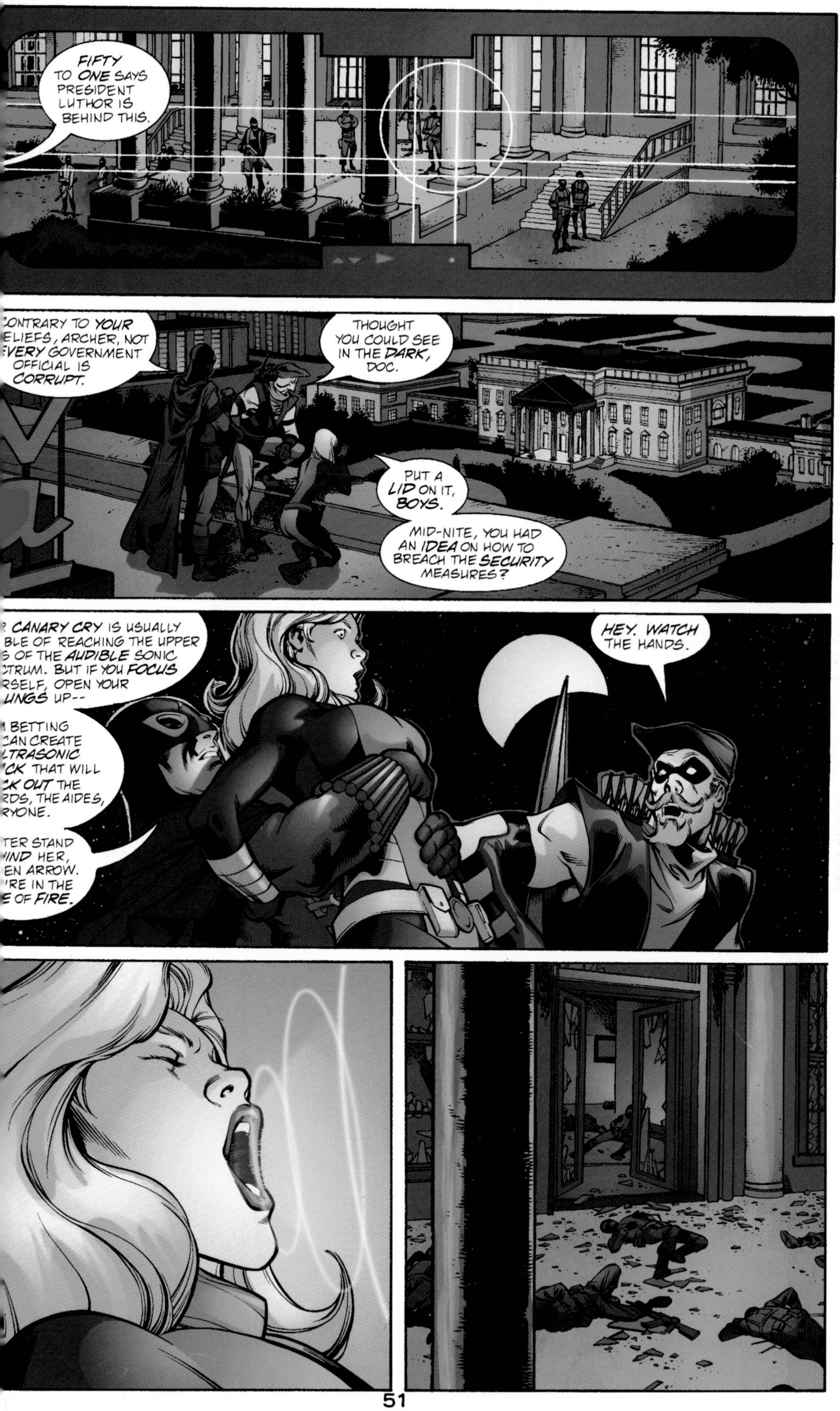
FIFTY TO ONE SAYS PRESIDENT LUTHOR IS BEHIND THIS.
ONTRARY TO YOUR ELIEFS, ARCHER, NOT EVERY GOVERNMENT OFFICIAL IS CORRUPT.
THOUGHT YOU COULD SEE IN THE DARK, DOC.
PUT A LID ON IT, BOYS.
MID-NITE, YOU HAD AN IDEA ON HOW TO BREACH THE SECURITY MEASURES?
CANARY CRY IS USUALLY BLE OF REACHING THE UPPER S OF THE AUDIBLE SONIC CTRUM. BUT IF YOU FOCUS RSELF, OPEN YOUR LUNGS UP--
I BETTING CAN CREATE LTRASONIC CK THAT WILL CK OUT THE RDS, THE AIDES, RYONE.
TER STAND HIND HER, EN ARROW. 'RE IN THE E OF FIRE.
HEY. WATCH THE HANDS.

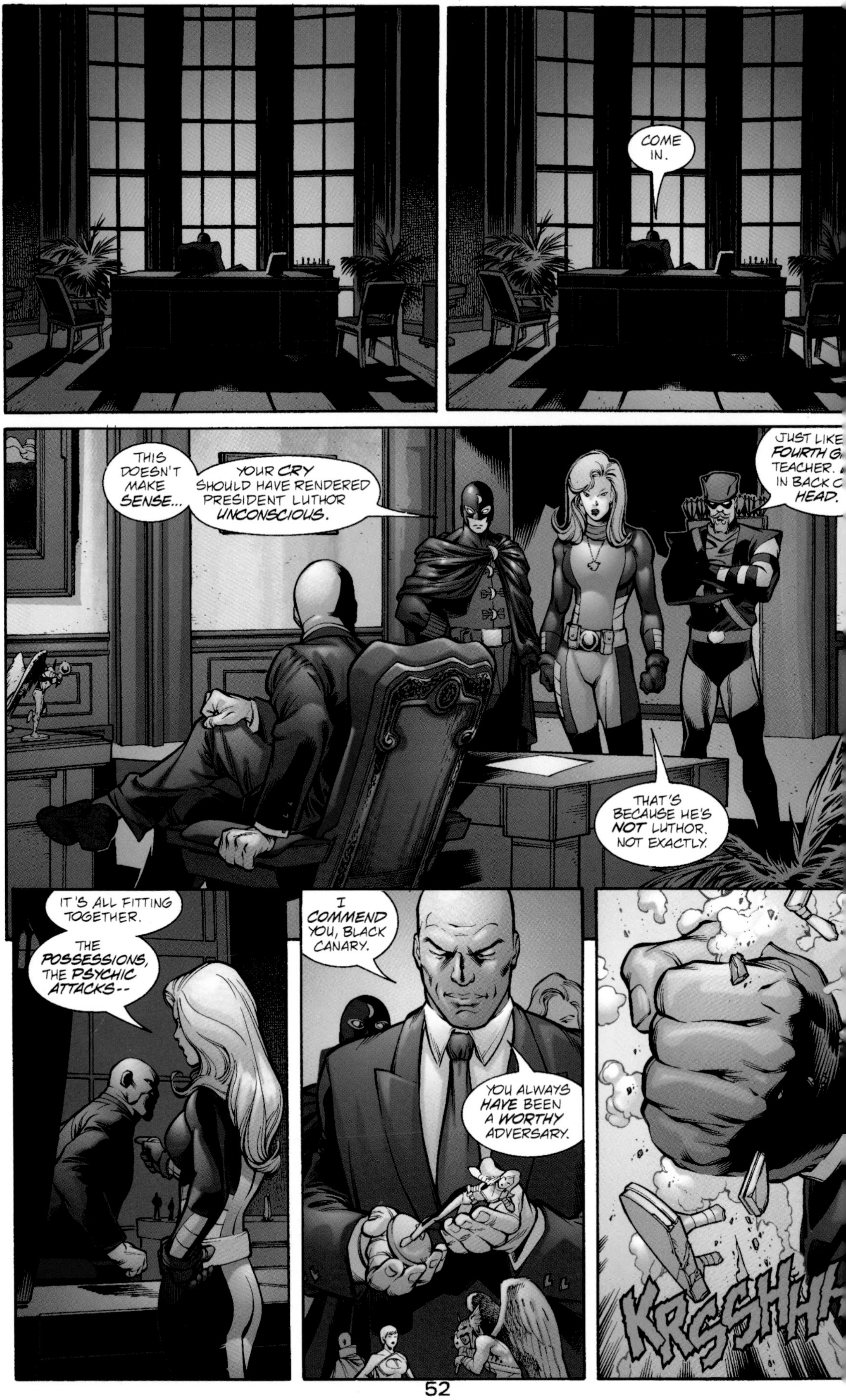
COME IN.
THIS DOESN'T MAKE SENSE...
YOUR CRY SHOULD HAVE RENDERED PRESIDENT LUTHOR UNCONSCIOUS.
JUST LIKE FOURTH G TEACHER. IN BACK O HEAD.
THAT'S BECAUSE HE'S NOT LUTHOR. NOT EXACTLY.
IT'S ALL FITTING TOGETHER.
THE POSSESSIONS, THE PSYCHIC ATTACKS--
I COMMEND YOU, BLACK CANARY.
YOU ALWAYS HAVE BEEN A WORTHY ADVERSARY.
KRSSH

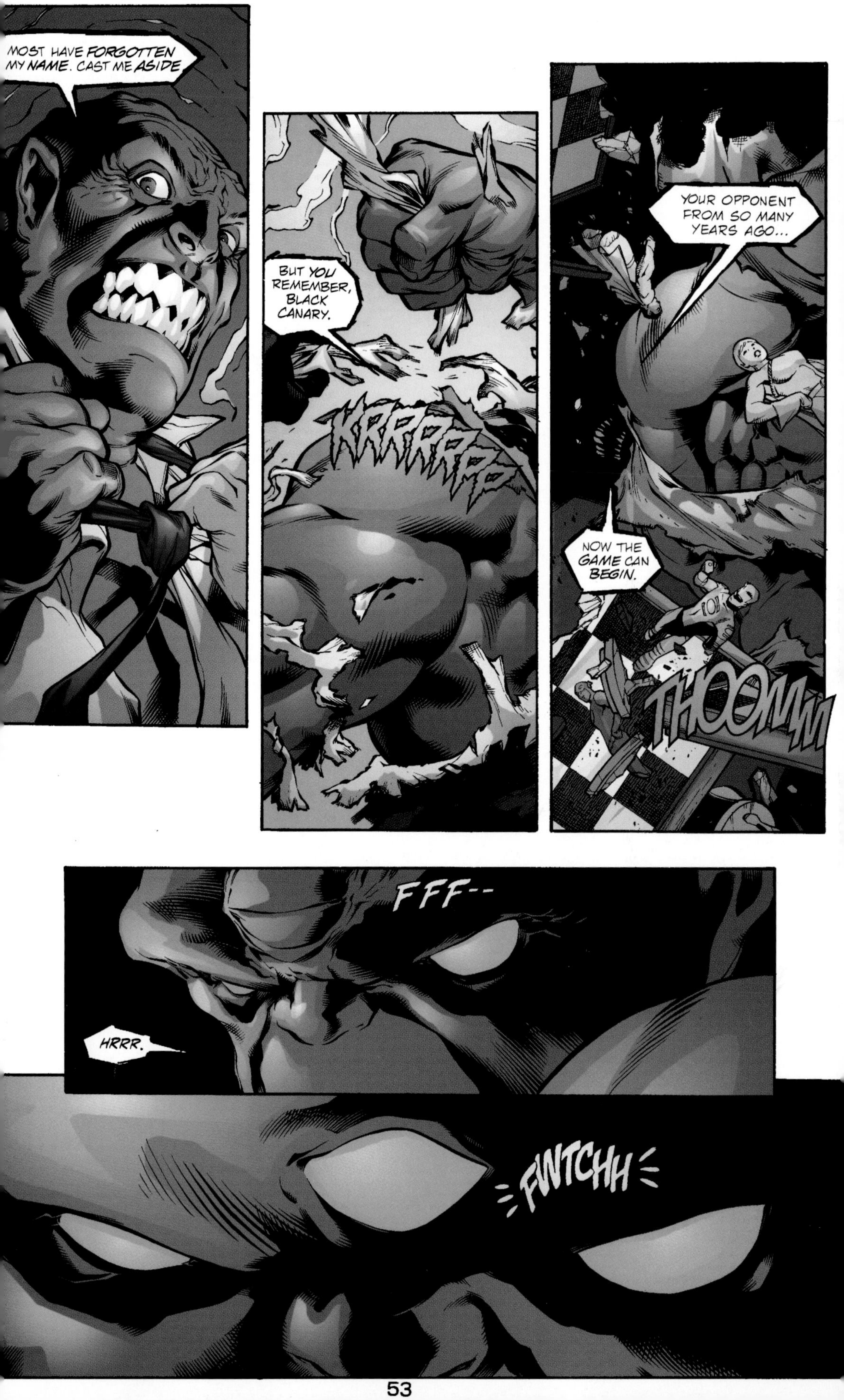
MOST HAVE FORGOTTEN MY NAME. CAST ME ASIDE
BUT YOU REMEMBER, BLACK CANARY.
KRRRRRP
YOUR OPPONENT FROM SO MANY YEARS AGO...
NOW THE GAME CAN BEGIN.
THOOMM
FFF--
HRRR.
FWTCHH

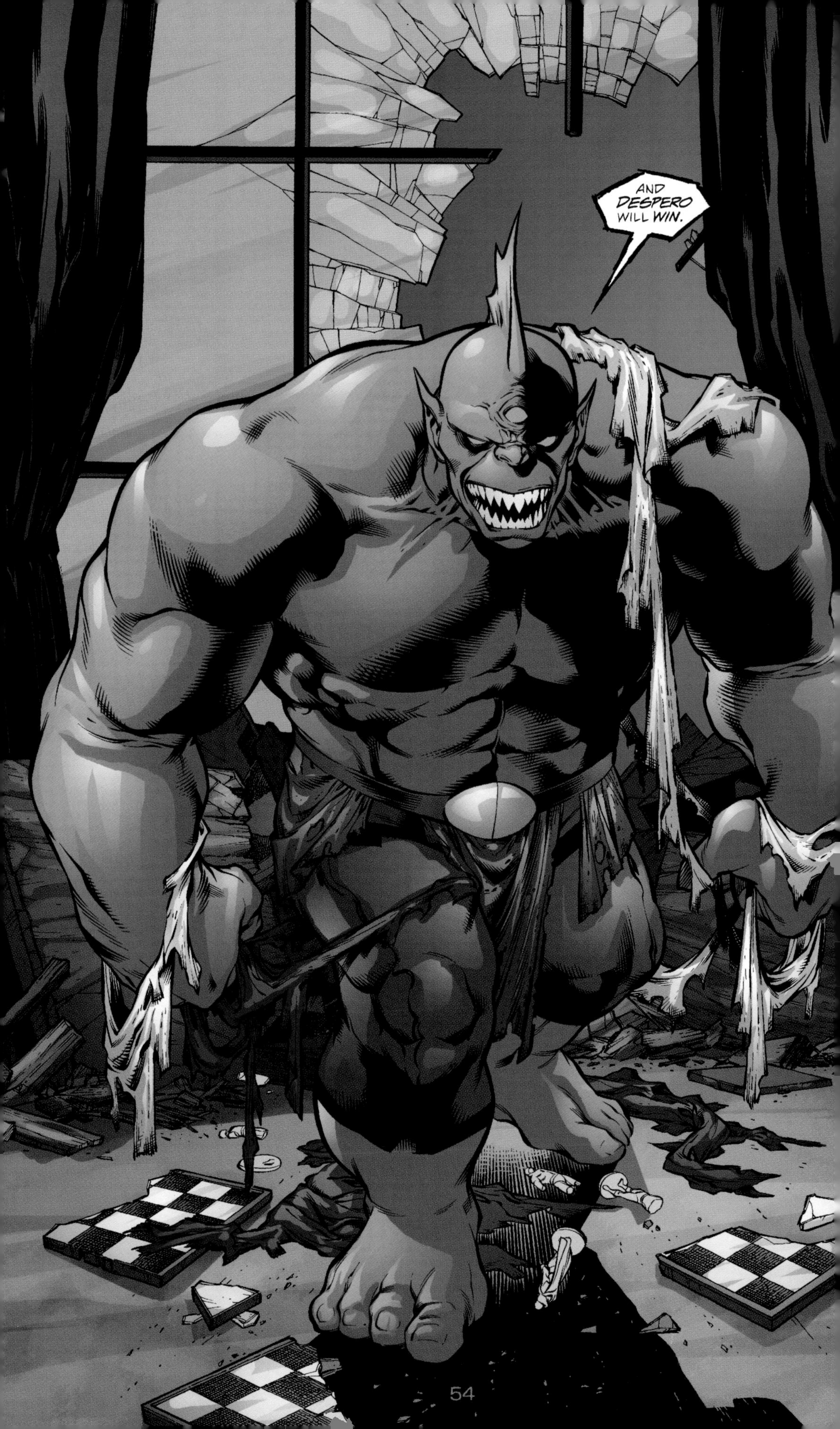
AND DESPERO WILL WIN.

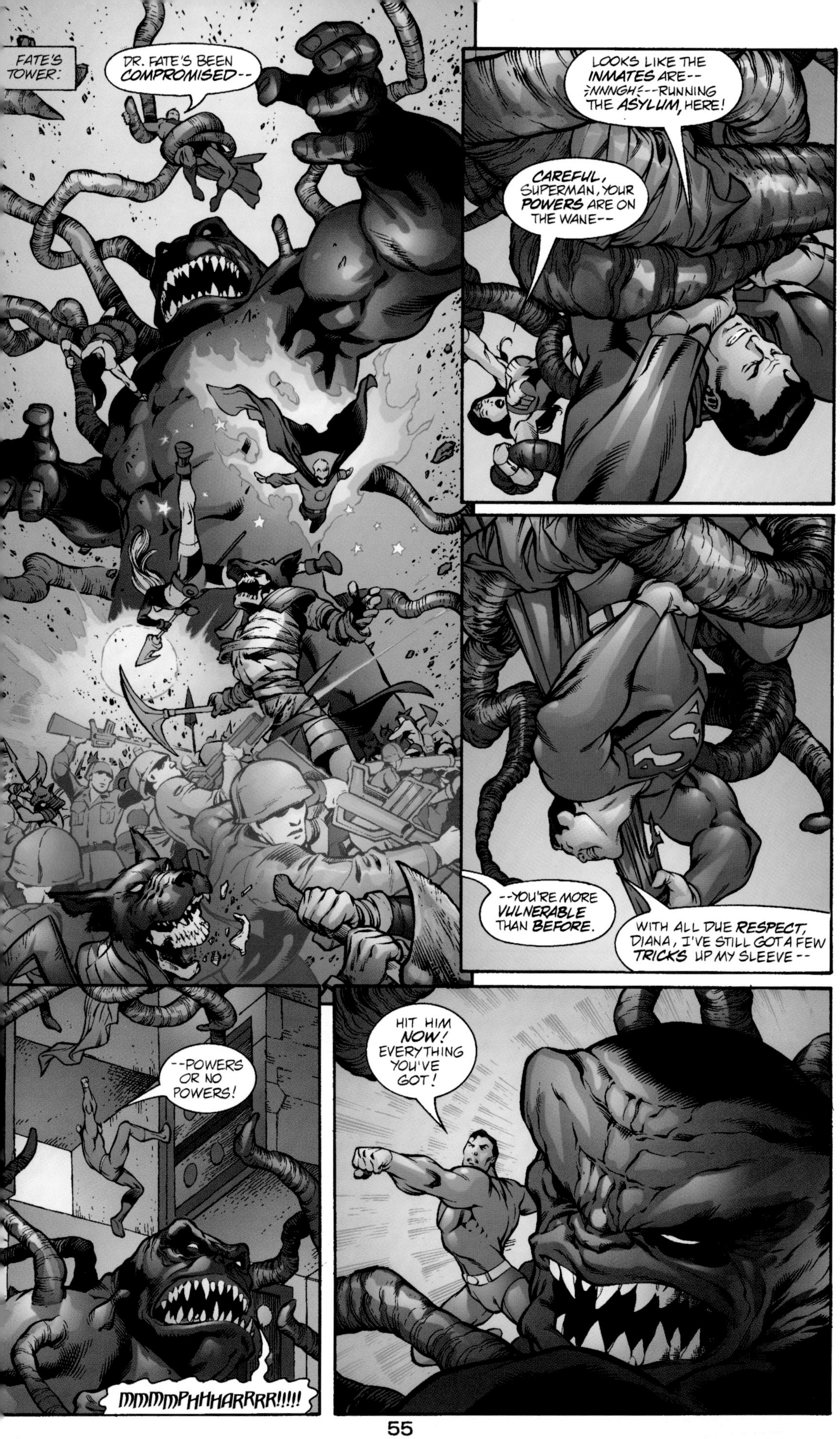
FATE'S TOWER:
DR. FATE'S BEEN COMPROMISED--
LOOKS LIKE THE INMATES ARE-- -NNNGH- --RUNNING THE ASYLUM, HERE!
CAREFUL, SUPERMAN, YOUR POWERS ARE ON THE WANE--
--YOU'RE MORE VULNERABLE THAN BEFORE.
WITH ALL DUE RESPECT, DIANA, I'VE STILL GOT A FEW TRICKS UP MY SLEEVE --
--POWERS OR NO POWERS!
MMMMPHHHARRRR!!!!!
HIT HIM NOW! EVERYTHING YOU'VE GOT!

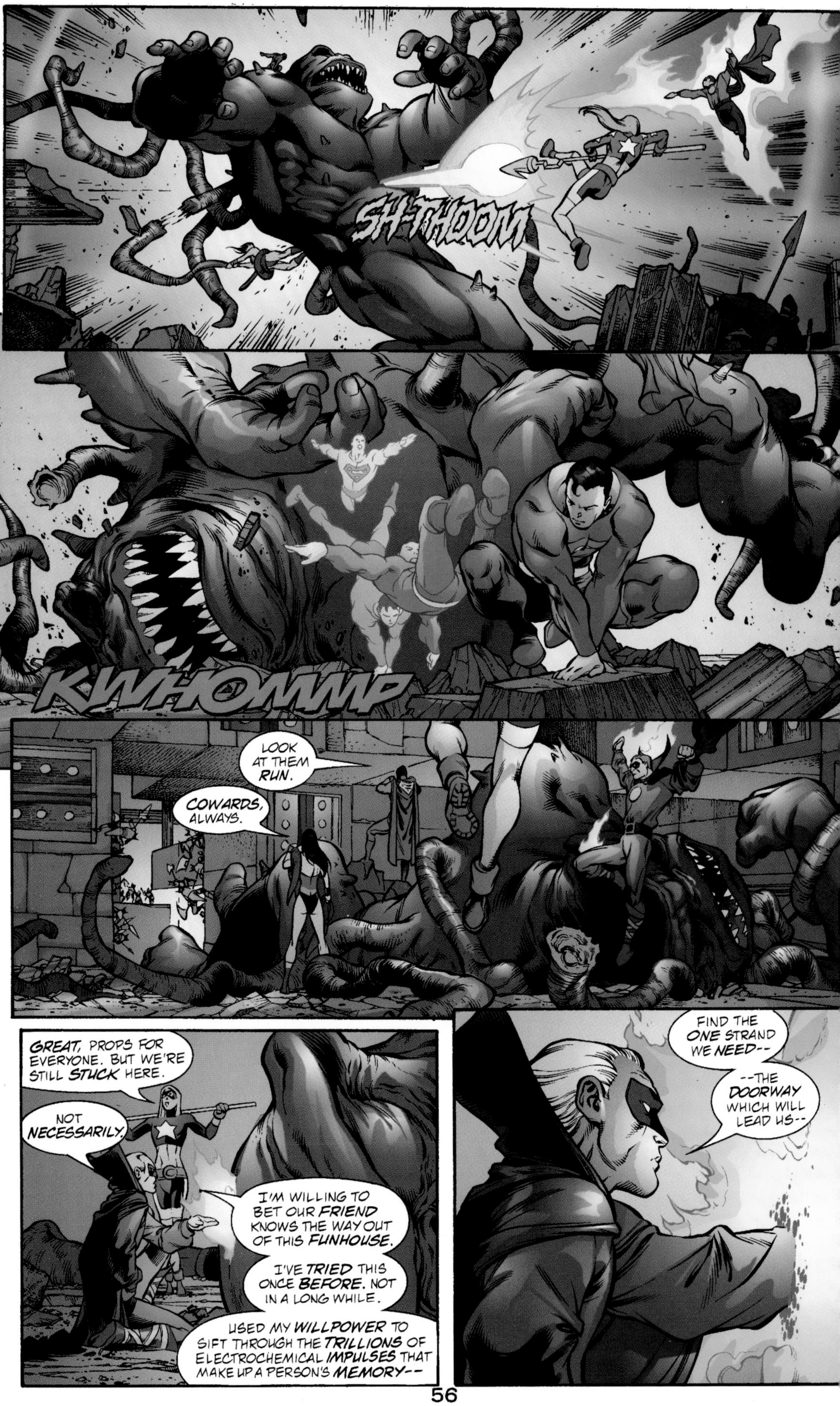
SH-THOOM
KWHOMMP
LOOK AT THEM RUN.
COWARDS, ALWAYS.
GREAT, PROPS FOR EVERYONE. BUT WE'RE STILL STUCK HERE.
NOT NECESSARILY.
I'M WILLING TO BET OUR FRIEND KNOWS THE WAY OUT OF THIS FUNHOUSE.
I'VE TRIED THIS ONCE BEFORE. NOT IN A LONG WHILE.
USED MY WILLPOWER TO SIFT THROUGH THE TRILLIONS OF ELECTROCHEMICAL IMPULSES THAT MAKE UP A PERSON'S MEMORY--
FIND THE ONE STRAND WE NEED--
--THE DOORWAY WHICH WILL LEAD US--

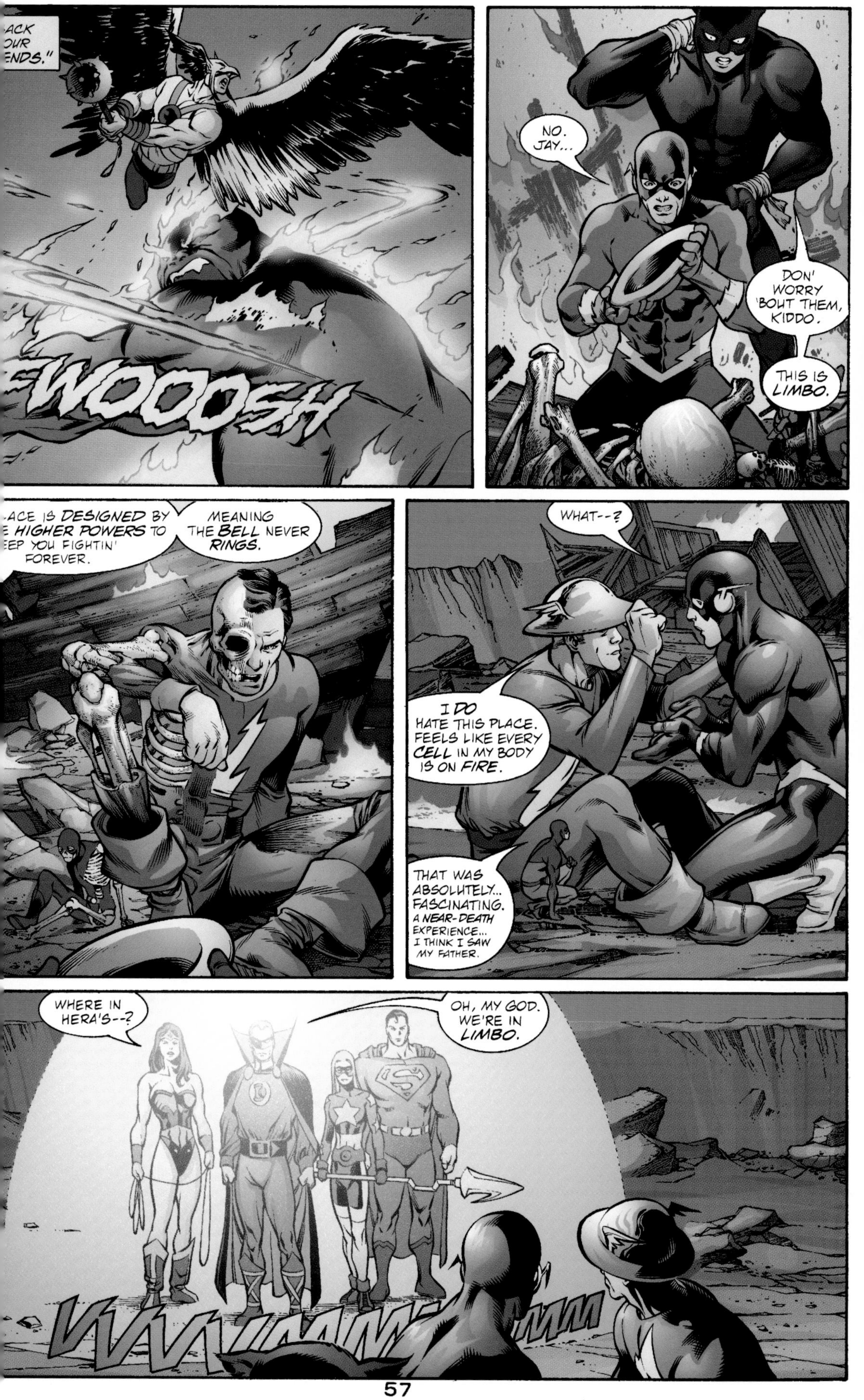

ACK
OUR
ENDS."
WOOSH
NO. JAY...
DON' WORRY 'BOUT THEM, KIDDO.
THIS IS LIMBO.
ACE IS DESIGNED BY
HIGHER POWERS TO
EP YOU FIGHTIN' FOREVER.
MEANING THE BELL NEVER RINGS.
WHAT--?
I DO HATE THIS PLACE. FEELS LIKE EVERY CELL IN MY BODY IS ON FIRE.
THAT WAS ABSOLUTELY... FASCINATING. A NEAR-DEATH EXPERIENCE... I THINK I SAW MY FATHER.
WHERE IN HERA'S--?
OH, MY GOD. WE'RE IN LIMBO.
VVVVAAAMMMMMM

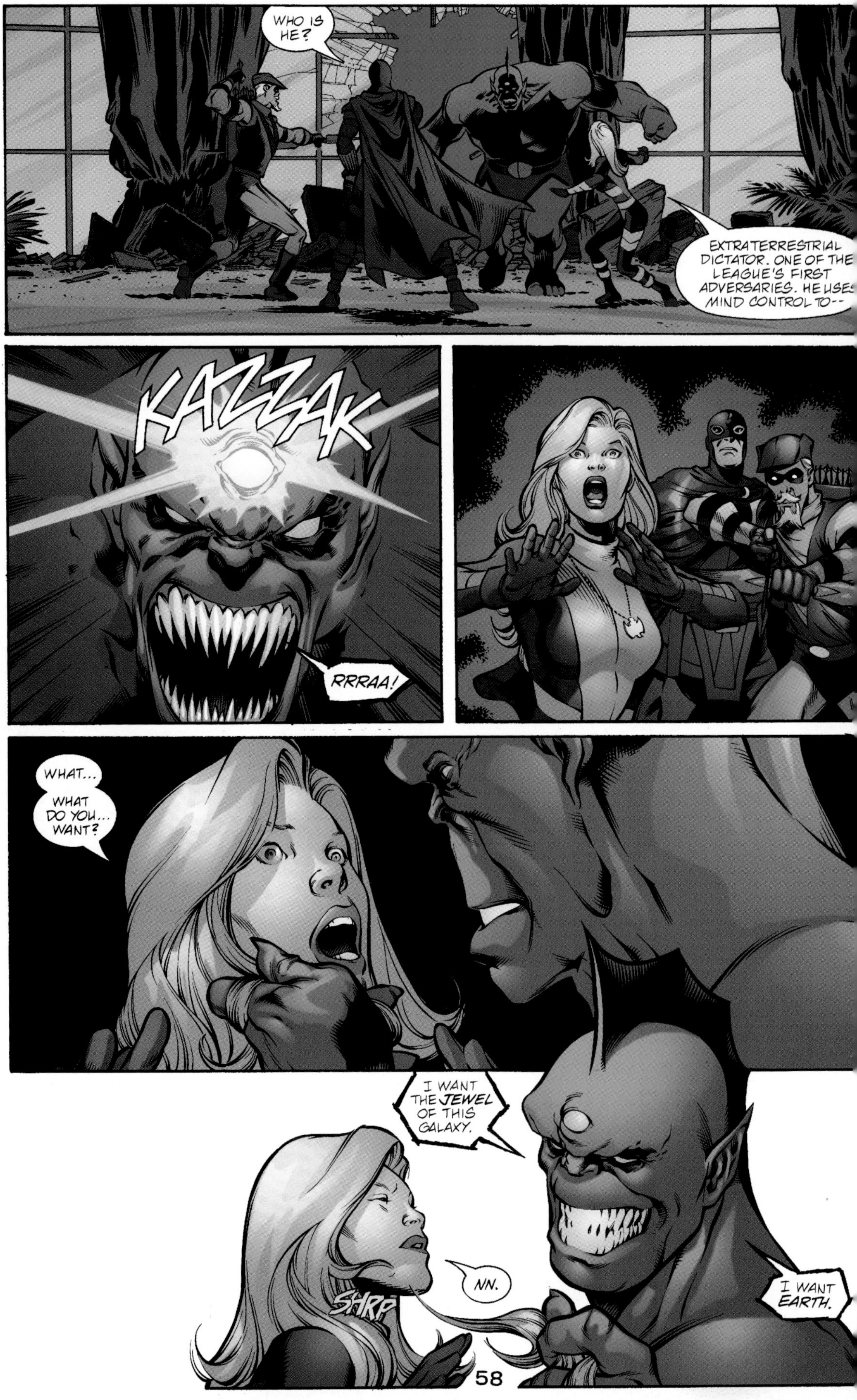
WHO IS HE?
EXTRATERRESTRIAL DICTATOR. ONE OF THE LEAGUE'S FIRST ADVERSARIES. HE USES MIND CONTROL TO--
KAZZAK
RRRAA!
WHAT...
WHAT DO YOU... WANT?
I WANT THE JEWEL OF THIS GALAXY.
NN.
SHRP
I WANT EARTH.

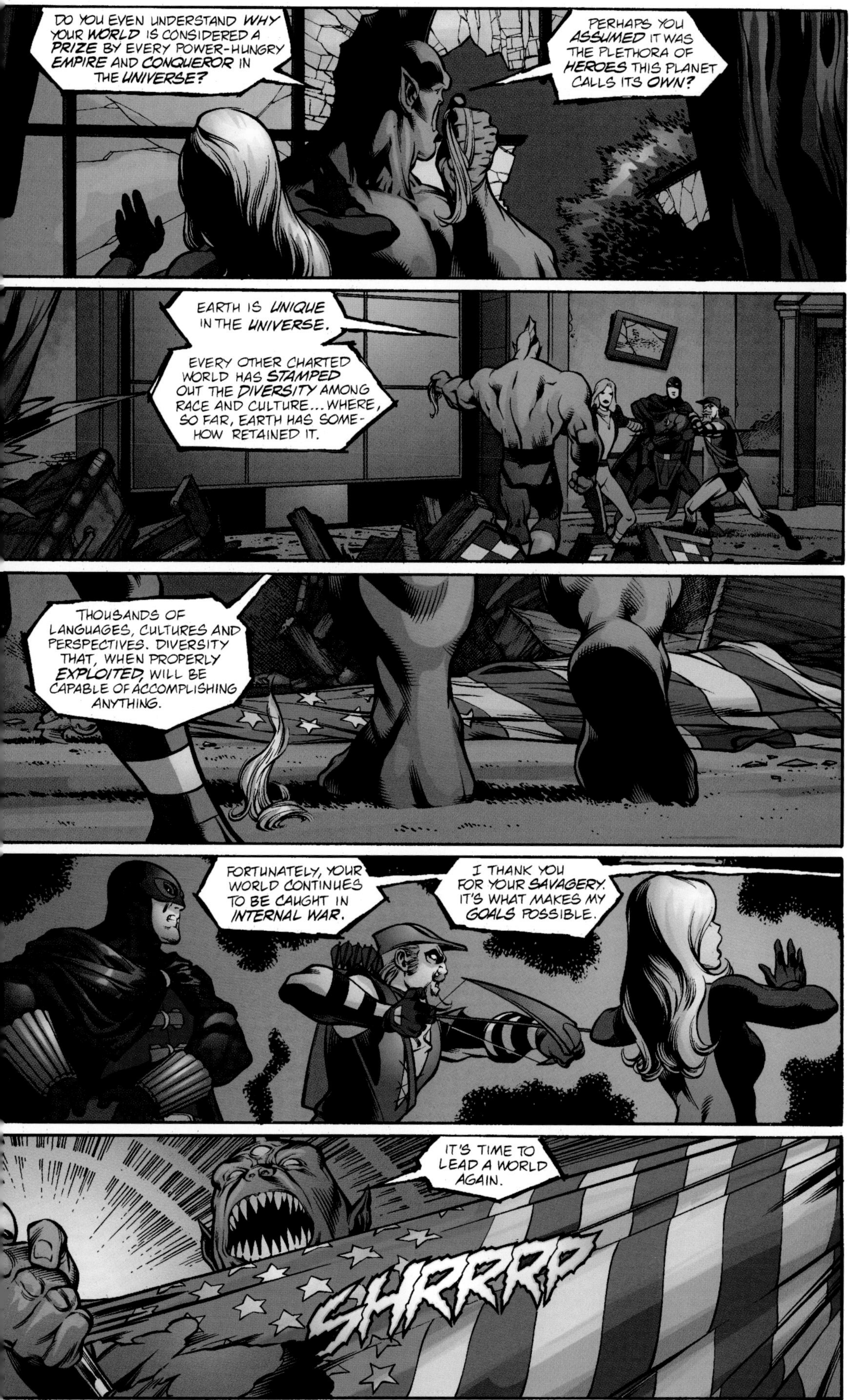
DO YOU EVEN UNDERSTAND WHY YOUR WORLD IS CONSIDERED A PRIZE BY EVERY POWER-HUNGRY EMPIRE AND CONQUEROR IN THE UNIVERSE?
PERHAPS YOU ASSUMED IT WAS THE PLETHORA OF HEROES THIS PLANET CALLS ITS OWN?
EARTH IS UNIQUE IN THE UNIVERSE.
EVERY OTHER CHARTED WORLD HAS STAMPED OUT THE DIVERSITY AMONG RACE AND CULTURE...WHERE, SO FAR, EARTH HAS SOME-HOW RETAINED IT.
THOUSANDS OF LANGUAGES, CULTURES AND PERSPECTIVES. DIVERSITY THAT, WHEN PROPERLY EXPLOITED, WILL BE CAPABLE OF ACCOMPLISHING ANYTHING.
FORTUNATELY, YOUR WORLD CONTINUES TO BE CAUGHT IN INTERNAL WAR.
I THANK YOU FOR YOUR SAVAGERY. IT'S WHAT MAKES MY GOALS POSSIBLE.
IT'S TIME TO LEAD A WORLD AGAIN.
SHRRRP

WHEN I WAS BANISHED FROM MY HOME PLANET OF KALANOR, I WAS BLINDED BY RAGE AND BLOODLUST.

FROM LEADER TO EXILE ALL BECAUSE OF EARTH'S HEROES. THE JUSTICE LEAGUE OF AMERICA.

I MAY HAVE CONTINUED TO EVOLVE--PHYSICALLY--BUT PSYCHOLOGICALLY I WAS FOUND LACKING.

I'D SQUANDERED MY ENERGIES ON PRIMITIVE FRONTAL ATTACKS. ALLOWED MYSELF TO BE OBSESSED WITH VENGEANCE.

AND IN ONE SUCH BATTLE, MY PHYSICAL FORM WAS FINALLY DESTROYED--

--LEAVING MY RUDDERLESS SPIRIT TO WANDER.

EVENTUALLY, MY PSYC[HIC] FORM COALESCED O[N] THE ABYSSAL PLANE, [A] DIMENSION NESTLE[D] BETWEEN THE CRACK[S] OF REALITY.

HE CALLED HIMSELF JOHNNY SORROW.

LIKE ME, HIS PHYSICAL FORM HAD BEEN SUNDERED FROM YOUR WORLD. APPARENTLY IT WAS HIS CRY FOR HELP THAT I HAD UNINTENTION-ALLY ANSWERED.

HE BLAMED ANOTHER TEAM OF HEROES--THE JUSTIC[E] SOCIETY--FOR HIS WRETCHED STATE.

IN THE CAULDRON OF OUR SHARED HATRED, A PACT WAS FORGED.

WE NEEDED AN ARMY. A HORDE THROUGH WHICH W[E] WOULD DISTRAC[T] EARTH'S HEROES.

60

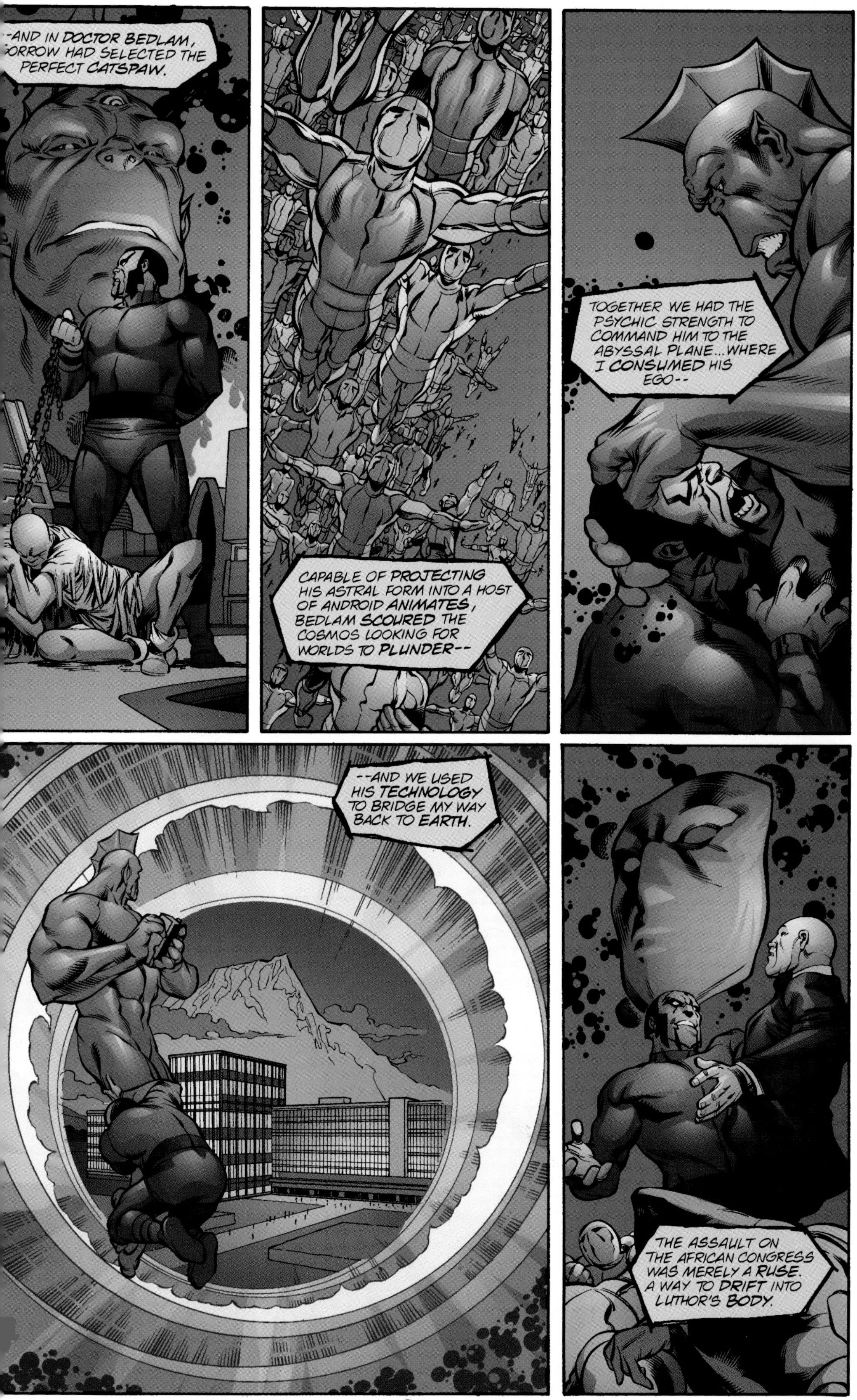
--AND IN DOCTOR BEDLAM, SORROW HAD SELECTED THE PERFECT CATSPAW.
CAPABLE OF PROJECTING HIS ASTRAL FORM INTO A HOST OF ANDROID ANIMATES, BEDLAM SCOURED THE COSMOS LOOKING FOR WORLDS TO PLUNDER--
TOGETHER WE HAD THE PSYCHIC STRENGTH TO COMMAND HIM TO THE ABYSSAL PLANE...WHERE I CONSUMED HIS EGO--
--AND WE USED HIS TECHNOLOGY TO BRIDGE MY WAY BACK TO EARTH.
THE ASSAULT ON THE AFRICAN CONGRESS WAS MERELY A RUSE. A WAY TO DRIFT INTO LUTHOR'S BODY.

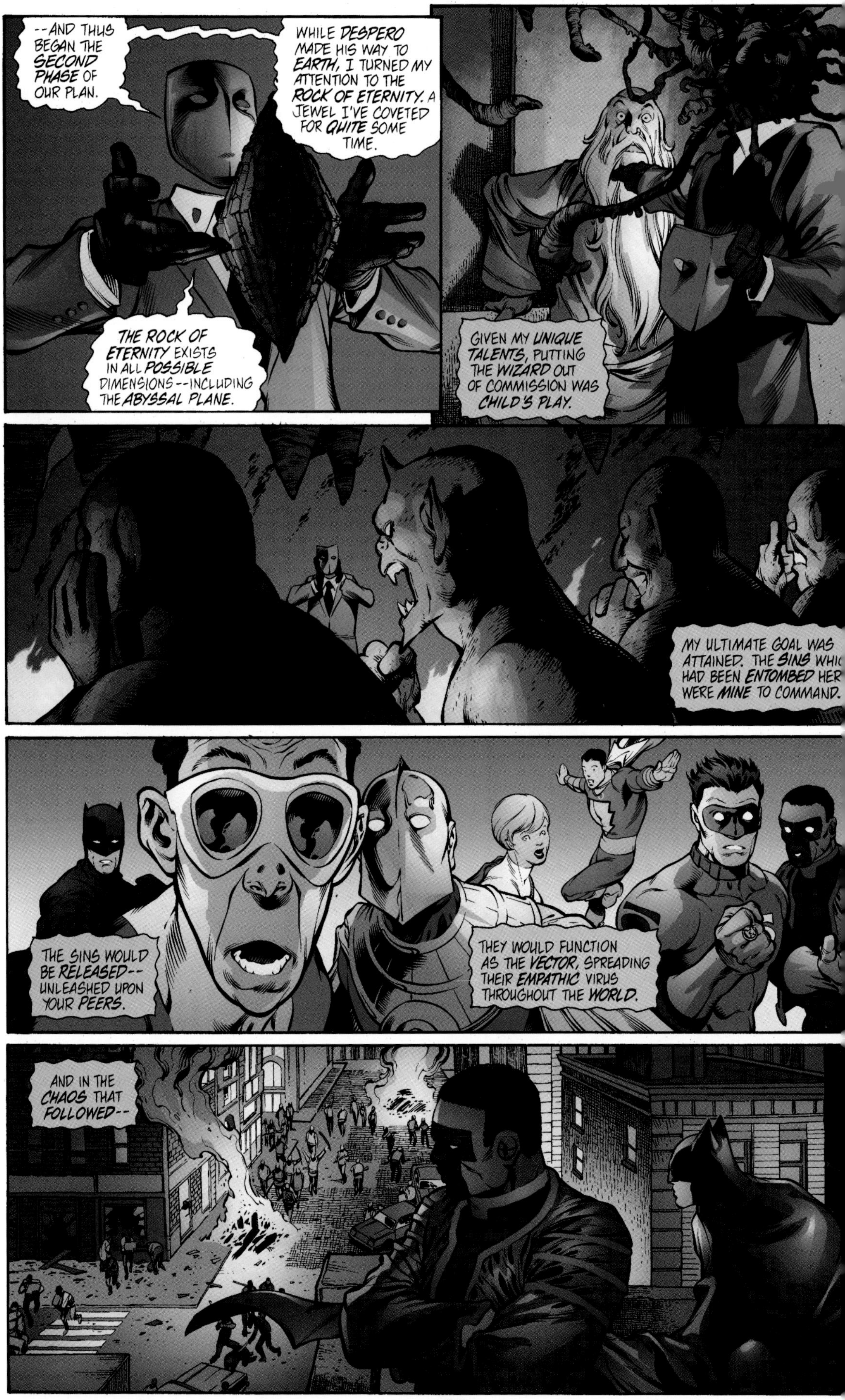
--AND THUS BEGAN THE SECOND PHASE OF OUR PLAN.
WHILE DESPERO MADE HIS WAY TO EARTH, I TURNED MY ATTENTION TO THE ROCK OF ETERNITY. A JEWEL I'VE COVETED FOR QUITE SOME TIME.
THE ROCK OF ETERNITY EXISTS IN ALL POSSIBLE DIMENSIONS--INCLUDING THE ABYSSAL PLANE.
GIVEN MY UNIQUE TALENTS, PUTTING THE WIZARD OUT OF COMMISSION WAS CHILD'S PLAY.
MY ULTIMATE GOAL WAS ATTAINED. THE SINS WHIC HAD BEEN ENTOMBED HER WERE MINE TO COMMAND.
THE SINS WOULD BE RELEASED-- UNLEASHED UPON YOUR PEERS.
THEY WOULD FUNCTION AS THE VECTOR, SPREADING THEIR EMPATHIC VIRUS THROUGHOUT THE WORLD.
AND IN THE CHAOS THAT FOLLOWED--

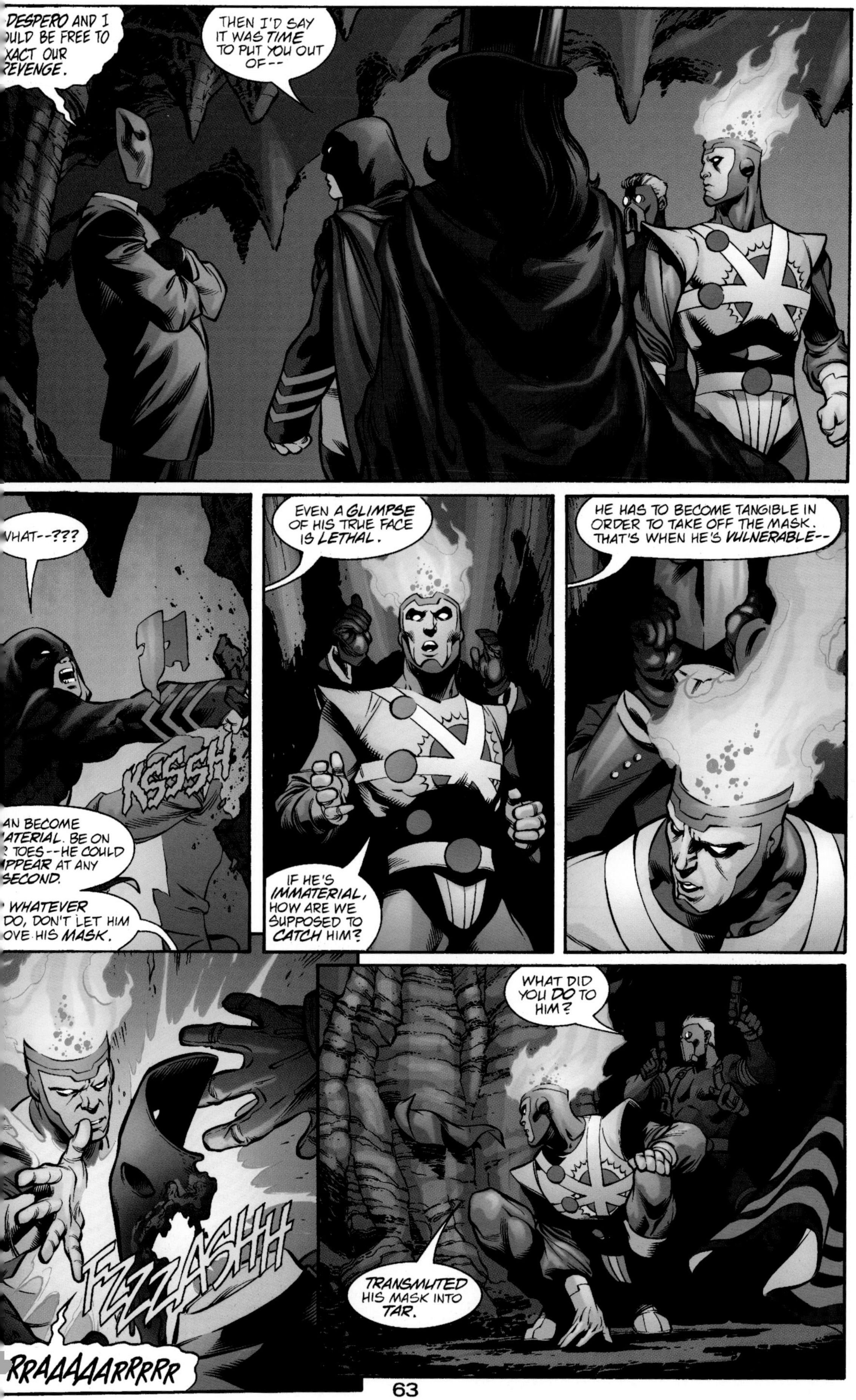
DESPERO AND I
OULD BE FREE TO
XACT OUR
REVENGE.
THEN I'D SAY IT WAS TIME TO PUT YOU OUT OF--
WHAT--???
EVEN A GLIMPSE OF HIS TRUE FACE IS LETHAL.
HE HAS TO BECOME TANGIBLE IN ORDER TO TAKE OFF THE MASK. THAT'S WHEN HE'S VULNERABLE--
KSSSH
AN BECOME
MATERIAL. BE ON
TOES--HE COULD
PPEAR AT ANY
SECOND.
WHATEVER
DO, DON'T LET HIM
OVE HIS MASK.
IF HE'S IMMATERIAL, HOW ARE WE SUPPOSED TO CATCH HIM?
FZZZASHH
RRAAAAARRRRR
WHAT DID YOU DO TO HIM?
TRANSMUTED HIS MASK INTO TAR.

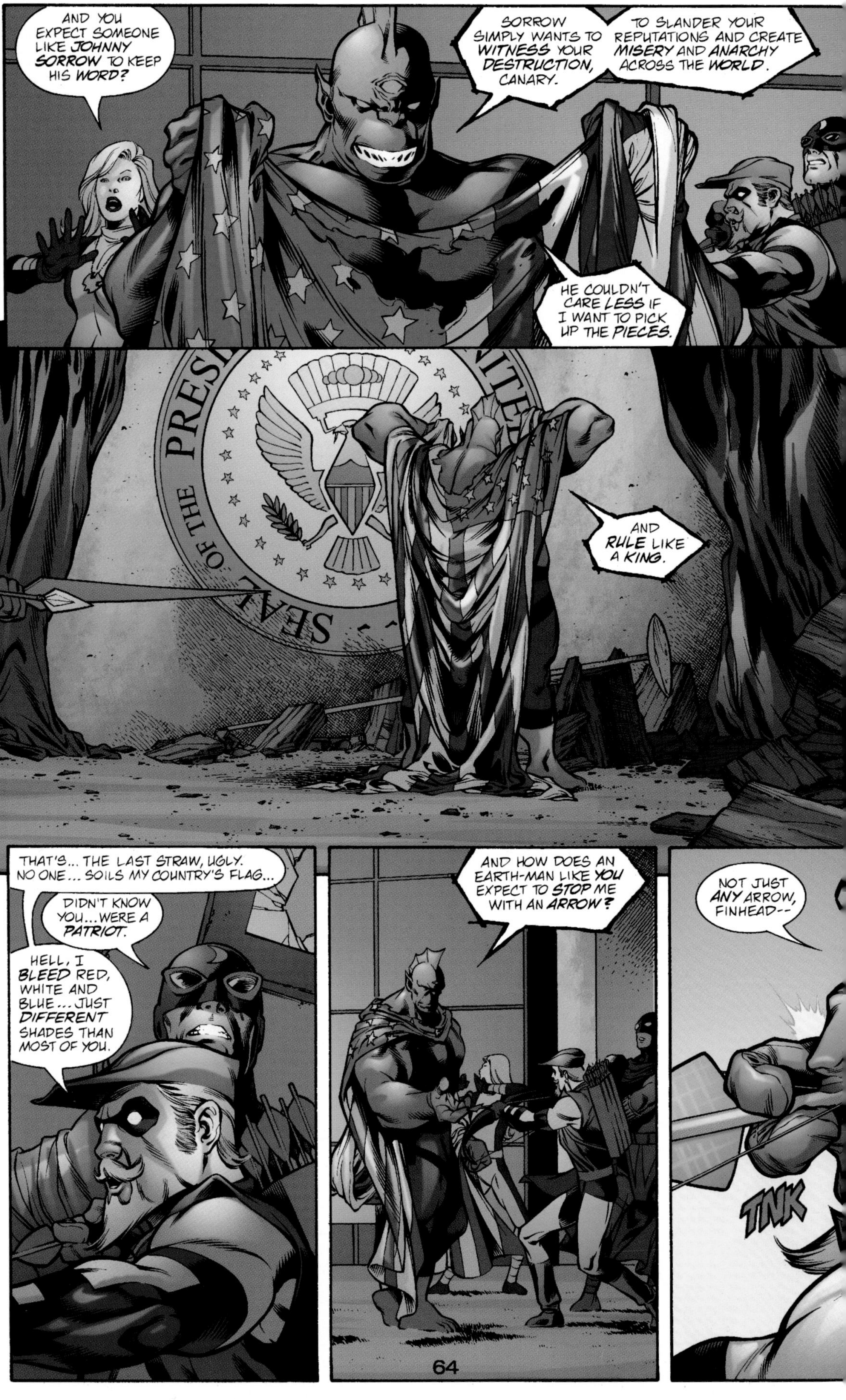
AND YOU EXPECT SOMEONE LIKE JOHNNY SORROW TO KEEP HIS WORD?
SORROW SIMPLY WANTS TO WITNESS YOUR DESTRUCTION, CANARY.
TO SLANDER YOUR REPUTATIONS AND CREATE MISERY AND ANARCHY ACROSS THE WORLD.
HE COULDN'T CARE LESS IF I WANT TO PICK UP THE PIECES.
AND RULE LIKE A KING.
THAT'S... THE LAST STRAW, UGLY. NO ONE... SOILS MY COUNTRY'S FLAG...
DIDN'T KNOW YOU...WERE A PATRIOT.
HELL, I BLEED RED, WHITE AND BLUE... JUST DIFFERENT SHADES THAN MOST OF YOU.
AND HOW DOES AN EARTH-MAN LIKE YOU EXPECT TO STOP ME WITH AN ARROW?
NOT JUST ANY ARROW, FINHEAD--
TNK

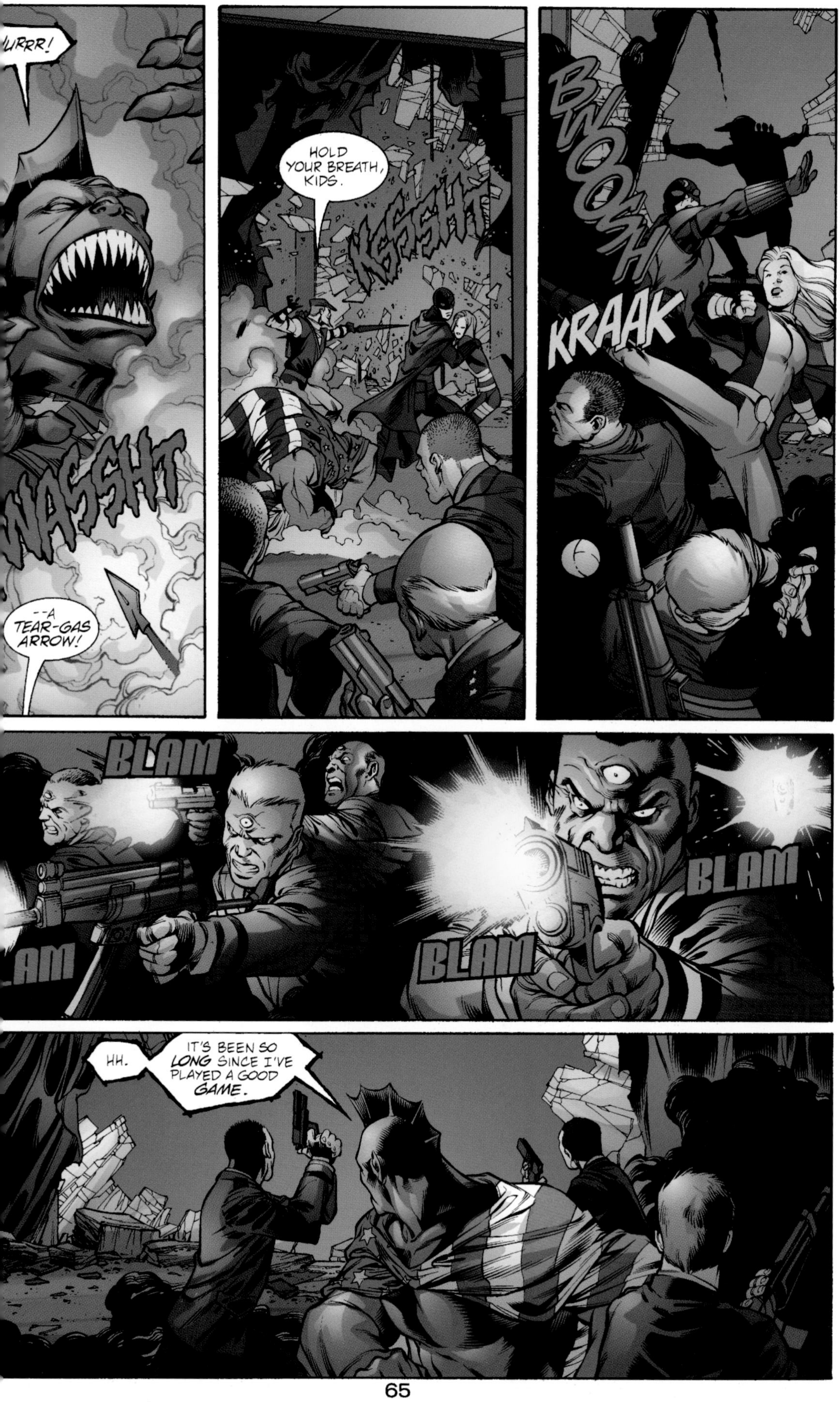

URRR!
WASSHT
--A TEAR-GAS ARROW!
HOLD YOUR BREATH, KIDS.
KSSSHT
BWOOMH
KRAAK
BLAM
AM
BLAM
BLAM
HH.
IT'S BEEN SO LONG SINCE I'VE PLAYED A GOOD GAME.

STAND BACK!

STAR?! WHAT ARE YOU DOING?

FASH

MY COSMIC ROD IS POWERED BY *SUNLIGHT.* I'M GIVING SUPERMAN'S POWERS A QUICK *RECHARGE.*

THANKS, STAR.

YO! NICE OF YOU FOLKS TO *DROP IN*--

SIT BACK. STAY A *WHILE.*

THE *ATOM'S* ABOUT TO TEACH THIS FLAMING MOOK A *LESSON* IN *THERMODYNAMICS.*

THE JSA FOUGHT THAT THING FOR *CENTURIES*--THE BEST WE COULD ACCOMPLISH WAS A *STANDSTILL.*

THAT'S BECAUSE YOU DIDN'T HAVE PROFESSOR RAY PALMER PINCH-HITTING FOR YOU.

SURTUR'S A *FIRE DEMON,* RIGHT? IN A NUTSHELL, WHAT THAT MEANS IS--HE'S A WALKING BUNDLE OF INTERNAL *NUCLEAR REACTIONS.* A SENTIENT *STELLAR MASS.*

IF THE *FLASHES* CAN LEND HIM THEIR *VELOCITY,* I'M BETTING THEY'LL BE ABLE TO SPEED UP THE RATE OF HIS *STELLAR EVOLUTION.*

THEY KEEP PUSHING *HARD* ENOUGH, THEY'LL *EXHAUST* THE NUCLEAR FUEL AT HIS *CORE.* THE RESULTING GRAVITATIONAL CONTRACTION SHOULD TURN HIM INTO A *BLACK HOLE.*

SO?

SO THIS--BLACK HOLES AR *WORMHOLES.* SHORTCUTS THROUGH THE SPACE-TIME CONTINUUM. IF WE CAN FIGL OUT A WAY TO POINT OUR WO HOLE IN THE RIGHT *DIRECTI* WE MAY BE ABLE TO HITCH A RIDE BACK *HOME.*

AND THAT'S WHERE *SENTINEL* COMES IN.

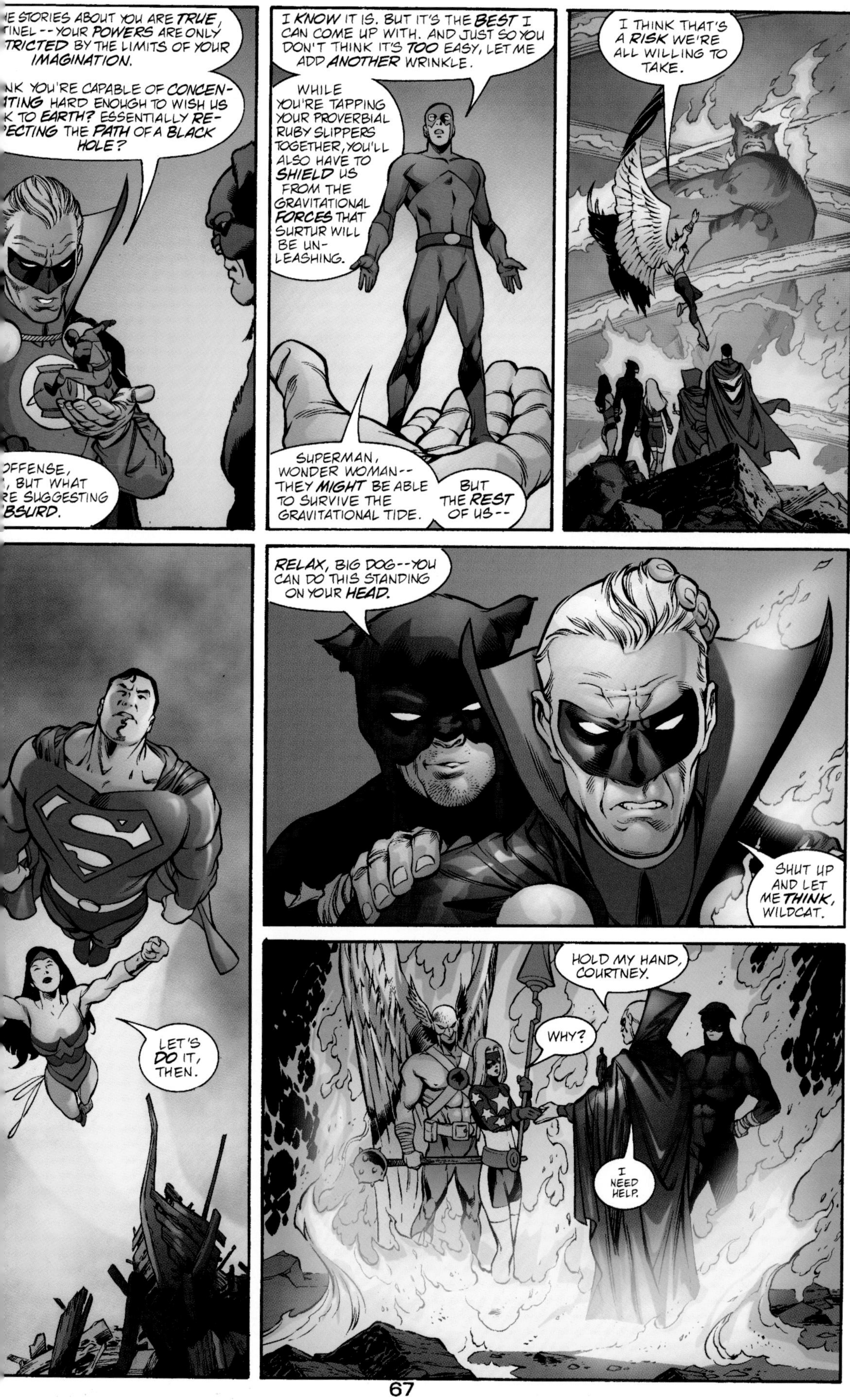
E STORIES ABOUT YOU ARE TRUE, TINEL--YOUR POWERS ARE ONLY TRICTED BY THE LIMITS OF YOUR IMAGINATION.
NK YOU'RE CAPABLE OF CONCEN-TING HARD ENOUGH TO WISH US K TO EARTH? ESSENTIALLY RE-ECTING THE PATH OF A BLACK HOLE?
OFFENSE, , BUT WHAT E SUGGESTING BSURD.
I KNOW IT IS. BUT IT'S THE BEST I CAN COME UP WITH. AND JUST SO YOU DON'T THINK IT'S TOO EASY, LET ME ADD ANOTHER WRINKLE.
WHILE YOU'RE TAPPING YOUR PROVERBIAL RUBY SLIPPERS TOGETHER, YOU'LL ALSO HAVE TO SHIELD US FROM THE GRAVITATIONAL FORCES THAT SURTUR WILL BE UN-LEASHING.
SUPERMAN, WONDER WOMAN--THEY MIGHT BE ABLE TO SURVIVE THE GRAVITATIONAL TIDE.
BUT THE REST OF US--
I THINK THAT'S A RISK WE'RE ALL WILLING TO TAKE.
LET'S DO IT, THEN.
RELAX, BIG DOG--YOU CAN DO THIS STANDING ON YOUR HEAD.
SHUT UP AND LET ME THINK, WILDCAT.
HOLD MY HAND, COURTNEY.
WHY?
I NEED HELP.

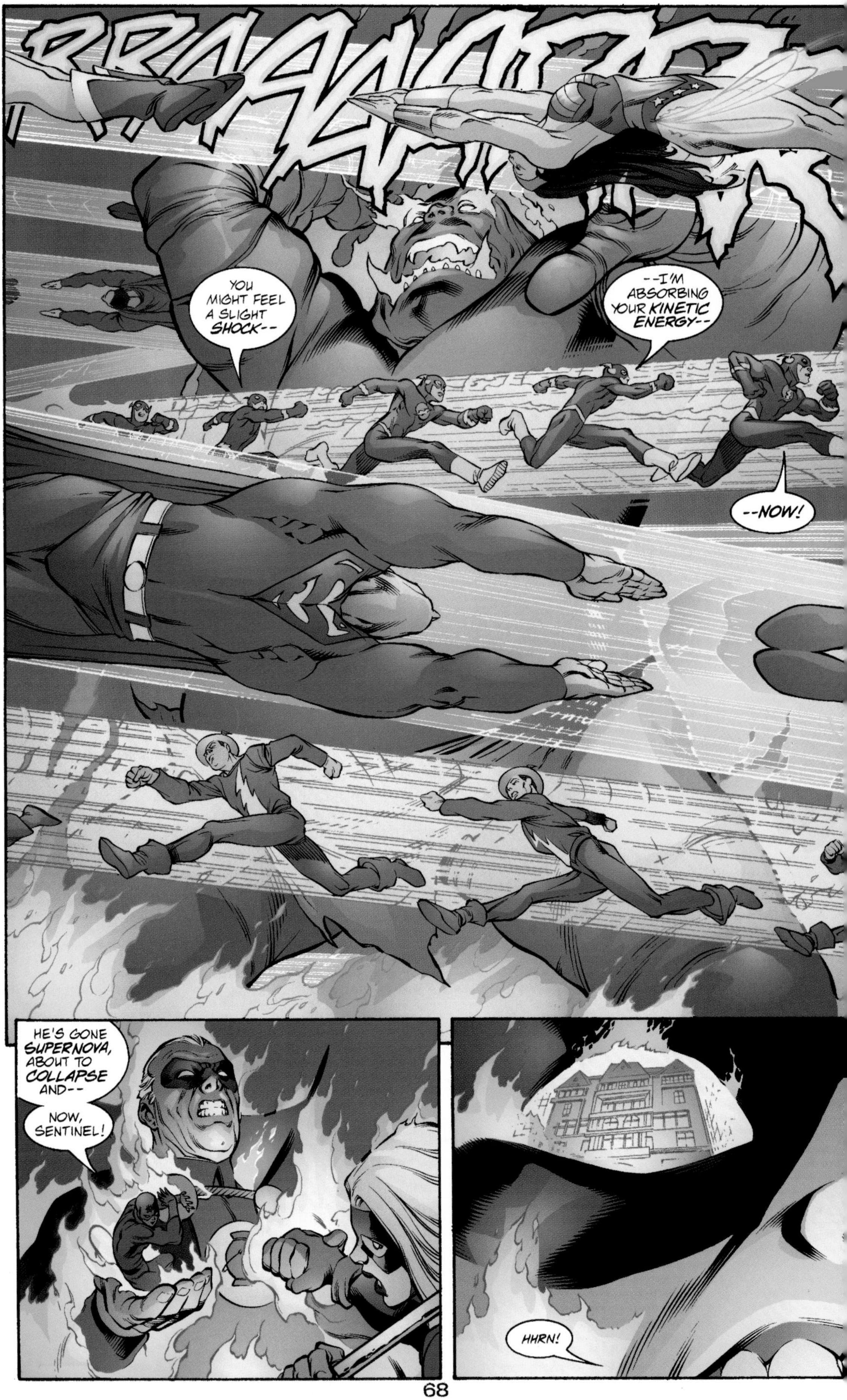
BRAAAKOOOM
YOU MIGHT FEEL A SLIGHT SHOCK--
--I'M ABSORBING YOUR KINETIC ENERGY--
--NOW!
HE'S GONE SUPERNOVA, ABOUT TO COLLAPSE AND--
NOW, SENTINEL!
HHRN!

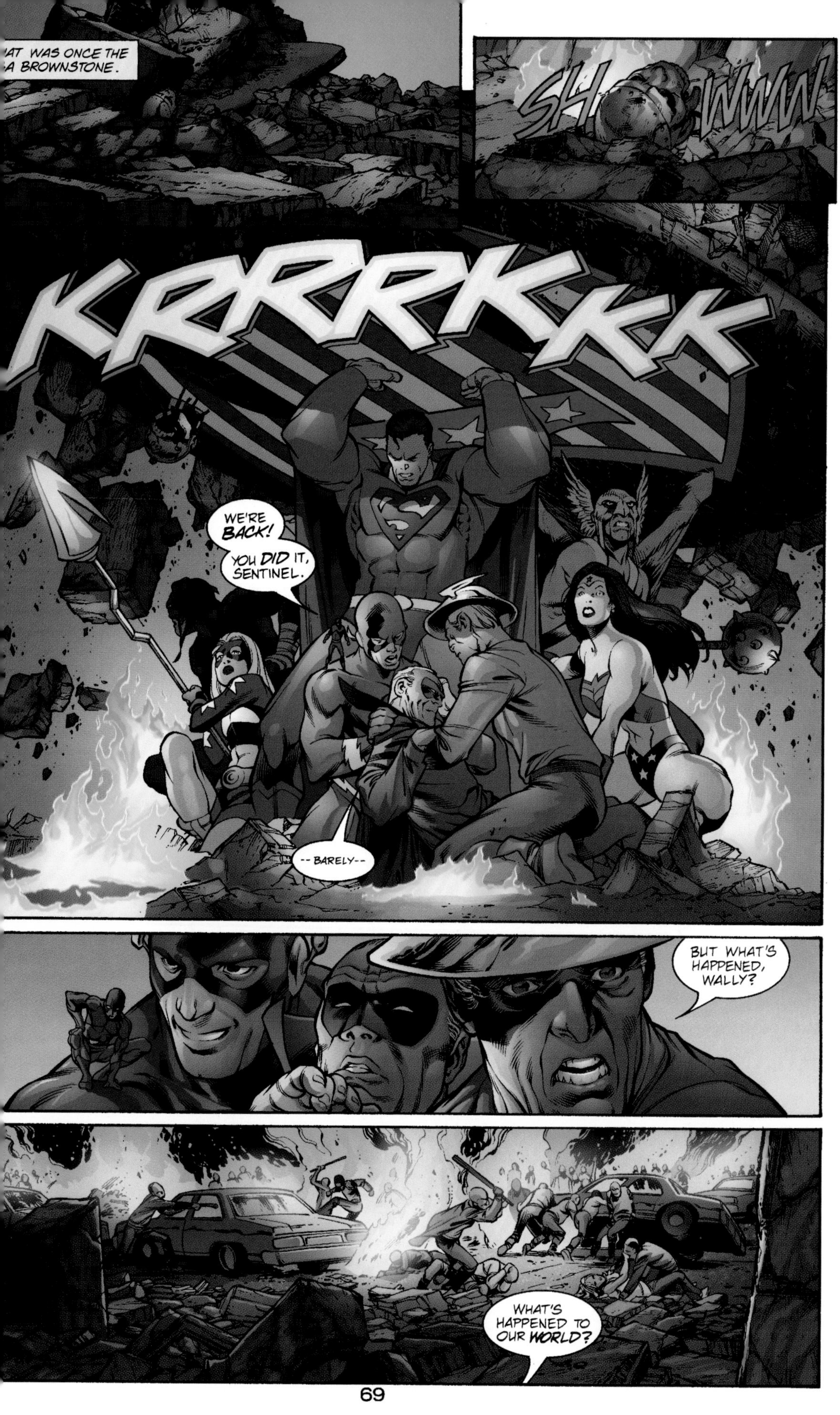

AT WAS ONCE THE
A BROWNSTONE.
SH WWW
KRRRKKK
WE'RE BACK!
YOU DID IT, SENTINEL.
--BARELY--
BUT WHAT'S HAPPENED, WALLY?
WHAT'S HAPPENED TO OUR WORLD?

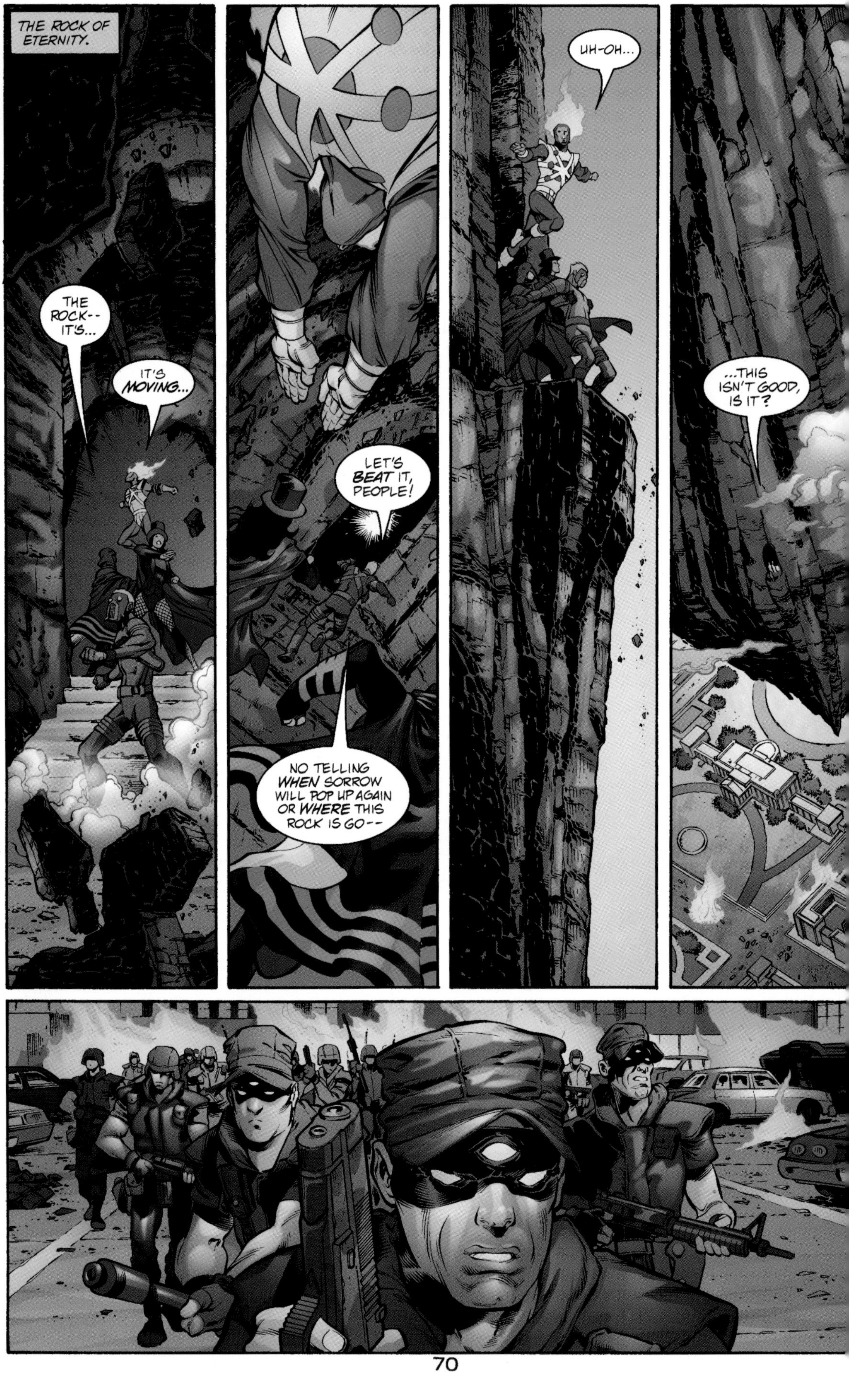
THE ROCK OF ETERNITY.
THE ROCK-- IT'S...
IT'S MOVING...
LET'S BEAT IT, PEOPLE!
NO TELLING WHEN SORROW WILL POP UP AGAIN OR WHERE THIS ROCK IS GO--
UH-OH...
...THIS ISN'T GOOD, IS IT?

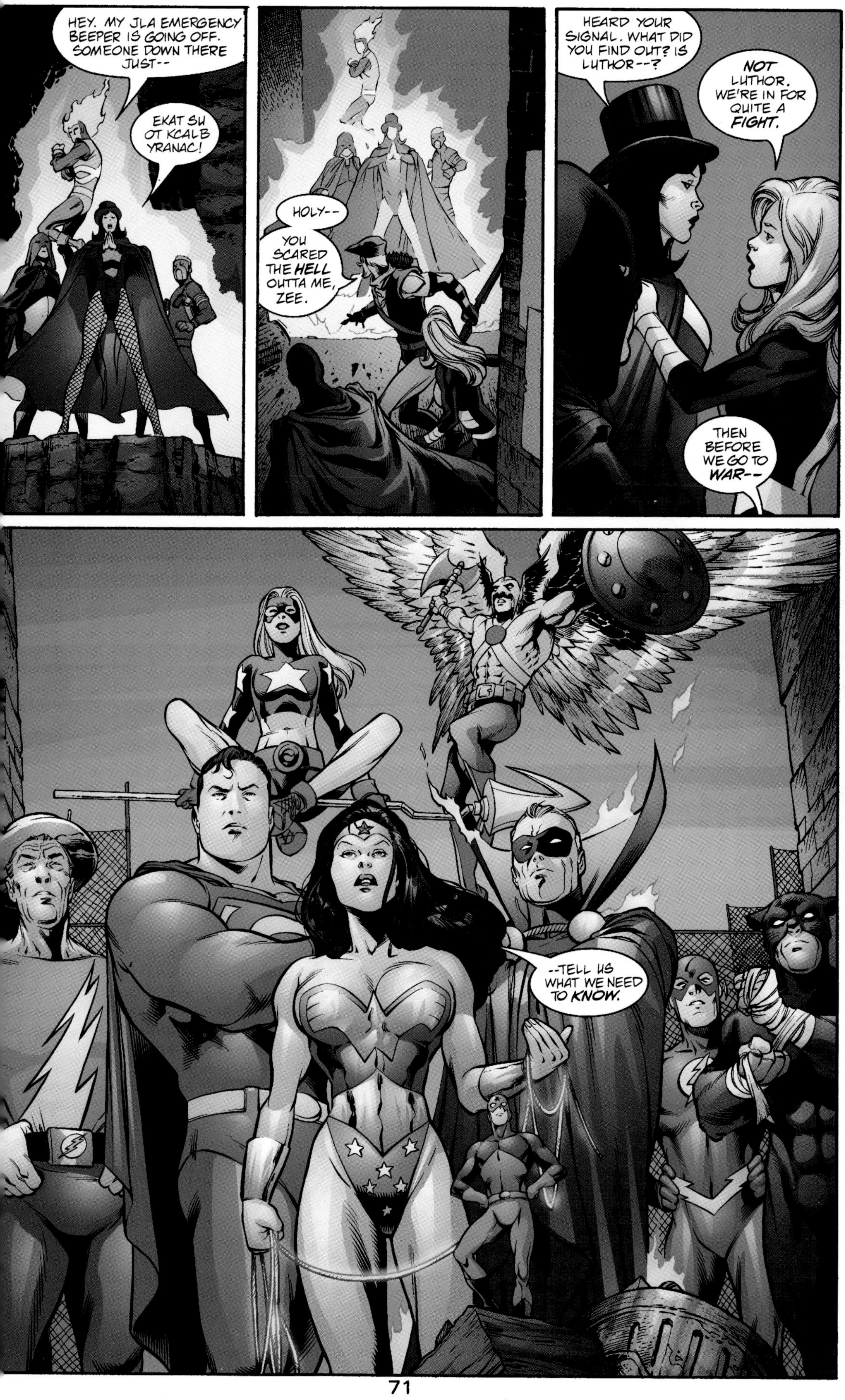
HEY. MY JLA EMERGENCY BEEPER IS GOING OFF. SOMEONE DOWN THERE JUST--
EKAT SU OT KCALB YRANAC!
HOLY--
YOU SCARED THE **HELL** OUTTA ME, ZEE.
HEARD YOUR SIGNAL. WHAT DID YOU FIND OUT? IS LUTHOR--?
NOT LUTHOR. WE'RE IN FOR QUITE A ***FIGHT***.
THEN BEFORE WE GO TO ***WAR***--
--TELL US WHAT WE NEED TO ***KNOW***.

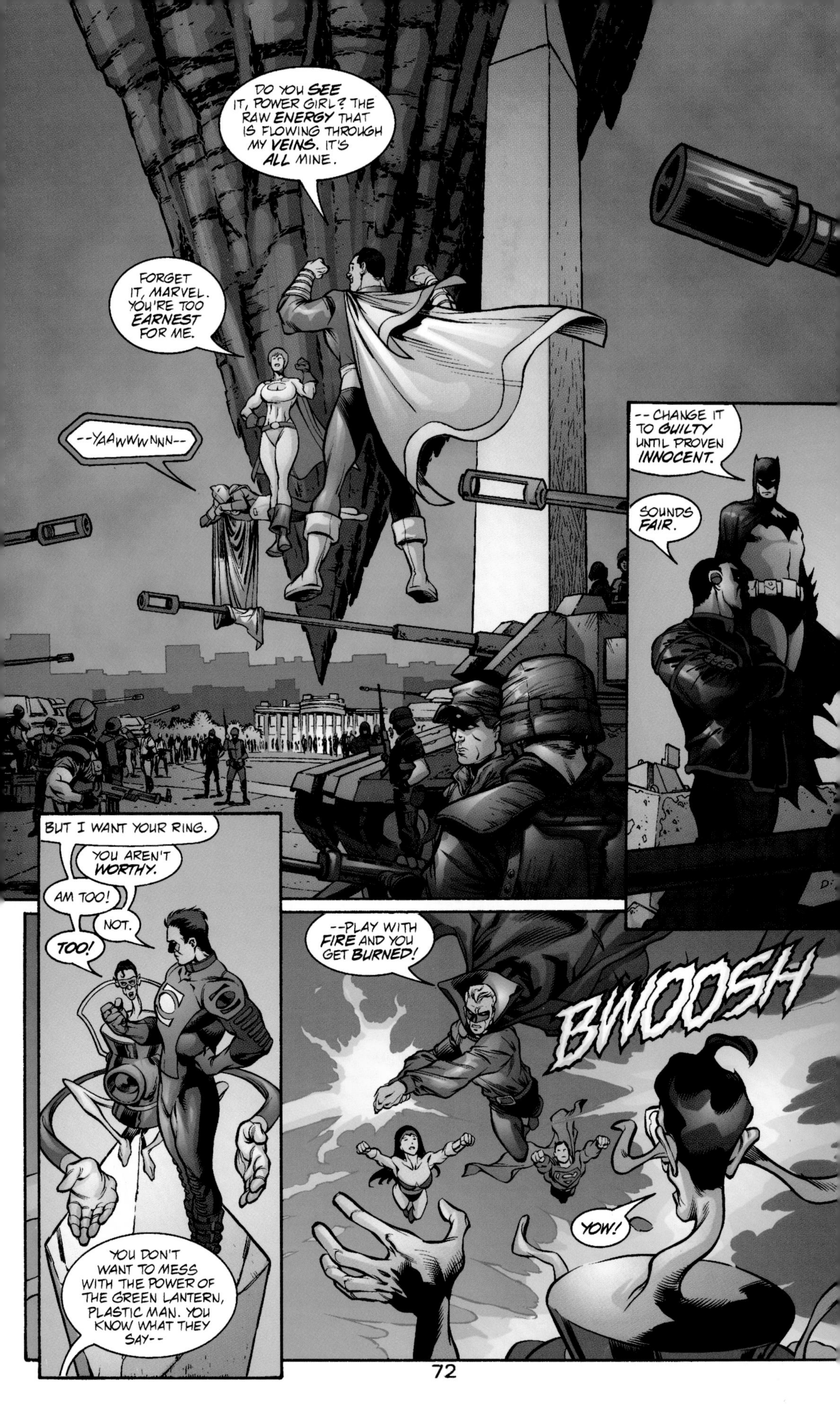
DO YOU SEE IT, POWER GIRL? THE RAW ENERGY THAT IS FLOWING THROUGH MY VEINS. IT'S ALL MINE.
FORGET IT, MARVEL. YOU'RE TOO EARNEST FOR ME.
--YAAWWWNNN--
--CHANGE IT TO GUILTY UNTIL PROVEN INNOCENT.
SOUNDS FAIR.
BUT I WANT YOUR RING.
YOU AREN'T WORTHY.
AM TOO!
NOT.
TOO!
YOU DON'T WANT TO MESS WITH THE POWER OF THE GREEN LANTERN, PLASTIC MAN. YOU KNOW WHAT THEY SAY--
--PLAY WITH FIRE AND YOU GET BURNED!
BWOOSH
YOW!

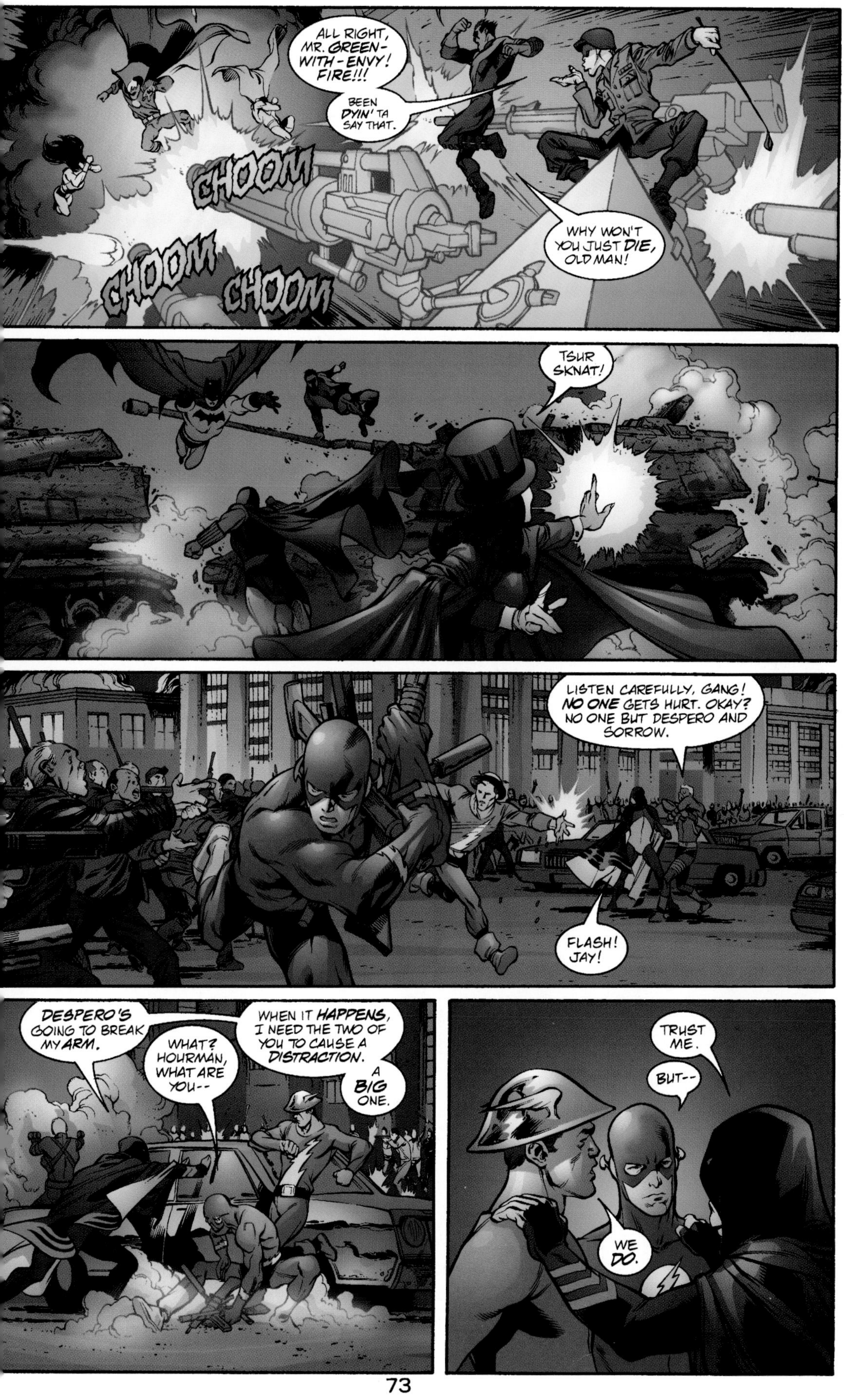
ALL RIGHT, MR. GREEN-WITH-ENVY! FIRE!!!
BEEN DYIN' TA SAY THAT.
CHOOM
CHOOM
CHOOM
WHY WON'T YOU JUST DIE, OLD MAN!
TSUR SKNAT!
LISTEN CAREFULLY, GANG! NO ONE GETS HURT. OKAY? NO ONE BUT DESPERO AND SORROW.
FLASH! JAY!
DESPERO'S GOING TO BREAK MY ARM.
WHAT? HOURMAN, WHAT ARE YOU--
WHEN IT HAPPENS, I NEED THE TWO OF YOU TO CAUSE A DISTRACTION.
A BIG ONE.
TRUST ME.
BUT--
WE DO.

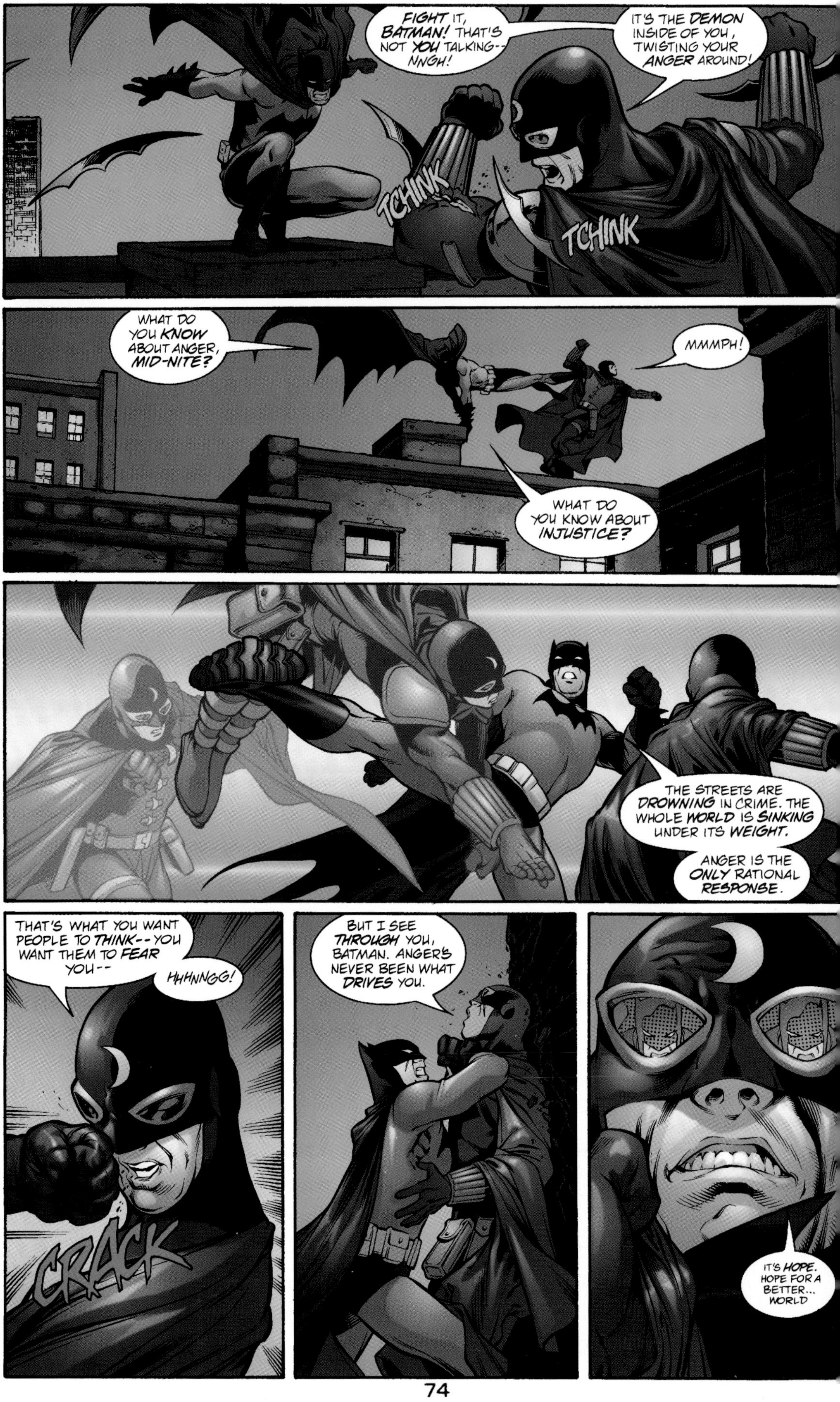
FIGHT IT, BATMAN! THAT'S NOT YOU TALKING-- NNGH!
IT'S THE DEMON INSIDE OF YOU, TWISTING YOUR ANGER AROUND!
TCHINK
TCHINK
WHAT DO YOU KNOW ABOUT ANGER, MID-NITE?
MMMPH!
WHAT DO YOU KNOW ABOUT INJUSTICE?
THE STREETS ARE DROWNING IN CRIME. THE WHOLE WORLD IS SINKING UNDER ITS WEIGHT.
ANGER IS THE ONLY RATIONAL RESPONSE.
THAT'S WHAT YOU WANT PEOPLE TO THINK-- YOU WANT THEM TO FEAR YOU--
HHHNNGG!
CRACK
BUT I SEE THROUGH YOU, BATMAN. ANGER'S NEVER BEEN WHAT DRIVES YOU.
IT'S HOPE. HOPE FOR A BETTER... WORLD

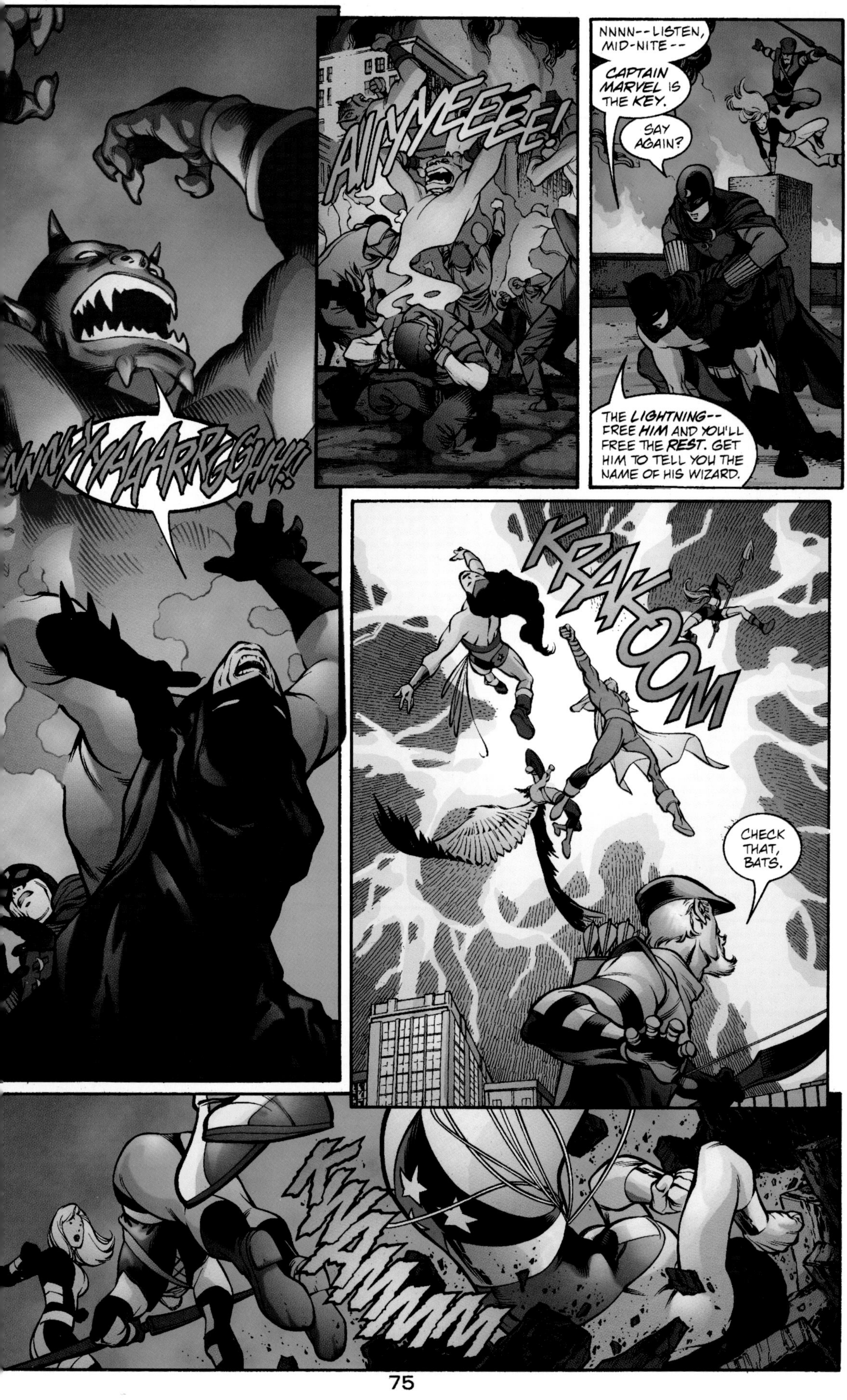
AIIYEEEEE!
NNNN--LISTEN, MID-NITE--
CAPTAIN MARVEL IS THE KEY.
SAY AGAIN?
THE LIGHTNING--FREE HIM AND YOU'LL FREE THE REST. GET HIM TO TELL YOU THE NAME OF HIS WIZARD.
NNNYYAAARRGGHH!!
KRAKOOM
CHECK THAT, BATS.
KWAMMMM

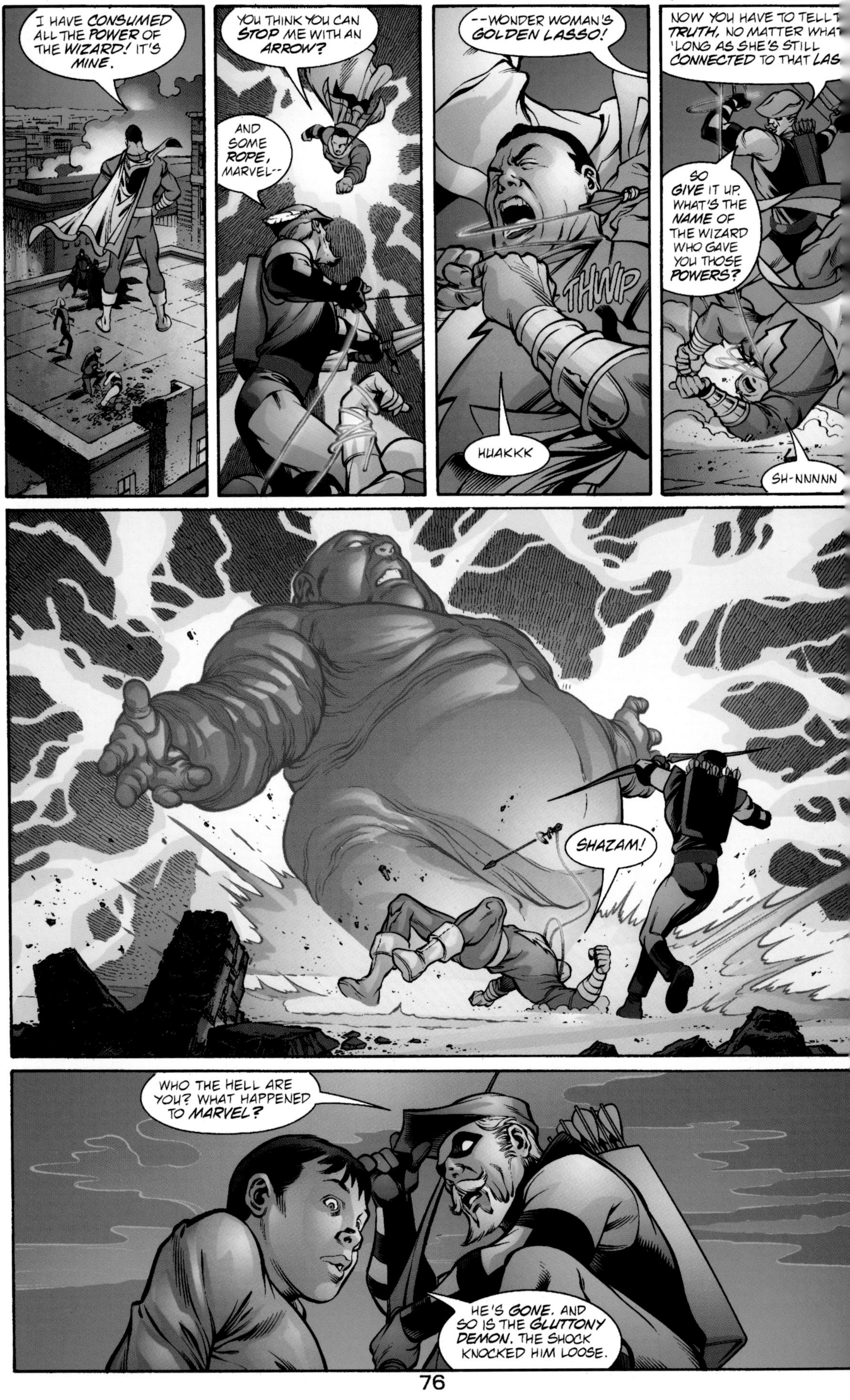

I HAVE CONSUMED ALL THE POWER OF THE WIZARD! IT'S MINE.
YOU THINK YOU CAN STOP ME WITH AN ARROW?
AND SOME ROPE, MARVEL--
--WONDER WOMAN'S GOLDEN LASSO!
THWIP
HUAKKK
NOW YOU HAVE TO TELL T TRUTH, NO MATTER WHAT 'LONG AS SHE'S STILL CONNECTED TO THAT LAS
SO GIVE IT UP. WHAT'S THE NAME OF THE WIZARD WHO GAVE YOU THOSE POWERS?
SH-NNNNN
SHAZAM!
WHO THE HELL ARE YOU? WHAT HAPPENED TO MARVEL?
HE'S GONE. AND SO IS THE GLUTTONY DEMON. THE SHOCK KNOCKED HIM LOOSE.

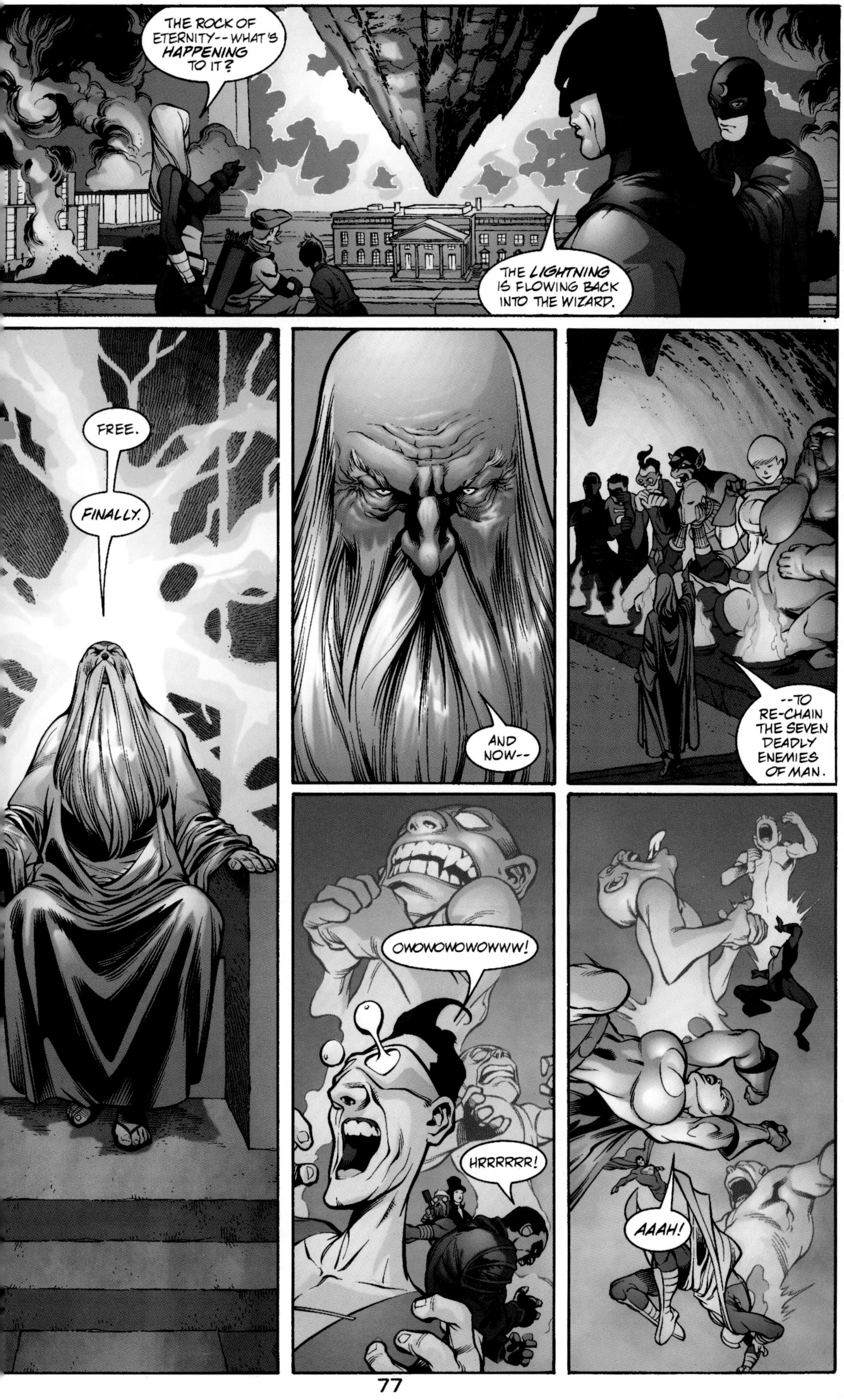
THE ROCK OF ETERNITY--WHAT'S HAPPENING TO IT?
THE LIGHTNING IS FLOWING BACK INTO THE WIZARD.
FREE.
FINALLY.
AND NOW--
--TO RE-CHAIN THE SEVEN DEADLY ENEMIES OF MAN.
OWOWOWOWOWWW!
HRRRRRR!
AAAH!

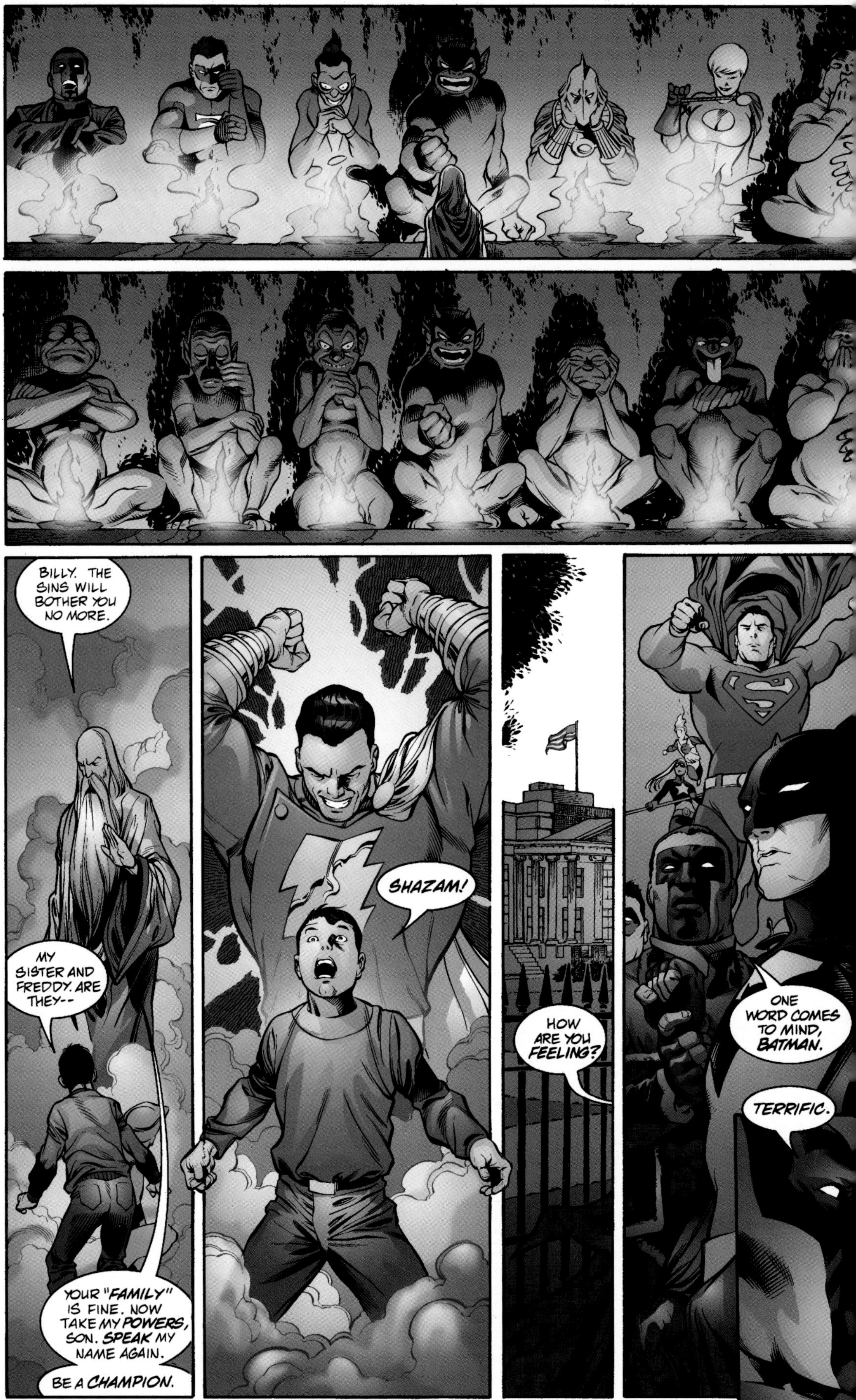
BILLY. THE SINS WILL BOTHER YOU NO MORE.
MY SISTER AND FREDDY. ARE THEY--
YOUR "FAMILY" IS FINE. NOW TAKE MY POWERS, SON. SPEAK MY NAME AGAIN.
BE A CHAMPION.
SHAZAM!
HOW ARE YOU FEELING?
ONE WORD COMES TO MIND, BATMAN.
TERRIFIC.

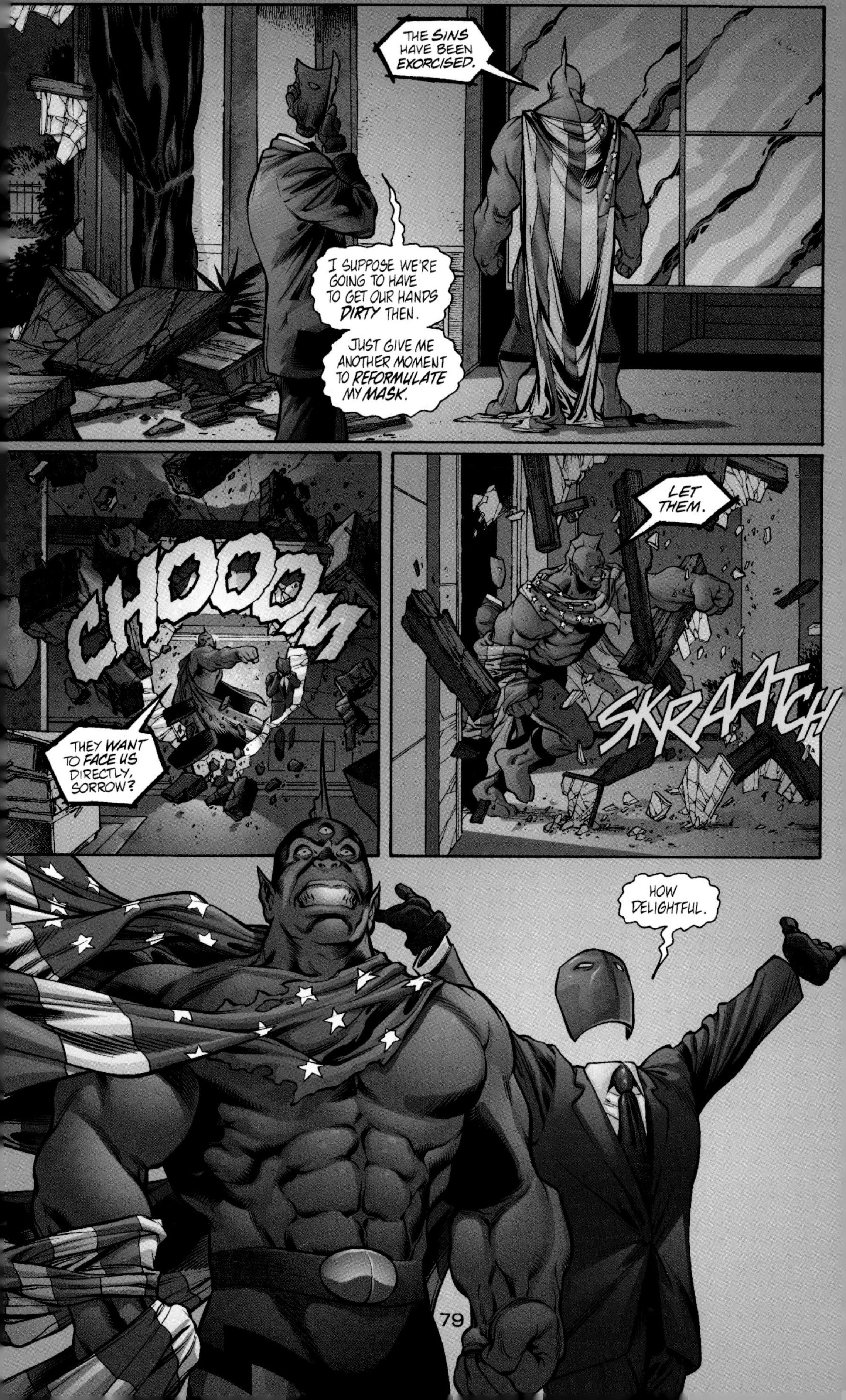
THE SINS HAVE BEEN EXORCISED.
I SUPPOSE WE'RE GOING TO HAVE TO GET OUR HANDS DIRTY THEN.
JUST GIVE ME ANOTHER MOMENT TO REFORMULATE MY MASK.
CHOOOM
THEY WANT TO FACE US DIRECTLY, SORROW?
LET THEM.
SKRAATCH
HOW DELIGHTFUL.

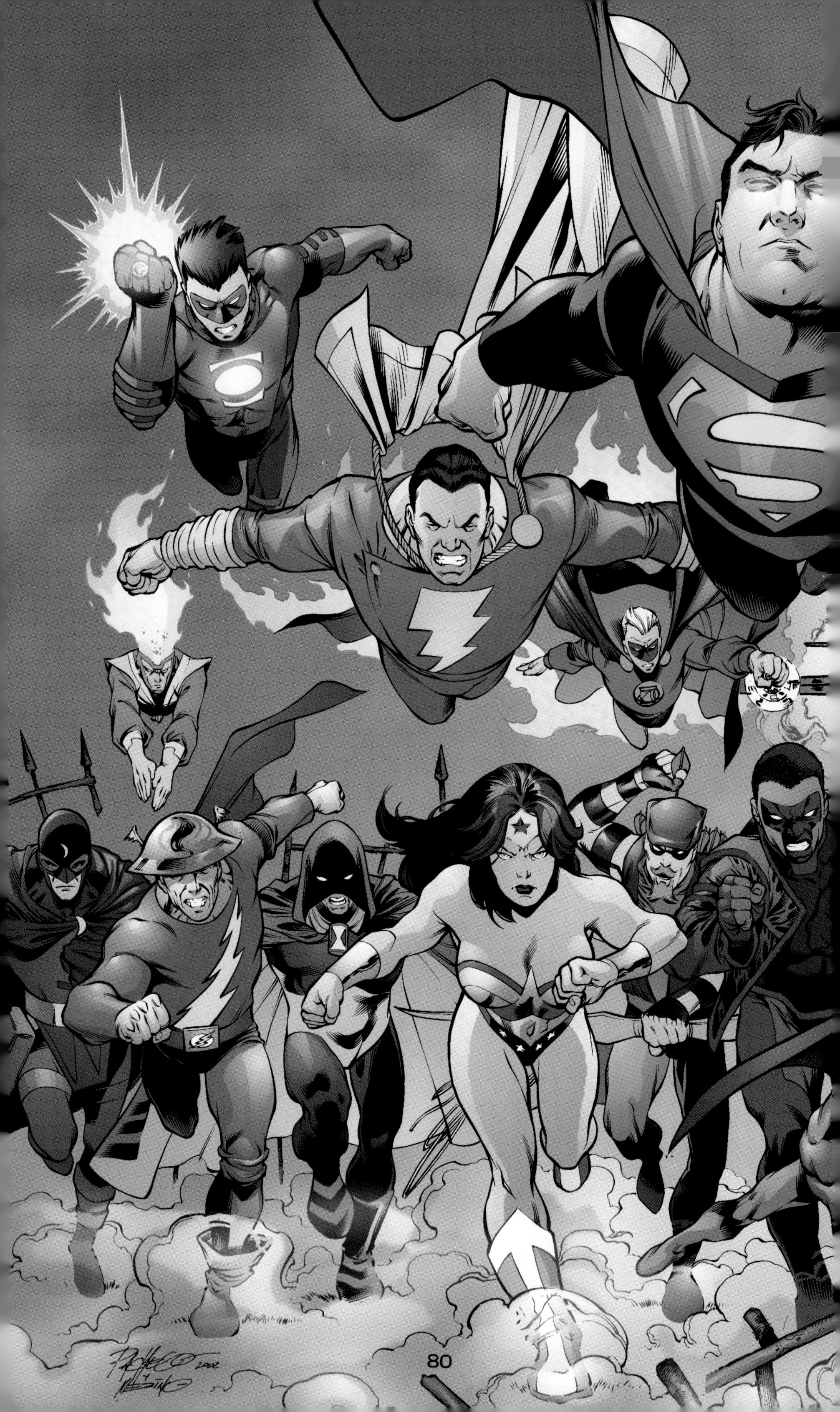

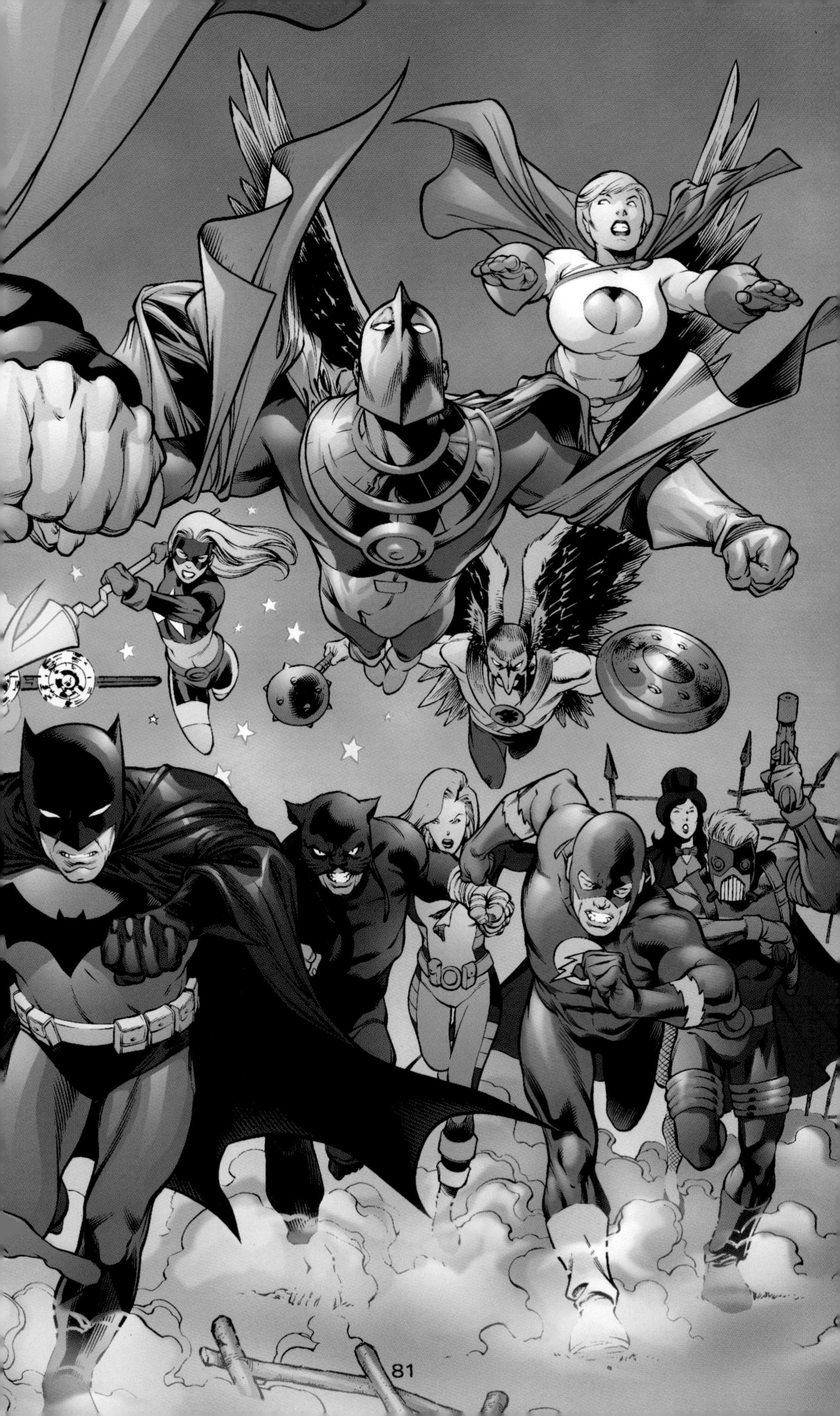

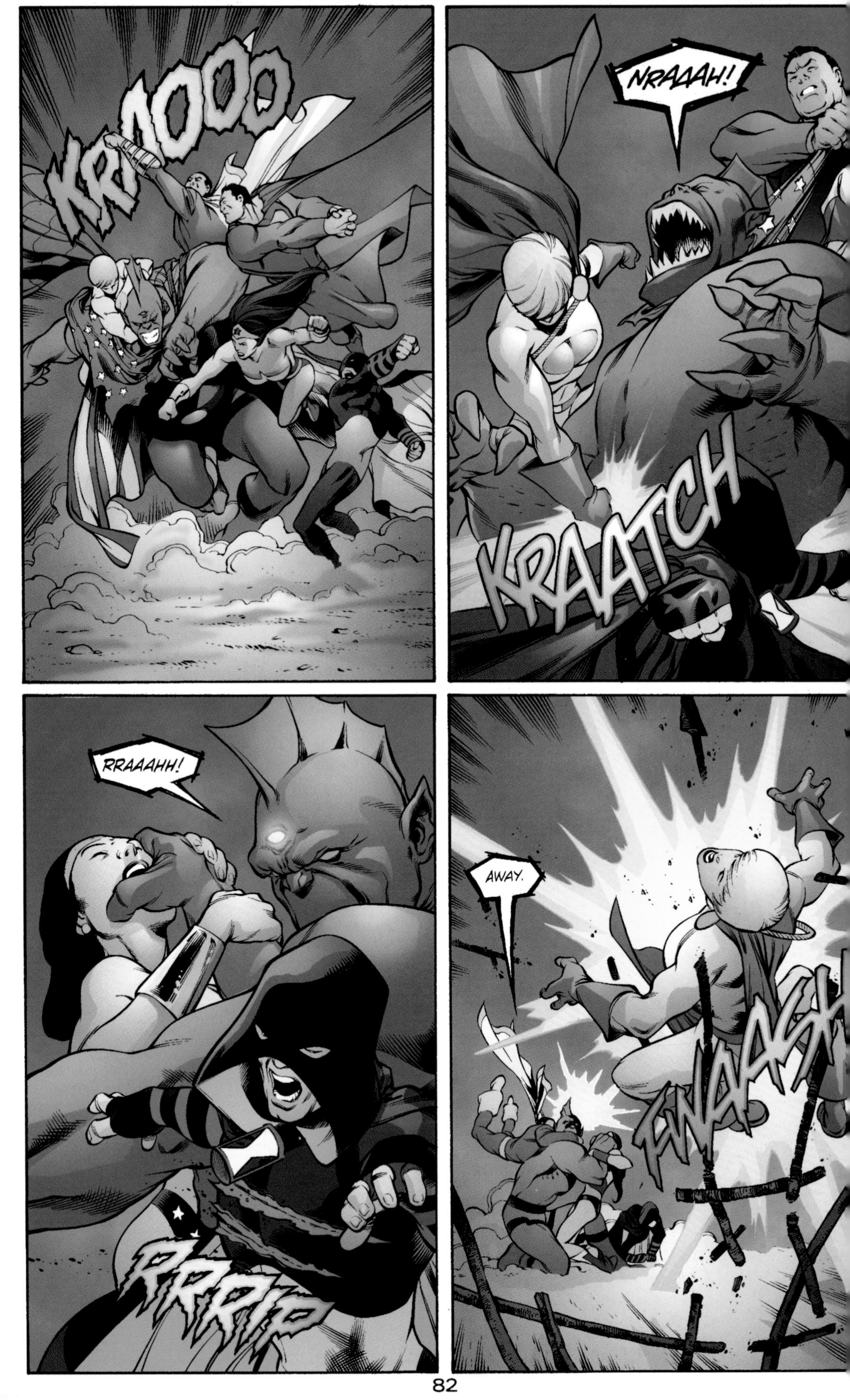
KRAOOO
NRAAAH!
KRAATCH
RRAAAHH!
RRRIP
AWAY.
FWAAS

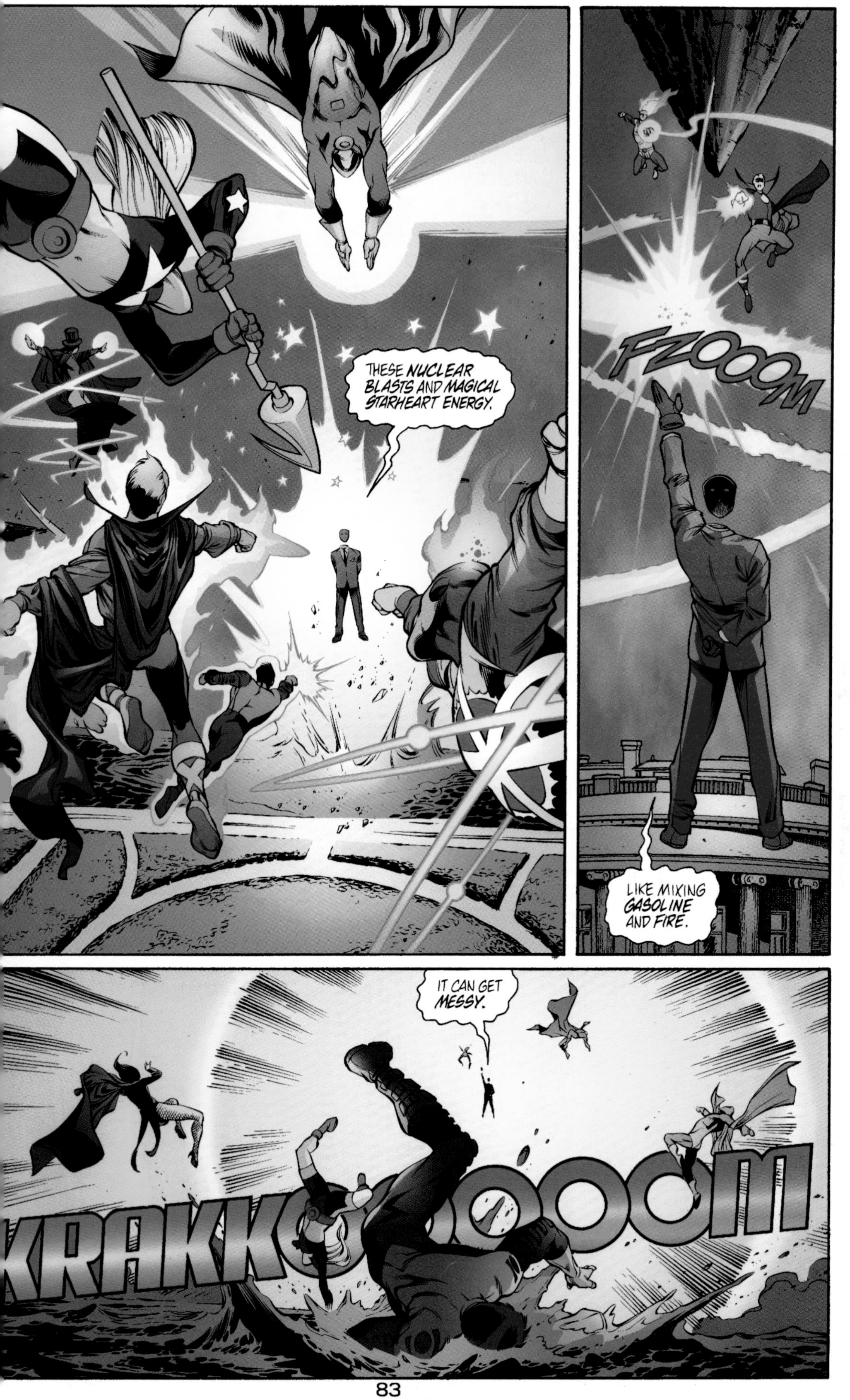
THESE NUCLEAR BLASTS AND MAGICAL STARHEART ENERGY.
FZOOOM
LIKE MIXING GASOLINE AND FIRE.
IT CAN GET MESSY.
KRAKKOOOOM

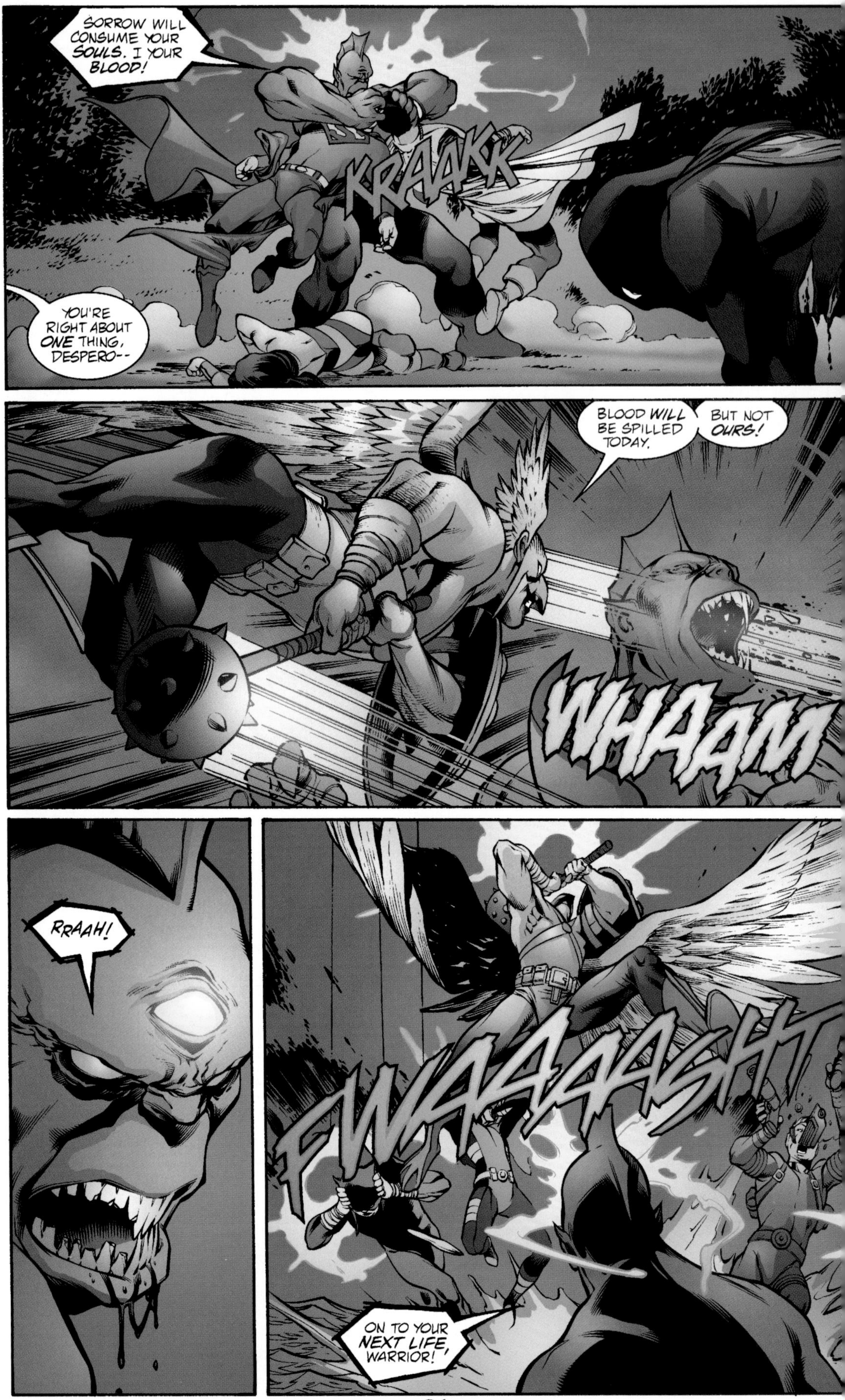
SORROW WILL CONSUME YOUR SOULS. I YOUR BLOOD!
KRAAKK
YOU'RE RIGHT ABOUT ONE THING, DESPERO--
BLOOD WILL BE SPILLED TODAY.
BUT NOT OURS!
WHAAM
RRAAH!
FWAAAASH
ON TO YOUR NEXT LIFE, WARRIOR!

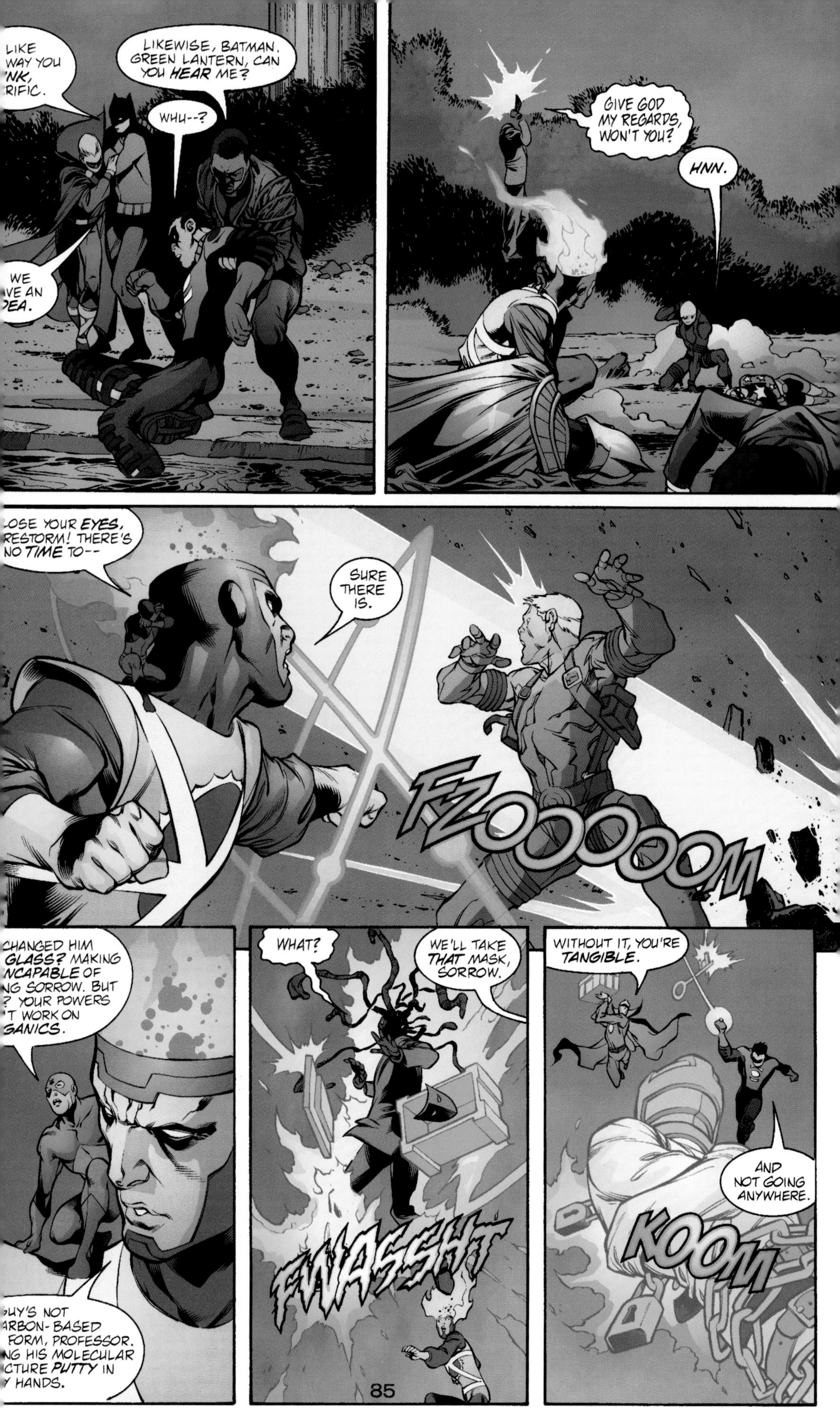
LIKE WAY YOU NK, RIFIC.
LIKEWISE, BATMAN. GREEN LANTERN, CAN YOU HEAR ME?
WHU--?
WE VE AN DEA.
GIVE GOD MY REGARDS, WON'T YOU?
HNN.
OSE YOUR EYES, RESTORM! THERE'S NO TIME TO--
SURE THERE IS.
FZOOOOOOM
CHANGED HIM GLASS? MAKING NCAPABLE OF NG SORROW. BUT ? YOUR POWERS 'T WORK ON GANICS.
GUY'S NOT ARBON-BASED FORM, PROFESSOR. NG HIS MOLECULAR CTURE PUTTY IN Y HANDS.
WHAT?
WE'LL TAKE THAT MASK, SORROW.
FWASSHT
WITHOUT IT, YOU'RE TANGIBLE.
AND NOT GOING ANYWHERE.
KOOM

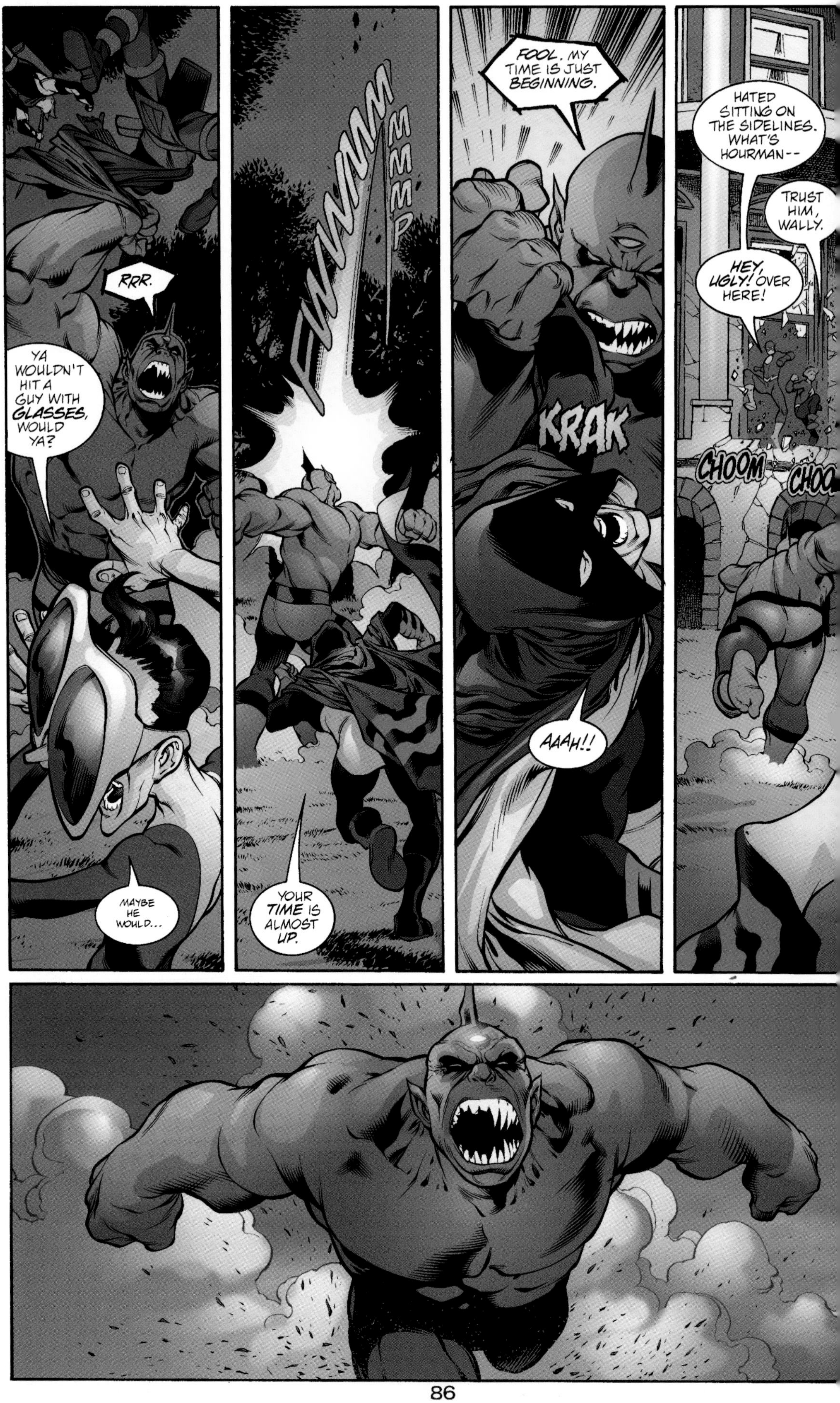
RRR.
YA WOULDN'T HIT A GUY WITH GLASSES, WOULD YA?
MAYBE HE WOULD...
FWWMMMMMMP
YOUR TIME IS ALMOST UP.
FOOL. MY TIME IS JUST BEGINNING.
KRAK
AAAH!!
HATED SITTING ON THE SIDELINES. WHAT'S HOURMAN--
TRUST HIM, WALLY.
HEY, UGLY! OVER HERE!
CHOOM

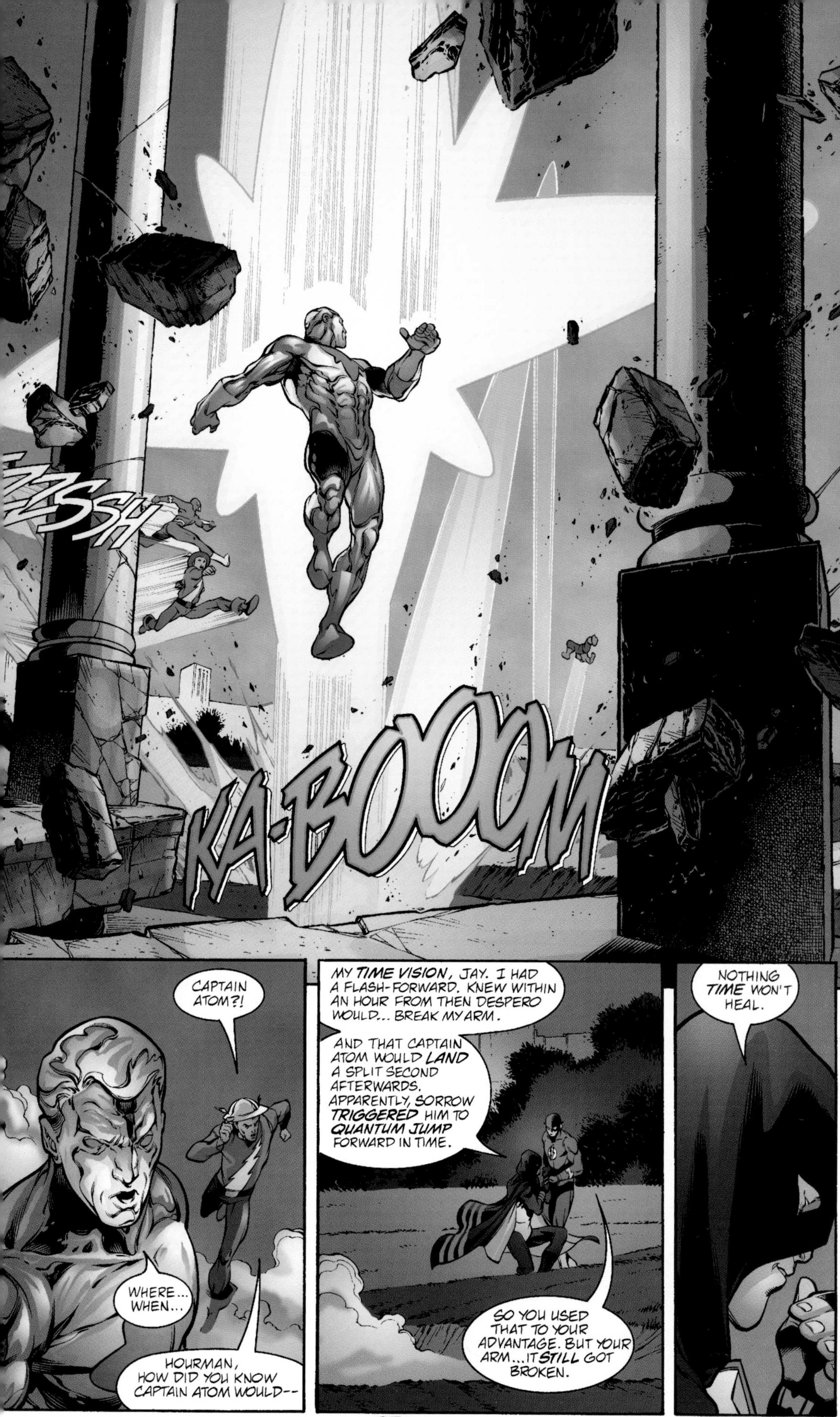
ZZSSH
KA-BOOOM
CAPTAIN ATOM?!
WHERE... WHEN...
HOURMAN, HOW DID YOU KNOW CAPTAIN ATOM WOULD--
MY TIME VISION, JAY. I HAD A FLASH-FORWARD. KNEW WITHIN AN HOUR FROM THEN DESPERO WOULD... BREAK MY ARM.
AND THAT CAPTAIN ATOM WOULD LAND A SPLIT SECOND AFTERWARDS. APPARENTLY, SORROW TRIGGERED HIM TO QUANTUM JUMP FORWARD IN TIME.
SO YOU USED THAT TO YOUR ADVANTAGE. BUT YOUR ARM... IT STILL GOT BROKEN.
NOTHING TIME WON'T HEAL.

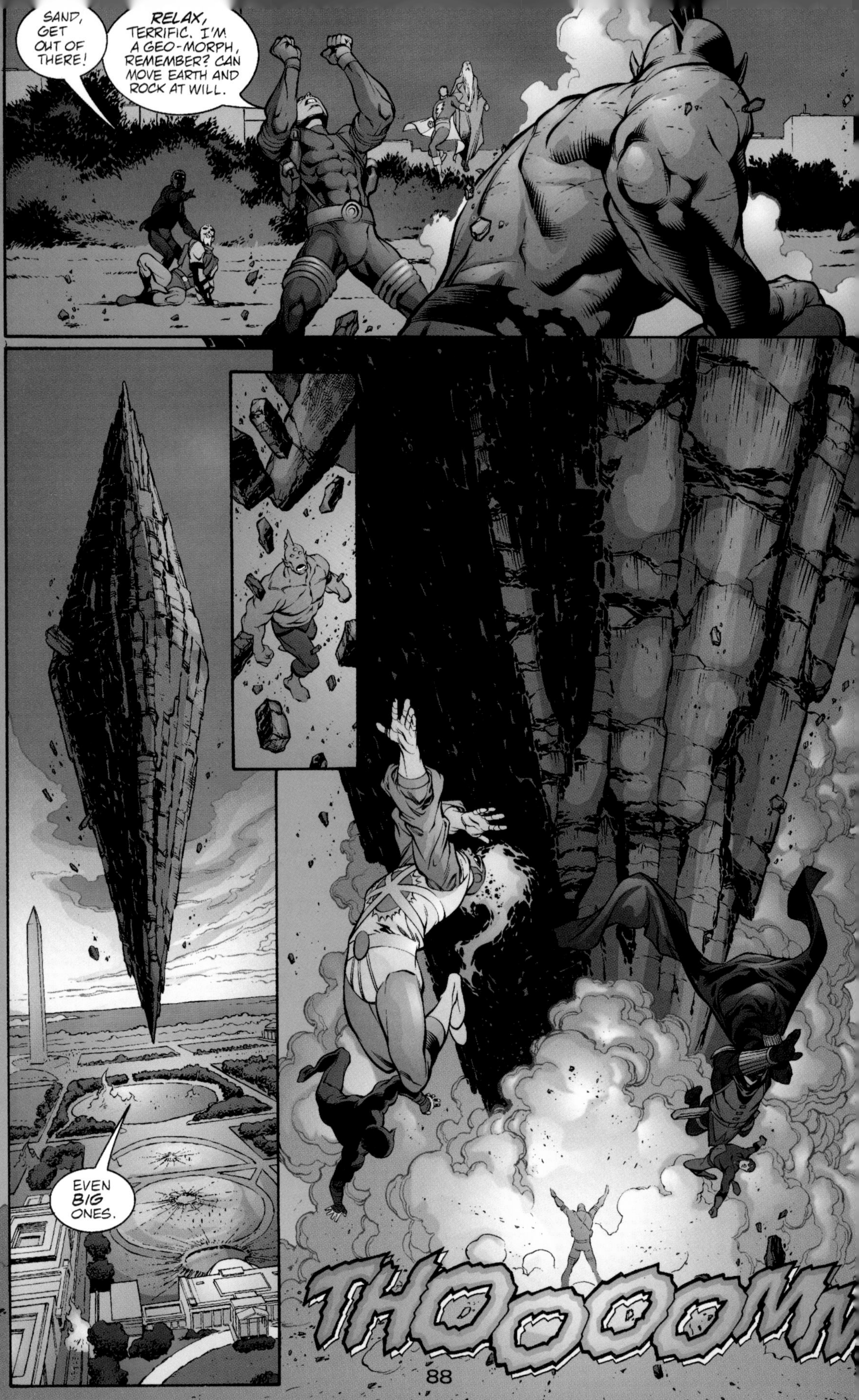
SAND, GET OUT OF THERE!
RELAX, TERRIFIC. I'M A GEO-MORPH, REMEMBER? CAN MOVE EARTH AND ROCK AT WILL.
EVEN BIG ONES.
THOOOOM

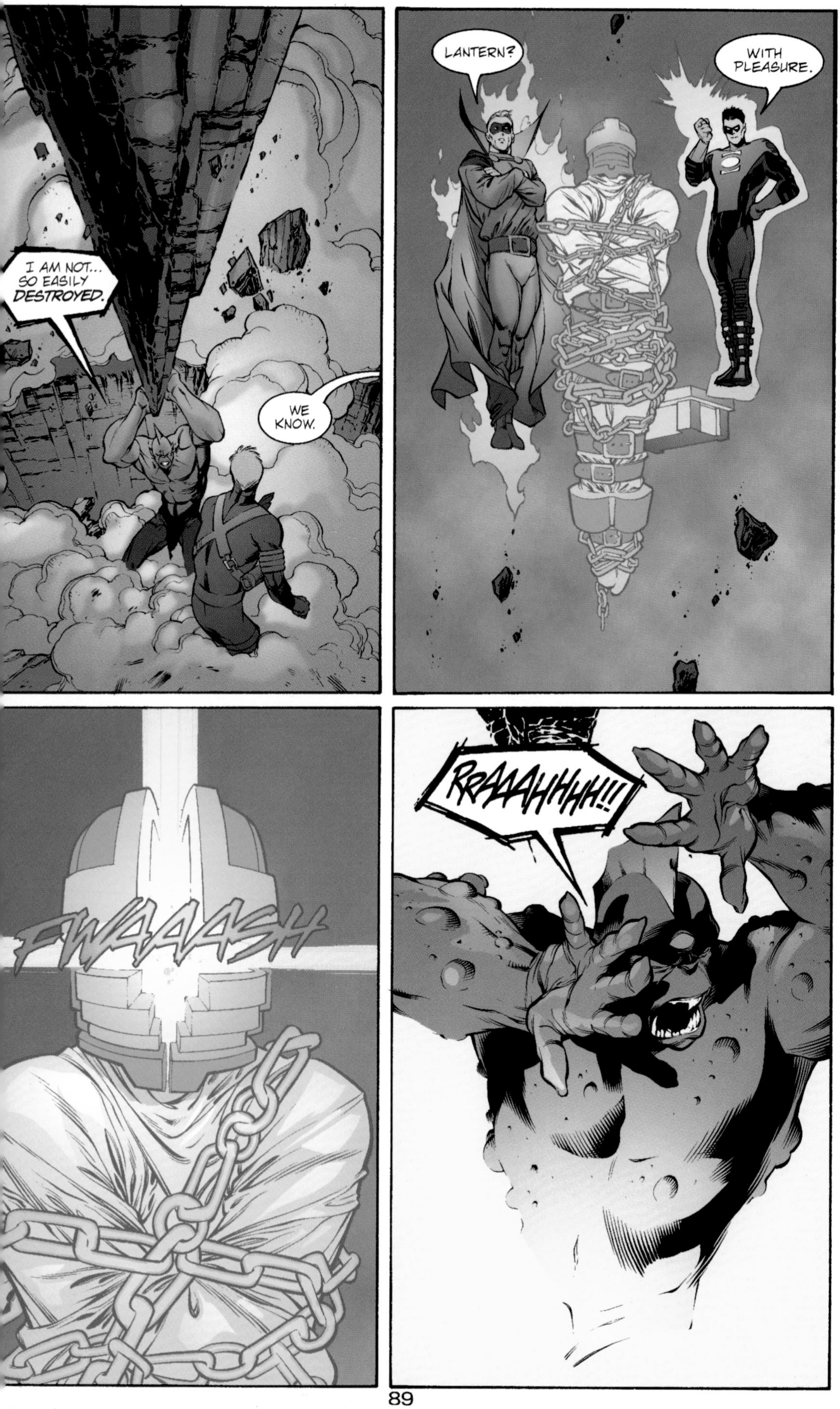
I AM NOT... SO EASILY DESTROYED.
WE KNOW.
LANTERN?
WITH PLEASURE.
FWAAAASH
RRAAAHHHH!!

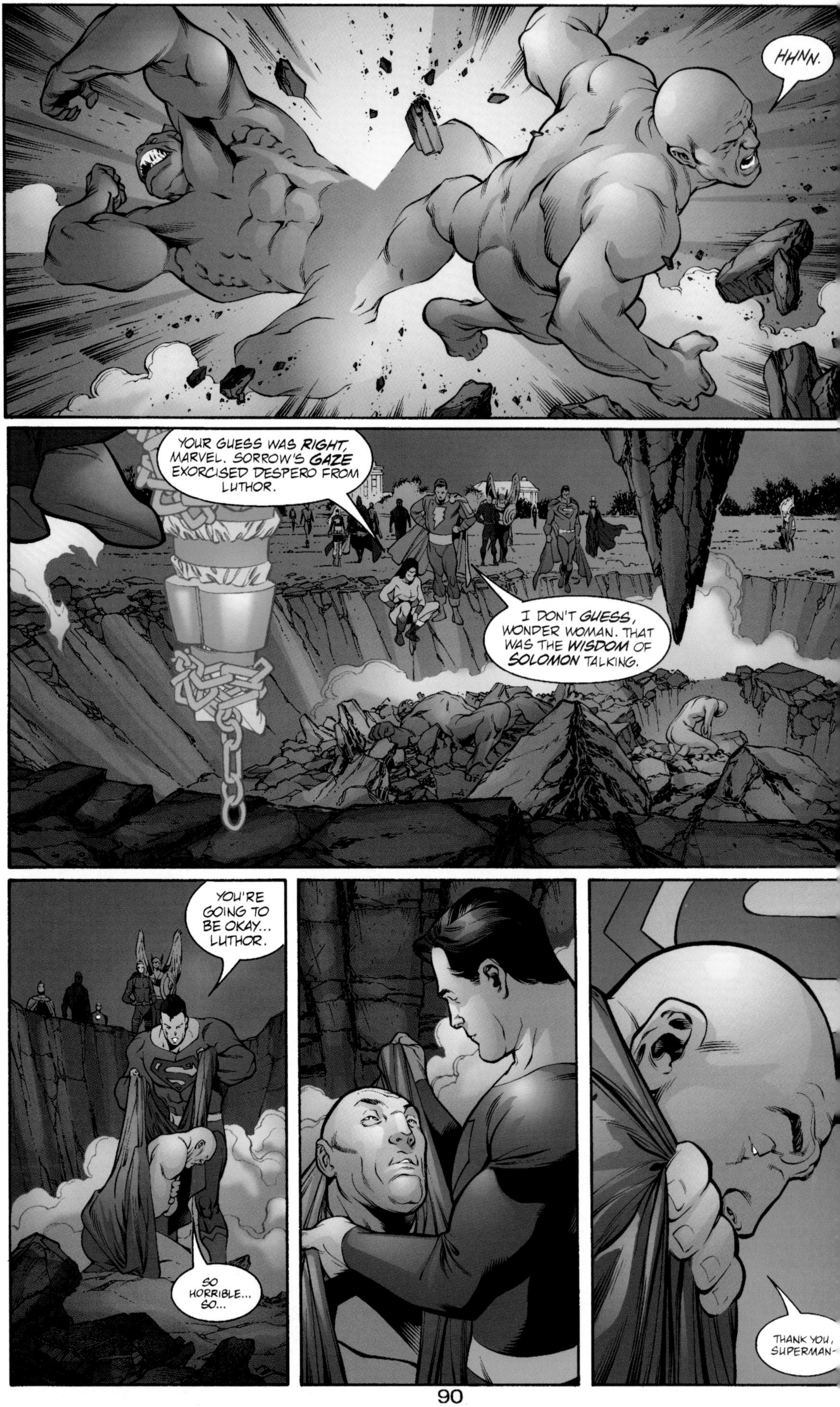
HHNN.
YOUR GUESS WAS RIGHT, MARVEL. SORROW'S GAZE EXORCISED DESPERO FROM LUTHOR.
I DON'T GUESS, WONDER WOMAN. THAT WAS THE WISDOM OF SOLOMON TALKING.
YOU'RE GOING TO BE OKAY... LUTHOR.
SO HORRIBLE... SO...
THANK YOU, SUPERMAN-

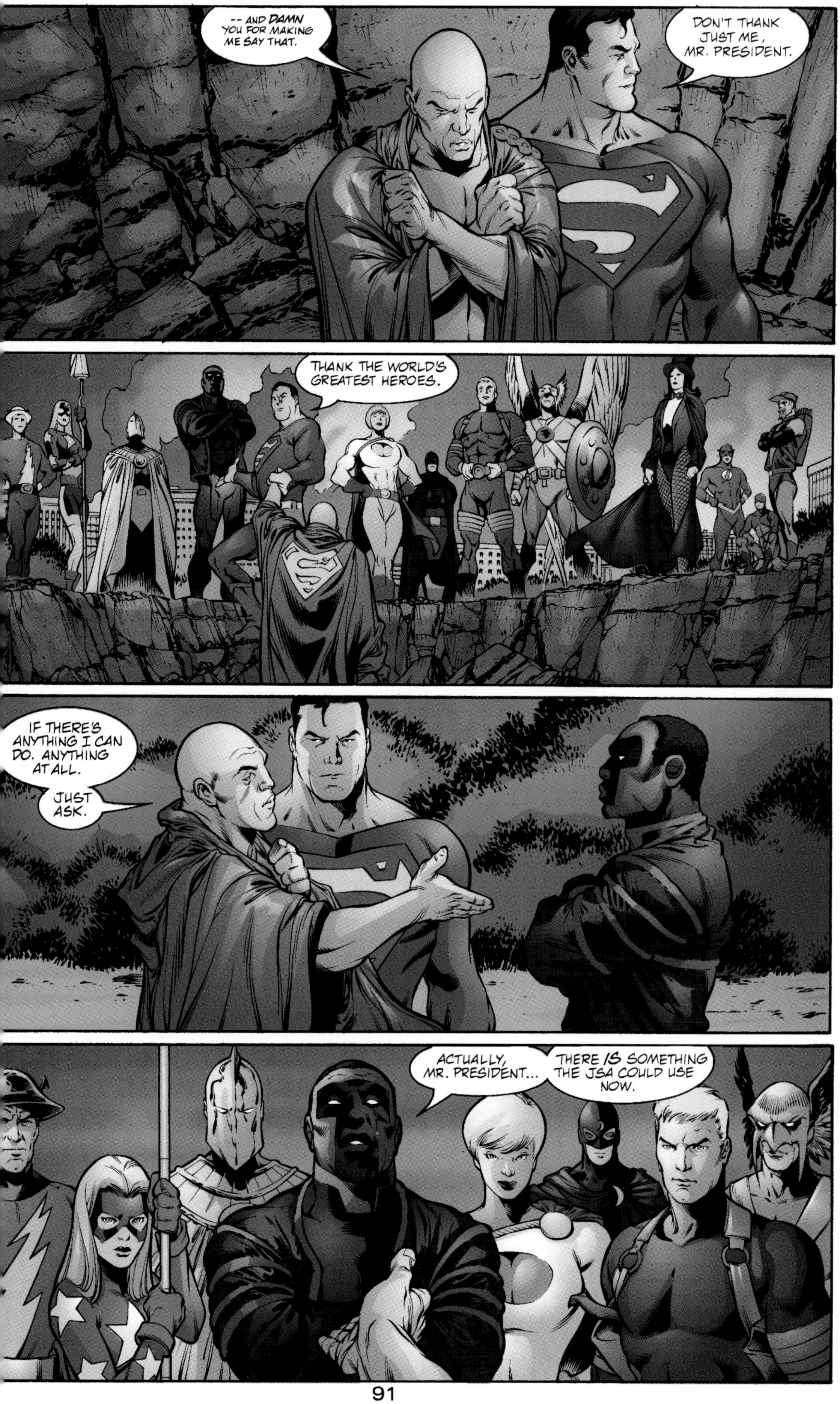
-- AND DAMN YOU FOR MAKING ME SAY THAT.
DON'T THANK JUST ME, MR. PRESIDENT.
THANK THE WORLD'S GREATEST HEROES.
IF THERE'S ANYTHING I CAN DO. ANYTHING AT ALL.
JUST ASK.
ACTUALLY, MR. PRESIDENT...
THERE IS SOMETHING THE JSA COULD USE NOW.

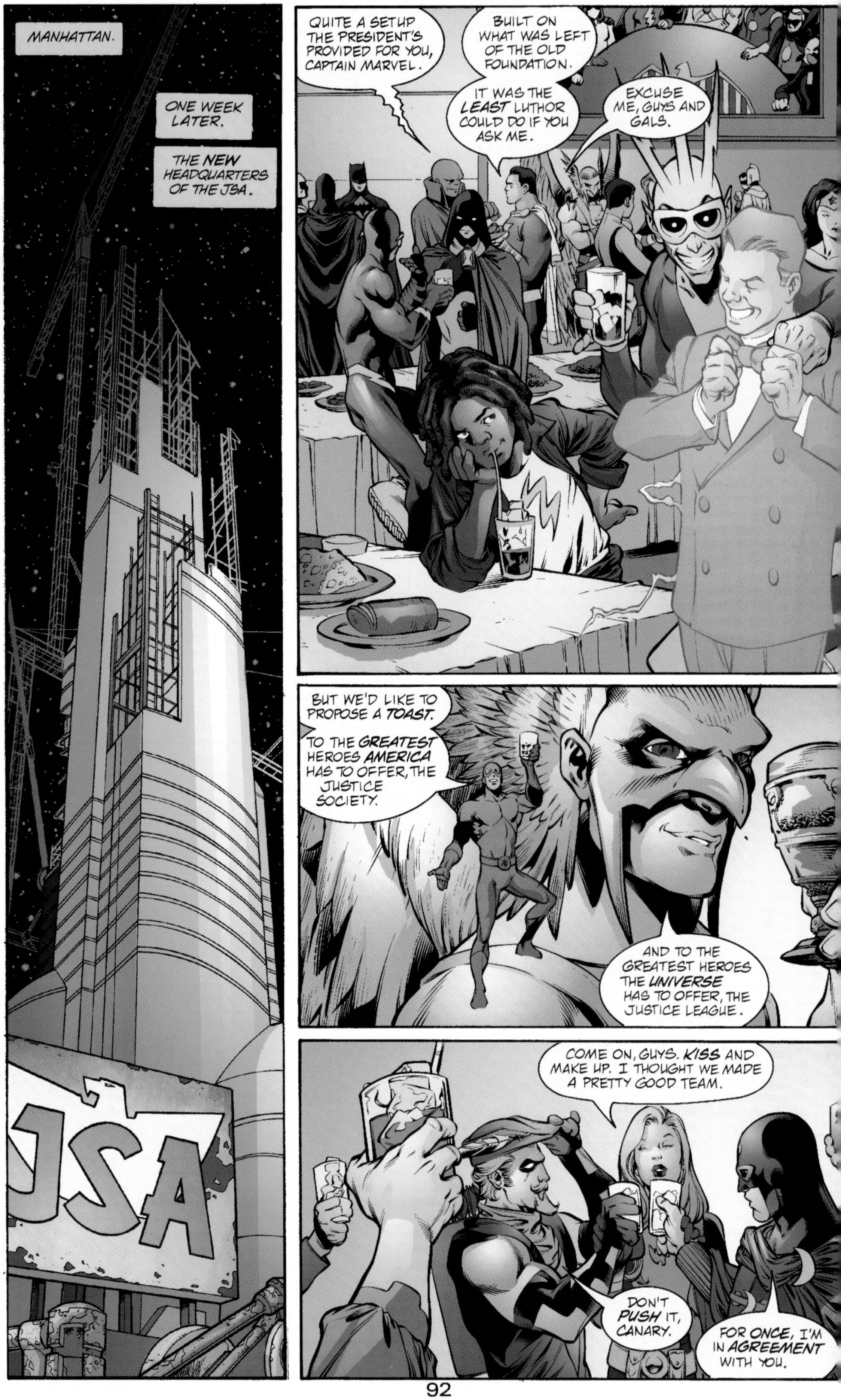

MANHATTAN.
ONE WEEK LATER.
THE NEW HEADQUARTERS OF THE JSA.
JSA
QUITE A SETUP THE PRESIDENT'S PROVIDED FOR YOU, CAPTAIN MARVEL.
BUILT ON WHAT WAS LEFT OF THE OLD FOUNDATION.
IT WAS THE LEAST LUTHOR COULD DO IF YOU ASK ME.
EXCUSE ME, GUYS AND GALS.
BUT WE'D LIKE TO PROPOSE A TOAST.
TO THE GREATEST HEROES AMERICA HAS TO OFFER, THE JUSTICE SOCIETY.
AND TO THE GREATEST HEROES THE UNIVERSE HAS TO OFFER, THE JUSTICE LEAGUE.
COME ON, GUYS. KISS AND MAKE UP. I THOUGHT WE MADE A PRETTY GOOD TEAM.
DON'T PUSH IT, CANARY.
FOR ONCE, I'M IN AGREEMENT WITH YOU.

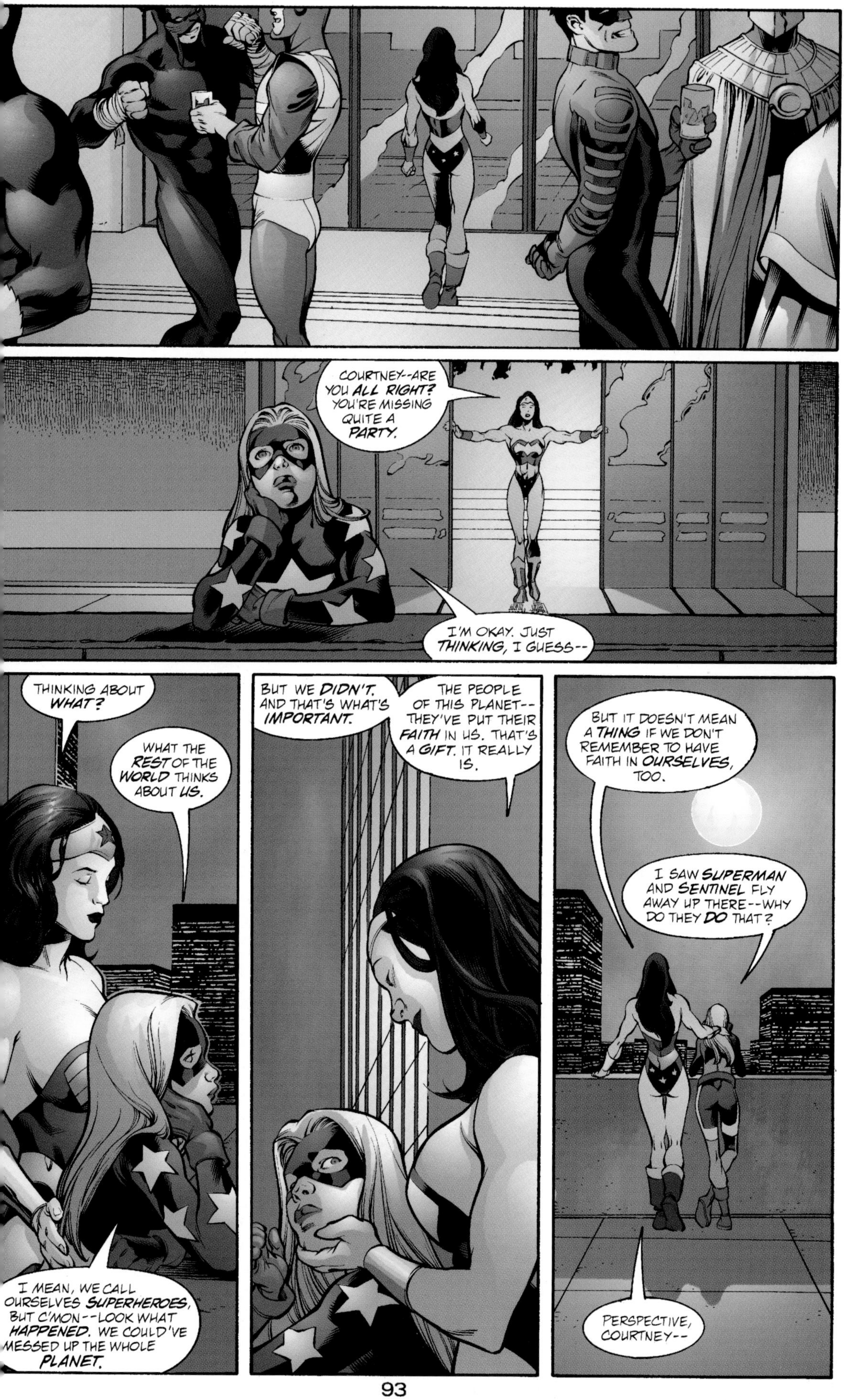
COURTNEY--ARE YOU ALL RIGHT? YOU'RE MISSING QUITE A PARTY.
I'M OKAY. JUST THINKING, I GUESS--
THINKING ABOUT WHAT?
WHAT THE REST OF THE WORLD THINKS ABOUT US.
I MEAN, WE CALL OURSELVES SUPERHEROES, BUT C'MON--LOOK WHAT HAPPENED. WE COULD'VE MESSED UP THE WHOLE PLANET.
BUT WE DIDN'T. AND THAT'S WHAT'S IMPORTANT.
THE PEOPLE OF THIS PLANET--THEY'VE PUT THEIR FAITH IN US. THAT'S A GIFT. IT REALLY IS.
BUT IT DOESN'T MEAN A THING IF WE DON'T REMEMBER TO HAVE FAITH IN OURSELVES, TOO.
I SAW SUPERMAN AND SENTINEL FLY AWAY UP THERE--WHY DO THEY DO THAT?
PERSPECTIVE, COURTNEY--

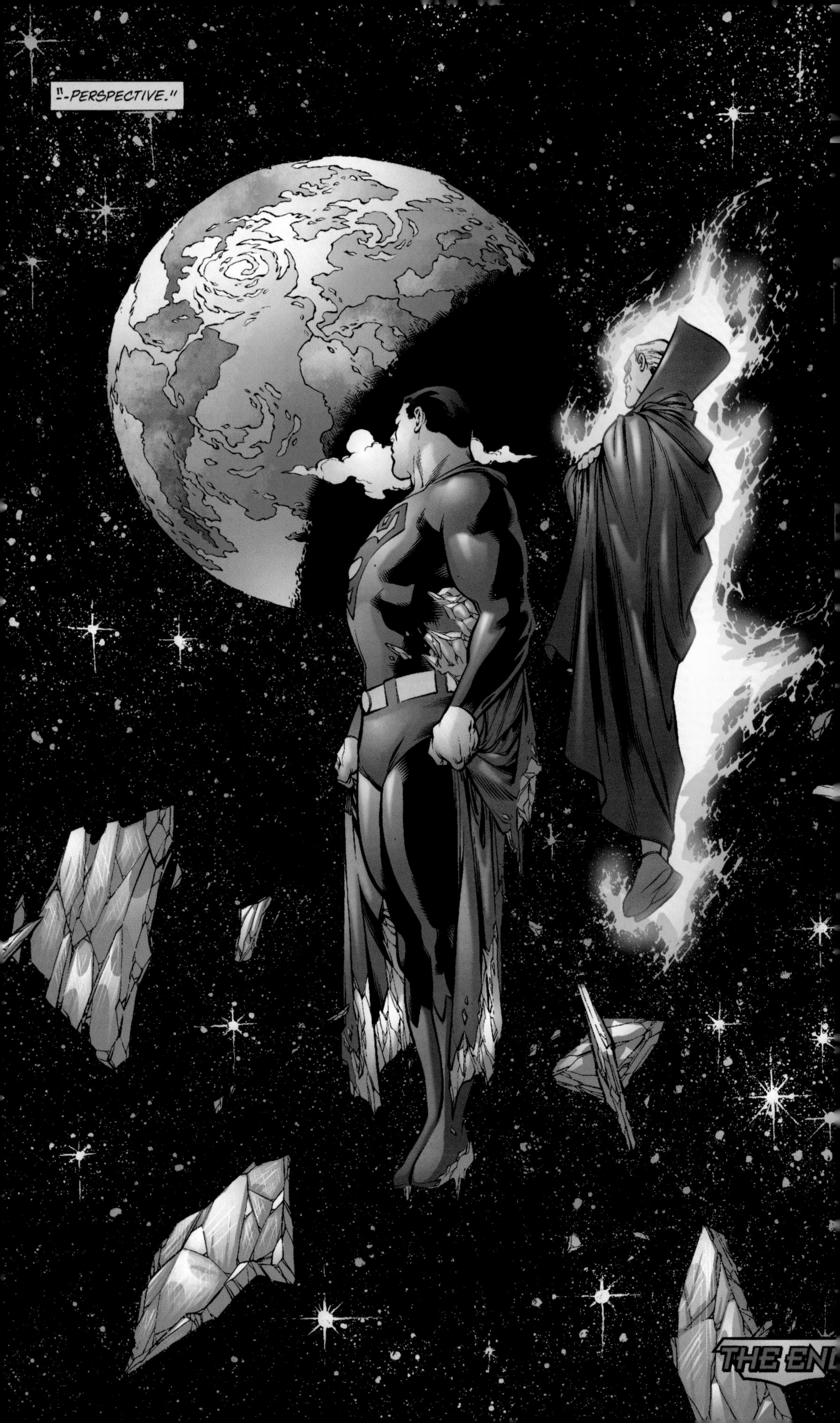
"--PERSPECTIVE."
THE EN